BAYOU WHISPERS

THE BAYOU SABINE SERIES

BAYOU WHISPERS

The Bayou Sabine Series

LAUREN FAULKENBERRY

Blue Crow Books

Bayou Whispers is a work of fiction. Names, characters, places, and incidents either are the product of the author's imagination or are used fictitiously. Any resemblance to actual persons, events, or locales is coincidental.

Publisher's Cataloging-in-Publication Data
Faulkenberry, Lauren 1978-.
Bayou Whispers : A Bayou Sabine Novel / Lauren Faulkenberry.
p.____ cm.____
ISBN 978-1-947834-19-4 (Pbk) | ISBN 978-1-947834-20-0 (eBook)
1. Women—Louisiana—Fiction. 2. Love—Fiction. 3. TK—Fiction. I. Title.
813'.6—dc23 | 2017955777

Blue Crow Books

Published by Blue Crow Books
an imprint of Blue Crow Publishing, LLC, Chapel Hill, NC
www.bluecrowpublishing.com
Cover Photograph by Aimee Junnila/Shutterstock.com
Cover Design by Lauren Faulkenberry

First published by Velvet Morning Press as
Bayou, Whispers from the Past: A Novel
First Blue Crow Books Edition 2017

Praise for The Bayou Sabine Series

Beautifully descriptive and engaging. A delightful story about learning to let go of who you think you need to be and take a risk on happiness.

—Orly Konig, author of THE DISTANCE HOME and founding president of the Women's Fiction Writers Association.

Faulkenberry is a gifted storyteller with the ability to capture the most human side of relationships. *Bayou Whispers* is a rich and emotional story that will draw readers into the heat of the bayou and leave them wanting more.

-Tina Ann Forkner, award-winning author of THE REAL THING and WAKING UP JOY

I'd read this book again, and I recommend it to others who love a fast-paced romantic mystery. I give this book five stars.

-Dayna Leigh Cheser, author of the TIME series

I loved this book. It has so many different dimensions that you will literally be glued to the pages...There's mystery, intrigue, and unexpected pieces to the story. PICK UP THIS BOOK. It's a MUST READ.

– Pretty Little Book Reviews

From the moment Jack spoke in that French/Creole drawl he and Faulkenberry had me hook, line and sinker. I was a goner, and I didn't surface until the novel's end. I may be in love.

– Page One Books

Faulkenberry creates a world of magic, suspense, and desire. An engrossing romance with just the right amount of heat!

- Julie C. Gardner, author of LETTERS FOR SCARLET

Also by Lauren Faulkenberry

The Bayou Sabine Series:

TROUBLE IN BAYOU SABINE

BACK TO BAYOU SABINE

BAYOU WHISPERS

JUST THE TROUBLE I NEEDED

Other Fiction:

BENEATH OUR SKIN and Other Stories

sign up for Lauren's author newsletter,

Writing Down South at laurenfaulkenberry.com and get a free book!

For my grandmothers, Jean and Lula Mae

Chapter One

IT'S hard to start a new life when you're living in a house full of ghosts.

My house, for example, used to be my grandmother Vergie's. Now that I was sharing it with Jack, I'd imagined that we'd make it into our own, and fill it with our own memories. I'd never loved anyone the way I loved him, and for the first time in a long while, it felt like I had a family again.

Making the house our own had turned out to be more difficult than I'd expected, though. Five months after moving all of my belongings here, I still couldn't break the habit of calling this house Vergie's. There were pieces of her everywhere.

This was also house my mother grew up in. The kitchen she'd had breakfast in, the clawfoot tub she'd used for baths. My mother was everywhere in this house, and I could barely remember her.

This wouldn't be so bad if my mother hadn't disappeared without a trace.

Being here in Bayou Sabine stirred up all kinds of feelings

for me, which sometimes felt like being tossed around in a hurricane. There were good memories attached to this place, too, but there was an awful lot of hurt and regret spliced into them. After inheriting Vergie's house, I'd expected to fix it up a little and sell it—and then never set foot in this town again.

But then I'd met Jack, and all of that had changed. He was like no man I'd ever met, who loved me fiercely, just as I was.

Because of him, I'd stuck around. Ghosts and all.

"Hey," Jack said. "You ready to head over?" He wore a thin plaid shirt and jeans that were snug in all the right places. I never got tired of seeing him in those.

"What's the hurry?" I said. "You got a hot date later?"

He flashed a mischievous grin and came closer, then nudged me against the kitchen counter. "I do," he said, placing his hands on my hips. "She's a total fox, and she hates it when I'm late." His lips moved against my ear as he spoke, and then they moved along my neck, and down to my collarbone.

And just that fast, my skin was tingling and I was less interested in staining floors.

"Maybe you should take the day off," I said, raking my hands through his hair. "Do something fun instead."

His hands slipped beneath my shirt, sliding along my waist. "I would, but my boss would have my hide. She rides my ass like you wouldn't believe."

I snorted. "I'm not your boss, and you know it."

He grinned. "Sure you are, you. And I like it." He kissed me hard on the lips and then said, "Come on, let's go finish those floors. Then we'll come back, have a hot shower, a nice dinner, and I'll let you wear me out all over again."

"I'm sorry. You'll *let* me?"

He smiled that crooked smile that had disarmed me the

moment we met. "I'll ask you very, very nicely." His hand was warm against the small of my back, pulling me against him.

Jack Mayronne was more tempting than the devil himself, with his chiseled body, cool blue eyes, and thick dark hair that was just this side of unruly. He had this particular way of gazing at me, full of mischief and want, that made my heart race.

He'd set that gaze on me when we'd first met, and I'd been a goner.

"Deal," I said, running my fingers through his hair. "But I'm going to need more coffee."

He reached into the cabinet behind me and grabbed two to-go mugs. "On it," he said. "I'll drive."

THE HOUSE JACK and I were renovating now was our third flip. The first had been Vergie's, and when I decided I wanted to stop working for my father and run my own house-flipping business, Jack had been one hundred percent supportive. Mostly because that meant I wasn't leaving him to return to North Carolina, but also because it meant I was working for myself now, and not my overbearing father. Jack had been working as a firefighter for a few years now, but he'd quickly learned he liked restoring houses, too. He liked to build and create, just like I did.

As it turned out, we made a solid team.

After selling my home in North Carolina, I'd used the money to invest in the second house we flipped. Jack's uncle and aunt—Buck and Josie—owned a hardware store in Bayou Sabine, and Buck had a hobby of building furniture out of salvaged wood. He also had enough friends around that he could find us things like original windows and carved doors that were being tossed out with new renovations. He could sniff out clawfoot tubs, stained glass windows and heart pine floorboards—beautiful pieces from historic houses that brought an extra level of uniqueness to our remodels.

Sometimes, those flips felt more like resurrection than renovation.

It was a good feeling, to save a home that had been left to die, to make it into something beautiful again. Not everything that was abandoned was garbage—but sometimes it took patience and a careful eye to see how it could be salvaged.

We'd made a good profit on the second house, and now we were working on our third—a cute river style home just on the outskirts of Bayou Sabine, situated on a small lot along one of the canals. I worked on the house almost every day, and Jack helped me on most of his days off from the fire station. We'd hoped to finish in a couple of months, but we were taking our time.

If nothing else, Jack was teaching me that I didn't always have to be in a hurry. He took his time with the house and did repairs the right way; he took his time with me and made my head spin. It wasn't a bad skill to have.

My favorite thing about the river house was the huge front porch with its tall shuttered windows. Along the front and spaced a couple of feet apart, they were eight feet high and opened out to a forty-five degree angle with poles in the bottoms to prop them open. The house was painted dove gray, the shutters a light blue. The inside was filled with dark-colored wood, and a second screened-in porch on the back faced the canal. Jack and I had already stripped the wallpaper and repainted, and Buck had replaced some broken banister rails and put up crown molding where it was missing. There wasn't much left to do on the house, so I expected our deadline to be a snap.

Once inside, Jack turned on the air conditioning so the floors would dry faster. It was always hot here, even in November. Thanksgiving was less than a week away, and I was still wearing shorts and a tank top.

Jack turned on the stereo and vacuumed the floor as I opened a can of stain and began to stir. It would take us all afternoon to stain the last of the floors, but I didn't mind—I'd finally found my place here, and found the things that I loved.

If only I could focus on them and make the ghosts go away.

Some night I still awoke with a start, drawing panicked breaths and clutching the sheets in my fists. Sometimes I dreamed of the night Vergie's house nearly burned down around me. Other times I dreamt of my mother, disappearing into the woods like a shadow. I always woke feeling empty and afraid.

Ghosts are persistent that way.

WHEN WE'D FINISHED the floors, Jack said, "You know, I had my doubts about this place at first, but now I see why you liked it so much."

Then sun was hanging low in the sky, settling in just over the canal. The big picture window in the living room had a perfect view, and the whole room was filled with golden light.

"You always see things that I don't," he said, slipping his arm around my waist.

"We just see different things," I said, running my fingers through his hair, and he smiled.

We left the air conditioning on and locked up, and then

climbed into his truck. As we headed back toward home, he said, "You thought any more about going home for Thanksgiving?" When he said *home*, he meant Raleigh, where my dad was. But now, this felt like home, and I didn't want to be anywhere else.

"Don't think I'm ready for that," I said. "Plus, I'd rather spend it with you."

He shrugged. "I could go with you to see your dad."

"That's like throwing yourself into a tiger cage. And besides, it would break Josie's heart if you were't here."

"She knows that might have to change someday." He smiled so his dimples showed.

Jack had spent every holiday with his aunt and uncle since he was ten. He'd never missed a Thanksgiving with them— they were basically like his parents. I'd spent most Thanksgivings with Dad, too, but this year would be different. It had been two months since I'd spoken to him. True to our bargain, I'd paid him back everything he'd loaned me to finish Vergie's house. My house in Raleigh hadn't brought as much as I'd hoped, but it was enough to pay off my debt and allow me to keep my other promise, too—the one I'd made to myself to quit working for my father and move here.

Those two things didn't sit well with him.

"You could invite him here," Jack said.

I laughed. "That's a recipe for complete disaster." We had plans to go to Buck and Josie's, along with Jack's best friend Andre. Plus, my best friend Kate was coming the next day. We'd only seen each other once since I've moved here in the summer, and she was dying to meet Jack and see my new life here.

Jack shrugged. "It might be good for him. And it would give me another chance to win him over."

"You do not need to impress my father." Their first meeting hadn't been a friendly one, and I wasn't ready to have another one yet.

"I know, but I'd like to at least meet him under normal circumstances."

"He was horrible to you," I said.

Jack shrugged. "He was worried about you, and he probably thought I was taking advantage. I'd like to show him otherwise."

He wasn't going to let this go.

"All right," I said. "I'll ask him. But I want our first holiday here to be a quiet one. No drama, no fighting, no flames on the sides of my face."

He smirked and reached over to squeeze my thigh, "Can't promise you that one. You know I like to bring a flush to your cheeks every now and then."

I snorted. "Jack Mayronne, you're relentless."

He grinned. "You love it."

We pulled into the drive, and as we got up to Vergie's house, I saw a young woman sitting on the porch. Jack's dog, Bella, sat right by her side, enjoying a head scratch. For a moment, I froze—the last time a strange woman had stood on this porch, it had been a disaster.

"Well, I'll be damned," Jack said, and hopped out of the truck like his feet were on fire.

Chapter Two

WHEN JACK GOT a few steps away from the truck, the woman jumped to her feet and ran towards him. She threw her arms around him and he laughed as he spun her around.

"I didn't think you were coming," he said, setting her down.

"Surprise," she said.

He stepped towards me and said, "Enza, this is Lucille. Buck and Josie's daughter." Lucille was tall and lean, with legs that went on forever. Her wavy red hair was cut into a stylish bob, and she wore skinny jeans and a tight tee shirt with the name of a bar I'd seen in the French Quarter.

At her feet, Bella pranced, wagging her bobbed tail. That dog hated to be ignored.

Lucille smiled and shook my hand. "Finally, I get to meet the mysterious Enza," she said. Her green eyes were bright. "I've heard a lot about you."

"Likewise," I said.

"Lucy's in grad school over at UT Austin," Jack said. "Full scholarship."

She looked embarrassed. "Yeah. I took a few years off to work and just started the arts management program last year."

"That's great," I said.

"It's pretty cool," she said. "I'm finishing up next semester. It's hard work, but it's the most fun I've ever had."

"Come on in," Jack said. "Catch us up."

She followed us as we walked up to the porch. Right by the door there was a big cardboard box addressed to me, the words written on it by hand, with a black marker.

"That's weird," I said, studying it as I unlocked the door.

Jack grunted as he lifted the box and carried it inside. "What'd you order, chère? Bricks?" He set it down on the kitchen table and then pulled three beers from the fridge.

"You've been busy," Lucille said. "This place looks great."

"I'll show you around," he said, and handed her a beer. He led her down the hall, going on about some of the repairs and additions we'd made with the house, including how the roofer had fallen through the ceiling.

Curious, I cut the box open. It had a handwritten return address in New Orleans, but no name. Inside, there was a pile of small books, some brightly colored fabric, and an envelope addressed to me.

Inside the envelope was a handwritten note.

Dear Enza-

These are some of Vergie's things. I thought you might like to have them. She spoke of you fondly, and often. I almost brought these to you myself, but I didn't want to intrude. She thought the world of you.

George

Carefully, I emptied the contents onto the table. There were a dozen small leather-bound books, a few novels, an old 35 mm film camera, a small jewelry box, and two brightly colored floral scarves.

"What's all that?" Jack said, leaning against the doorframe.

"The man Vergie lived with—his name was George?"

"Yeah," he said. "That's right."

"He mailed a box of her things."

His brow arched. "Oh?"

The books were filled with Vergie's small cursive handwriting. "These are more of her journals." A photo and a postcard slipped out of the book, and I glanced at them before placing them back inside.

"Wow," he said, picking up one of the journals. "That was nice of him."

Lucille bounded into the kitchen, Bella at her heels. "Hey," she said. "Want to go grab something at Brenda's? I'm starved."

Jack glanced at me over her shoulder and I gave him a tiny shrug. It was clear what he was thinking: *so much for our date night and all those wicked plans.*

"Come on," she said, grabbing his arm. "You can meet Toph."

"I thought he wasn't coming." Jack's tone suggested he'd have preferred it that way.

She shrugged. "He changed his mind." She nudged his arm, teasing, until he relented.

"Okay," Jack said. "Sure."

"Great!" She slipped her phone from her pocket and walked out onto the porch as she dialed.

"Sorry," he whispered to me. "Raincheck on that quiet dinner?"

"Sure," I said. "She's excited to see you. And now there's a mystery guest."

He rolled his eyes. "He's not much of a mystery, from what I hear."

"Come on, she wants you to meet her new boyfriend. She wants you to like him."

"She's known this guy for like, five minutes."

"How'd you feel about me after you'd known me for five minutes?"

His brow arched and he fixed his big blue eyes on mine. "That's exactly what I'm afraid of."

BRENDA'S RESTAURANT was just a few miles down the road, nestled in a grove of trees. If you didn't know it was there, it was difficult to find. It was clapboard on the outside, with a big porch on the front that held a few tables and rocking chairs. Inside, it was crammed with tables and booths, with a diner-stye counter at the front. Brenda had already strung twinkling lights up all around the windows and hung paper snowflakes from the ceiling. People around here decorated early and often, and took their celebrating seriously.

Jack, Lucille, and I sat at a booth in the back. It was quiet tonight, with some of the regulars spread out through the room. If it were Saturday, it would be packed. Jack had proudly told me that Brenda served the best gator tail in all of Louisiana, and her prize-winning pecan pie was nothing to sneeze at, either.

"He said he was on his way," Lucille said, checking her phone.

Jack furrowed his brow, sipping his beer. "Who's this guy again?"

"Be nice," Lucille said.

He smirked. "We'll see."

Frowning, she said, "He probably just got lost. It's not hard to do out here."

Bayou Sabine was about half an hour from New Orleans, if you drove fast, but it was out on a two-lane highway that felt like it was leading you to the middle of nowhere. When I'd arrived back in the summer, I'd been certain the GPS was sending me clear off the edge of the earth.

Buck and Josie's house was just a ten minute drive from our place, and Brenda's was a couple of miles further down the road. Once it got dark around here, though, it was like being inside an ink bottle. The narrow roads ran like ribbons through the swamps and cypress groves, and I'd made plenty of wrong turns when I was still learning my way around.

Lucille's phone buzzed and she checked the screen. "He's outside." She stood up from the table and waved toward the door until the man she was watching headed our way.

He wore a button-down shirt with the sleeves rolled to his elbows, jeans with that expensive kind of excessive stitching on the pockets, and boat shoes that looked like they'd never seen a dock. His hair was restrained by some sort of pomade and was molded like a Ken doll's. He looked older than Lucille —thirty-five or so, and had a lean build. When he rested his hand on the back of the booth, I saw a watch on his wrist that likely cost more than my annual car insurance.

He also looked dissatisfied.

"Enza, Jack," Lucille said, "this is Toph."

He shook my hand, squeezing it too tightly, and flashed a

too-big smile with too-white teeth. After shaking Jack's hand, he sat in the booth next to Lucille. His eyes darted past us, around the corners of the room, like he couldn't decide what to focus on.

"Toph's from Dallas," she said. "But he's working in Austin now."

"What do you do?" I asked him.

"This and that," he said, his eyes shifting back to me. "Mostly investment in startups."

"Toph's into entertainment and media," Lucille said. "He also writes scripts."

"Screenplays, babe," he corrected.

"He's got one under consideration with an agent right now," she said.

Jack sipped his beer, his eyes narrowed. It didn't take him long to size a person up.

"How interesting," I said. If Jack wasn't going to say anything, I felt like I had to.

"He's super talented," Lucille said.

"I don't need talent," Toph said, smirking. "I just need friends in the right places. And enough people who owe me favors. Luckily, I have both."

Lucille said, "Toph got me this awesome job with the city theater. They weren't hiring, but somehow he convinced them to give me a chance. Seems like he knows somebody everywhere."

"I'm going to get a drink," Toph said, standing. "Since it seems we don't have a waitress."

When he stalked towards the bar, Lucille sighed. "He's just cranky from the drive. We drove straight through and traffic was horrible. Apparently I woke him from a nap, but I wanted him to meet you before the big dinner."

Jack muttered something about manners as he sipped his beer. Lucille shot him a warning look.

"What?" he said, daring her to press him.

"How long are you staying?" I asked her.

"Just a few days," she said. "I've got a week long break, but Toph has to be in Dallas for the weekend."

"You're going with him?" Jack said. "Thought you hated big metro areas with rush hour traffic."

She shrugged. "I'm trying to get used to it."

Jack's brow furrowed, as if he didn't like that implication.

When Toph came back to the table, he had a tumbler with a clear drink and a lime floating on top.

Lucille eyed him, as if that were unusual, and he said, "They didn't have Macallan's."

She snorted. "Honey, nobody drinks that around here. The 18 would be 30 by the time Brenda sold the whole bottle."

He squeezed the lime into his drink and scanned the room, as if taking in every detail.

Jack stared at Toph, as if doing the same.

Lucille managed to tie the conversation together through the course of our meal. It was artful for sure, since she was stuck with Toph, who was trying—and failing—to be charming, and Jack, who was studying his every move and taking notes that he'd no doubt tell me about later. It wasn't hard to imagine what was rolling around in his head—Jack had no patience for pretentiousness.

Things Jack would dislike: Toph was twelve years older than Lucille; Toph's family were bazillionaires who made their fortune in oil; Toph squeezed Lucille's thigh under the table in a way that was showy and possessive.

Things he would like: Toph was leaving in seven days.

When dinner was over, Toph grabbed the check and said,

"Please, I insist." He slipped a gold credit card into the tray with the bill and winked at me in that way that usually means you're being had.

Jack didn't miss that, either.

"Be right back," Toph said, and headed toward the restrooms in the back.

As soon as he was out of earshot, Lucille said to Jack, "Come on, cut him some slack. He's been driving all day and met my entire family in the span of three hours." She nudged his leg under the table until his lip curved up with a hint of a smile.

"I'm just trying to keep him on his best behavior," Jack said.

"Jesus, you sound like Dad."

Jack smirked, finishing his beer. "I'm sorry, Luce, but you know that no man will ever live up to my standards for you. Especially some dude in skinny jeans."

She looked at me and said, "He's hopeless. How do you stand this?"

BY THE TIME we got back to our house, it was nearly eleven. Toph had followed us in his car—a sporty red BMW that looked brand new. Lucille hopped out and waved to us as she climbed into Josie's little Honda that she'd driven here earlier, and then led him back to the highway.

"What on earth does she see in that guy?" Jack said. "I was hoping he'd be a quick phase, like that time she dyed her hair blue."

"He seemed a little aloof, but maybe he's just nervous about meeting her family."

"He's an entitled little prick." Jack's big brother status meant he could hate him just for being the guy who was dating the girl he thought of as his sister.

"Lucille seems like a smart woman," I said. "He must be doing something to make her happy."

"I'd rather not think about those particulars." He leaned against the kitchen counter, his arms crossed over his chest.

I laughed. "I mean, like the job she's so excited about."

Frowning, he said, "The last thing she needs is to be indebted to a guy like that."

Jack was protective of Lucille in ways I'd been envious of my whole life. Part of me had always wanted a sibling, one who would look out for me the way he did with her. One who would never leave me.

"People have to learn in their own ways," I said. "You just have to trust her to make her own decisions."

He sighed. "I still think he's a prick."

"Fair enough. You don't have to like him."

"But I do have to sit through Thanksgiving dinner and not stab him with a fork."

"That would be my preference, yes." I leaned against him, running my fingers through his hair. "Now do you want to keep talking about Toph, or is there something more fun you'd like to do?"

He smirked as I wrapped my arms around his neck, pressing my body against his.

"I can think of a few things," he said, lifting me up onto the counter. His hands slipped under my shirt and pressed into my back as I wrapped my legs around his waist to pull him closer.

He kissed me, gently at first, and then caught my lip in his teeth in that way that he knew drove me completely wild. "I've been wanting to do this all day," he said, nuzzling my neck. His lips slid along my collarbone as he tugged at my hair.

"I should take a shower," I said. "I'm covered in stain and sawdust."

"I don't care." He pulled my tee shirt over my head and tossed it to the floor.

I laughed, feeling the roughness of his stubbled cheek against my neck. It was one of my favorite feelings in the world. "Want to join me?"

His fixed his eyes on mine and slipped his hands inside the waistband of my jeans. "Um, naturally."

There was a wicked flash in his eyes and then he scooped me up and carried me across the hall to his bedroom, his arms squeezing me tight against him.

He sat me on the bed and said, "Stay," and then unbuttoned his shirt as he went into the bathroom. I slipped out of my jeans as the shower came on, and when he appeared again, he'd stripped naked.

I never got tired of drinking in the sight of Jack Mayronne: six foot two inches of chiseled muscle, dark hair that always seemed perfectly tousled and always a hint of a five o'clock shadow. He had an intense gaze and a rakish smile that still melted me to the floor—and he knew it. It should be a crime to be that gorgeous.

"You are an absolute goddess," he said. "And I'm the luckiest man alive."

When I stood and kissed him, he leaned his body into mine and pulled me tight against him, his big hands squeezing my hips.

He nudged me towards the shower and said, "Last chance

before your friend gets here and we have to be on *our* best behavior. Better make it count."

"Who said anything about behaving? Kate travels with noise cancelling headphones."

He grinned as he pulled me into the hot spray, and then his hands and lips were everywhere, and I was lost.

IT WAS after lunch the next day when I heard Kate's car coming down the gravel lane. A cloud of dust followed her little black Audi as it curled along the meadow, and I stepped out on the porch to greet her.

"Good grief," she said, climbing out. "The damned GPS tried to send me straight into a swamp. Thought I was gator food for sure." She pulled a suitcase out of the backseat and trudged through the grass in a pair of impossibly high wedges. Kate was my best friend and had been since college. We agreed on a lot of things, but fashion was not one of them. Kate loved swishy skirts and high heels, and always had a trendy haircut that showed off her high cheekbones. She regularly experimented with hair color, but this time it was back to its natural blonde shade, cut just above her shoulders. She'd tried to make me appreciate fashion for the last ten years, but I preferred my vintage cowboy boots, tank tops and jeans. The most girly thing I could muster was some pale lipstick and a flat iron every now and then.

"That can't be the only bag you have," I said, nodding toward the tiny suitcase.

She rolled her eyes. "Oh please. This is overflow from the trunk."

She set the suitcase on the steps and hugged me, tighter

than she had in a long time. "Look at this house!" she shrieked. "It's adorable."

The old Victorian was the typical four-on-four style with a porch that stretched the entire length of the front. The master bedroom, bath, and living room were in the front, with a hall straight down the middle and the kitchen and study in the back. The kitchen had a back door and walk-in pantry that had some of the loveliest woodwork in the whole house. The upstairs had four big rooms and a small bathroom. We'd kept one as a guest bedroom, and the others we were still figuring out: Jack liked having a room just for his things, and I needed a room that was mine.

"I'm so glad you're here," I said.

She grinned. Her big vintage Ray-Ban sunglasses covered half her face. "You twisted my arm."

It hadn't been hard. She'd called me a few weeks before, swearing like a sailor because her jerk of a fiance had cheated on her and she'd kicked him out of her house.

"I just can't handle Thanksgiving with my family," she'd said. "My mom hated Benjamin and I'll never hear the end of this. She's like a dog on a bone."

"Then come see me," I'd told her. "Give yourself a vacation."

Kate never took vacations. She had a demanding job at one of the top research labs in Research Triangle Park. She was always on the verge of a breakthrough, and she felt like if she left that lab, someone else would make the discovery and she'd lose her place of honor in the pecking order. The lab where she worked rewarded ingenuity and efficiency, and there was always pressure to be better at both. She had enough vacation days accrued to stay here two weeks, but she wouldn't stay that long. Kate thought guests had an expiration date. For me, that rule didn't apply to friends, and sometimes I managed to convince her of it.

Also, she really loved her job. Sometimes I thought she liked looking through a microscope more than anything else. Studying patterns and behaviors was fascinating to her—whether they were human or microbial.

I grabbed her bag. "Come in. I'll make you a drink and show you around." She'd love seeing the house's features and all the work we'd done, but it was a long, boring drive from Raleigh, and I knew she'd be exhausted.

In the kitchen, I introduced her to Jack.

"Glad to have you with us," he said, shaking her hand.

"It's good to meet you for real this time." She smiled, nearly eye-level with him in her heels. Her gray eyes sparkled.

She'd met Jack briefly at Vergie's funeral, before I'd even met him. She'd teased me the rest of that weekend about the sexy man in the pale gray suit. It was one of those slim-cut tailored suits that hugged his shoulders and his hips in the most tantalizing way. When I'd told Jack about that later, he'd laughed and said, "I only wear a suit about twice a year, but if you like it that much, I'll wear it more often."

When he did, I thought, I'd be sure to trace my fingers over every single seam until he could barely breathe.

KATE and I sat on the porch swing for a long time, drinking vodka tonics and watching the clouds drift across the sky. From the porch, we had a clear view of the lagoon at the edge of the cypresses. The house was on a five-acre lot, which meant we had lots of solitude and no close neighbors.

Kate had piled her honey-blond hair high up on her head

and changed into a pair of jeans and a blouse. "Thanks for letting me stay with you," she said after a while.

"You know you're welcome anytime. Besides, it's been forever and you needed to get away."

"Understatement of the year." She held the glass against her face. She and Benjamin been going out a year and had set a date for May. A week ago, Kate had found his cell phone in a coat pocket, dead, and plugged it in to recharge it for him. The screen had lit up with a string of unread text messages from another woman he was seeing, and Kate had confronted him.

Benjamin wasn't the smartest man she'd ever dated.

He'd denied everything, but he couldn't make up enough lies to convince her she was wrong. Kate was a biologist, an observer of behavior patterns. It killed her to think she hadn't been able to see his.

"Why didn't you tell me I was being stupid?" she said, halfway through her third vodka.

"Because you weren't being stupid."

She grimaced, squeezing the lime into her drink. "A year was too soon to get engaged. I should have made him pay for the deposits on the vineyard and the cake."

"He's the one who was stupid. Let's get that straight."

She raised her glass. "Maybe I'll still get the cake. Chocolate raspberry. It was like heaven on a fork."

"Not all behaviors are predictable," I said. "You know that."

"I just feel like the worst cliché ever."

"He's the cliché."

"Maybe I'll just stick with single-celled organisms for a while."

I leaned back in the porch swing, feeling tipsy. "I never

really liked him anyway. He winked too much, like a car salesman."

"Enza Parker," she said, tossing her lime at me. "You said you liked him."

"You're practically my sister. You loved him. What did you expect me to say?"

"You should have told me," she said. "You're like a bomb-sniffing dog. I'd have listened to you."

"Kate," I said, resting my hand on her arm. "It was only important that you liked him. I figured whatever you saw that made him so wonderful, I'd see it someday, too."

She turned away, staring out into the field. Although the humidity lingered, the air was starting to turn chilly. "I thought I was past this part of my life," she said at last. "I thought I'd seen all the patterns and learned how to weed out the liars and the cheaters."

"I know you did. But you can't blame yourself. We've all had that one person who managed to find our blind spot and take advantage. And that's what he did—he took advantage of your trust."

"He totally blindsided me," she said. "But that's nature—full of surprises, always eager to humble us when we think we have her figured out."

"I can't argue with that."

"My mother used to tell me I should never get married. She told me I had expectations of loyalty that no man could live up to. Maybe I should take her advice."

"Mothers don't always have the answers," I said, but part of me thought I shouldn't get married either. My parents' marriage had ended in disaster. My mother had walked out and straight up disappeared, and my father refused to talk about her, even to this day.

Kate gazed out over the field, sipping her drink. It was impossible to read her mind, because her face so rarely revealed her thoughts.

"Do you ever wonder?" she said at last. "Do you ever want to find her?"

Back in the summer, I'd told her about the letters and journals I'd found in Vergie's closet. Most of them were from decades ago, when Vergie was in her twenties—they didn't span the period of time when my mother left us. As a teen, I'd been desperate to know where my mother had ended up. Coming back here for Vergie's funeral in the spring had dredged that up again, and I'd been overcome with curiosity. Had my mother kept up with Vergie after all this time? Could she have been at the funeral? She could live nearby, and I'd have no idea. She could bump into me at the grocery store, at the library, at a gas station. The thought of her being so close, and yet still outside of my orbit made me ache with sorrow. On that gloomy day in the church, it had occurred to me that she could be there, too—and though I'd spent years imagining what I'd say to her if I ever saw her, I'd had a full on panic attack and run outside into a raging thunderstorm. I'd have rather been struck by lightning than see her there.

It was easier to picture her long gone, living in another country halfway around the world. Because if she had been just a few states away from me all this time and had never reached out to find me, I wasn't sure I could forgive her for that. Had she kept up with me all these years somehow? Did she know I went to college, worked for my father? I needed to know if she had cut me out of her life completely, or if she had watched me from afar, scared and sad and unsure of how to be a part of my life again.

These choices mattered. If she hadn't cared enough to look

for me, then I didn't want to meet her again. But I did want to know what had happened to her. I wanted to see the life she had, the one she'd traded us to find.

"Sometimes," I said. The truth was, I wished I didn't want to find her. I wanted to not care anymore, to not wonder where she was, why she left, what she was like. But as hard as I tried to bury those thoughts, they still gnawed at me, down deep where I couldn't always reach. Though I desperately wanted to rip them from my head, like weeding a garden, it didn't work that way.

I didn't tell Kate about the box of things that George had sent over. She'd want to dig through them, like we had a mystery to solve—and I wasn't ready for that.

"Maybe you should find her," Kate said. "Just get it over with, and then you wouldn't wonder anymore."

"Some things might be better left unknown."

"Imagine my marriage with Benjamin if I hadn't found out he was cheating on me. The unknown never helped anybody. Trust me on that. I'm a scientist."

LATER, when Kate was sound asleep in the guest room upstairs, I slipped into my own bedroom downstairs, where Jack lay with his back toward me. Quietly, I stripped out of my clothes and settled into bed next to him. He rolled over and draped his arm around my waist, pulling me against him.

No matter how quiet I was, I always woke him.

"You two have a nice chat?" he mumbled, half asleep.

"Yeah."

"Figured I should make myself scarce, given the circumstances with her ex."

My head still buzzed from the alcohol. "Oh, please. She likes you. And I think you'll like her, too."

"I don't doubt that. I just figure right about now she's wishing there were four billion less of us fellas around."

Sliding my hand over his, I said, "She liked you from the get-go, remember?"

He muttered something I couldn't quite make out. He was drifting off again.

For a while I lay there thinking about what Kate had said. Why had I been so afraid of bumping into my mother at Vergie's funeral? For a ghost, she took up a lot of space in my mind. My memories felt fragmented, but being here made them keep trying to resurface. Now that Kate was here, I kept thinking back to the funeral, the way the little gray-haired lady had said I looked just like my mother, then said something like *It's been so long.* It made me wonder where she'd seen my mother last and how long ago. What if my mother really did live close to here? What would I do if that were true? If she was easier to find than I'd ever imagined?

My stomach clenched, and everything inside me seemed to squeeze tighter.

Easing out of the bed, I tiptoed out of the bedroom and down the hall to the study, where I'd left the journals that George sent.

The box contained sixteen diaries, all different sizes. Most were leather bound, but a few looked handmade with decorated papers. Opening to the first page of each one, I placed them in a pile in chronological order. There was a bundle of letters in the box, too, held together with a rubber band. Quickly, I sifted through them and arranged them in order by postmark. Some had no return address, but they were all addressed to Vergie.

They were all the same handwriting—a tiny cursive. When I opened the top one, I saw *Dear Mama*, and then flipped the page over to see the signature.

Martine.

My mother had written these letters to Vergie, and the one in my hand was dated the year before she left us.

For a long while, I stared at the stack of letters, trying to decide if I wanted to dive down this rabbit hole. If there were any clues to find about my mother's whereabouts—or about why she left me—I'd find them here.

Once I went down this road, there would be no going back.

Chapter Three

WHEN JACK ANSWERED HIS PHONE, his eyes widened in that way that meant something terrible was happening.

"What's wrong?" I said. It was seven-fifteen, and I was barely awake. Nothing good ever came from an early Sunday morning phone call.

He sat up in bed, placing his hand on my shoulder and I strained to hear the voice on the other end of the call.

"All right," he said into the phone. "I'm on my way. Sit tight."

He ended the call and said, "It's Buck. Josie said he fell off a ladder trying to clean out the gutters." He pulled on his jeans and grabbed a shirt from the nearest chair.

"I'll go with you," I said, reaching for the tee shirt and jeans I'd worn the day before. "Are they at the hospital?"

He snorted. "She'd have to hog-tie him for that. She thinks he just hurt his arm, but I'll go check him over and make sure it's not serious."

Because he worked as a firefighter, Jack was also an EMT.

He'd patched up all of his friends and family members more times than he could count.

When we went into the kitchen, there was no sign of Kate. No coffee brewing, which meant she was still sleeping.

"I hate to wake her," I said. She'd been exhausted from the drive and the late night.

"Just text her," he said, grabbing his keys and his first aid bag. "We won't be there long."

"She sleeps with that phone right by her head. It'll wake her." Instead, I scribbled a note telling her we were at Josie and Buck's and left it right by the coffee maker. No way she'd miss that.

As we hurried out the door and down the porch steps, Bella sat up and whined from her spot under the porch swing.

"Sorry girl," Jack said "Breakfast when we get back, I promise."

She huffed and lay back down.

We climbed into his truck and sped down the road, Jack going just a few miles over the speed limit. He was concerned but not frantic. Jack Mayronne hardly ever lost his cool.

WHEN WE GOT to Buck and Josie's, Buck was sitting on the sofa amongst a pile of throw pillows.

"Thanks for coming over," Josie said, intercepting us. "He's mad as a wet hen, and I think his arm might be broken, but he won't let me take him to the hospital." She hugged me while Jack made a beeline for Buck.

"You want some coffee, hon?" she said. "I just made a fresh pot." Her short gray hair, usually in a sleek bob, was tousled, her reading glasses pushed up into her hair.

"Sure," I said. "Thank you."

In the living room, Jack was taking Buck's blood pressure, checking his pulse.

"This is all unnecessary," Buck said. His glasses sat crooked on his face, one of the nose pads broken. There was a small bruise forming under his left eye.

"Just a precaution, Pop," Jack said, his voice calm.

"I told him to wait until I could help him," Josie told me. "But he insisted on getting up there early, before it got too hot. I was getting dressed and heard a crash, and went out there and found him on the ground. He said he got dizzy and fell right off."

"You able to walk OK?" Jack asked him.

"Sure," Buck grumbled. "Same as usual."

"Did you hit your head?"

"Don't think so."

"Did you black out?"

"No," he said, squinting his eyes. "I think I just felt a little light headed, and then I was on the ground."

He had a few scratches and bruises on his face and hands, which Jack had begun to clean with antiseptic.

"The only thing that hurts is my arm," Buck said. He was shaped like a pot-bellied stove, sturdy and stout. He got around good for sixty-eight, and seemed to be as tough as nails. He'd been helping us with repairs at the river house when he wasn't at the hardware store. Like Josie, he liked to keep himself busy—neither one of them could stand to sit still for long.

When Jack touched his arm, Buck winced.

Jack carefully moved his arm at the elbow and and pressed his fingers against his forearm. I could see some bruises and scrapes from where I stood in the doorway to the kitchen.

"I think it's broken," Jack said. "It's starting to swell. Maybe just a fracture, but you should go get x-rays. Maybe a cast."

Josie sighed, shaking her head. "Stubborn old goat."

Buck started to argue and Jack said, "Come on. I'll drive you. We'll get in and out in no time."

"I'm going, too," Josie said, grabbing her purse. "We can take my car."

We all piled into Josie's little Honda crossover, Jack and me in the front, and Josie fussing over Buck in the back. She'd brought a throw pillow for him to prop is arm on and was examining his glasses we pulled out of the driveway.

FIVE HOURS LATER, Buck had a cast and a sling and was back in his recliner at home. He had a prescription for pain medication and strict instructions to keep his arm immobilized and stay off of ladders.

"Thanks for coming," Josie said. "I don't think I could have gotten him to go by myself."

Jack hugged her and said, "Call us if you need anything."

She nodded, walking us to the door. "I just hate this happened. I feel like I need to watch him all the time because of these dizzy spells."

"It's happened before?" Jack said. He sounded worried.

"A few times," she said, keeping her voice low, and one eye on Buck in the living room. "But this is the first time he's fallen because of it."

Jack sighed. "I wish you'd told me."

She shrugged. "It's just part of getting old, chèrie. We don't want to worry you about every little thing that breaks down in these old bodies."

He frowned. "That one's sort of important." He hugged her again and said, "Please don't keep these things from me. Let me know how I can help. "

She nodded. "We'll be fine. Lucy can help us while she's here."

We were supposed to all get together for Thanksgiving dinner in just a few days, but now that would be a hardship on both Josie and Buck. Buck had been boasting about this new turkey recipe he was going to try, but no one wants to cook with a broken arm.

"Josie," I said. "Why don't you let us do dinner at our house? Then you and Buck can take it easy. You don't have to worry about a bunch of people being over here underfoot. You can keep an eye on Buck, and he can rest."

She glanced at him, now snoozing in the recliner.

"Yeah," Jack said. "Let's do it at our place. Come stay as long as you like, and when y'all get tired of us, you can leave and not have to worry about a house to clean up."

"You don't need to go to all that trouble," she said, but her mouth was drawn in a way that seemed like she was just saying what she thought she ought to.

"It's no trouble," I said. "We'd love to do it. We want to help."

She looked back at Jack and said to me, "OK, sweetie. That sounds really good." She hugged me then, her arms tight around me.

∾

As JACK and I turned onto the gravel lane that led to our house, I was startled to see blue lights flashing by the porch.

"Jack," I said. My chest tightened as I thought of the last time there had been flashing lights in this yard.

Those nightmares still haunted me.

Jack slowed the truck, his brow furrowed as we approached the house.

"Is that Andre's truck too?" I asked.

He nodded. Jack's best friend, Andre, was the sheriff, but he hadn't come in his patrol car. His red pickup truck was parked under the big oak tree by the porch. A police cruiser was parked several yards from it, the driver's door open.

"Wait here," Jack said.

I felt sick to my stomach, thinking of Kate inside. I'd called our landline from the hospital when she didn't reply to my texts. When she hadn't answered, I'd assumed she was sleeping in.

"No way," I said, grabbing his arm. "You're not going in there until we know what's going on."

Jack pointed toward the back of the house, where another officer held his arm up in greeting as he approached us. Jack waved out the window in response. "I think it's all right," Jack said. "That's Frankie." He climbed out and walked up to the porch before I could protest again.

When Jack shook the man's hand and smiled, it was clear that nothing serious had happened. I got out of the truck and walked over to them, curious.

"Enza," Jack said, this is Frankie."

Frankie, a tall Black man with wayfarer glasses, looked about twenty-five. He also looked like he could body slam Batman. The sleeves of his uniform shirt stretched tight across his biceps. He smiled, revealing perfect white teeth.

"Nice to meet you, Enza," he said, shaking my hand a bit too hard. "Sorry if we alarmed you. There was just a little misunderstanding. Everybody else is inside."

I bolted up the porch steps and into the house, Jack following close behind.

"Kate!" I called. "Where are you? What happened?"

The living room was empty, and the study, too. I hollered for her again, running though the hall and into the kitchen. By the sink, Andre was standing with a towel pressed to his forehead. A trickle of blood ran down his jaw. A drop of red splashed onto the white porcelain of the sink, and I felt my stomach twist into a knot, thinking of the last time there had been blood on that porcelain, filling the grooves of the old built-in counter top.

I felt like I might faint.

"Andre," I said, taking a step toward him. "What happened? Where's Kate?"

His lip turned up with a hint of a smile. He pulled the dishcloth away from his head to reveal a small cut at his hairline, the blood dappling his copper-colored hair. "She's fine," he said, sounding amused. "She locked herself in the bathroom after she tried to kill me."

From behind me, Jack asked, "What's going on?"

Andre ran some water on the cloth and wiped the side of his face, cringing when he saw the blood. "I came to borrow that fishing gear, and you weren't here," he said. "It looked like nobody else was either, so I let myself in."

"Oh no," Jack said. "I forgot you were coming." He pulled a chair out from the table and sat.

"When I went upstairs to get the gear," Andre said, "I quickly surmised that the house was not, in fact, empty when your friend walked out of the bathroom, um, not in her Sunday finest."

I chewed my lip. Poor Kate.

"I tried to explain I was a friend of yours, but she threw her hair dryer at me and then locked herself in the bathroom and called 911. Which is why Frankie's here."

Jack ran his hands through his hair, muttering something in patois. It was an endearing habit, though it meant he was annoyed. He rested his elbows on the dark wood of the table. "And?"

"I called dispatch on my cell and gave them my badge number," Andre said, "but they sent him over anyway. Strict policy." He sighed, folding the cloth neatly and placing it on the edge of the basin. "It's better for her they sent him over. I was having difficulty convincing her I wasn't an intruder."

Andre was just about six feet tall and built like a tank, with reddish-brown hair that, today, looked like he'd carefully sculpted it to look like bed-head. Wearing his plaid shirt and broken in jeans, he didn't exactly look like law enforcement. His stubbled beard and piercing eyes made him look more like a Viking. It was no surprise that Kate had panicked.

She was no doubt mortified.

Outside, the siren made one clipped sound, and the car door slammed. Tires crunched on the gravel as Frankie drove away.

"Your friend has excellent aim," Andre said to me, smiling. "A good arm too. And inch or two to the left, and she'd have broken my nose."

I went upstairs and knocked on the bathroom door. "Kate, are you in there?"

"Are you alone?" she said, her voice low.

"Yeah, just me."

She unlocked the door and pushed it partway open so I could slip inside. Behind her, the curtain in the open window rippled in the breeze.

Kate sat on the edge of the clawfoot tub, now wearing a silk bathrobe. One foot was planted on the blue and white tiles while she swung the other like a pendulum. Her lean arms were crossed tightly over her chest.

"Oh, honey," I said. "I'm sorry."

"That guy's really a friend of yours?"

"Andre," I said. "Jack's best friend. He's a good guy."

"He's an asshat. He barged in here and scared the shit out of me."

"I'm sure he didn't mean to. He said he came to borrow Jack's fishing gear."

"So he just walked right in without knocking?"

"He has a key. He thought we were gone, and Jack had forgotten he was coming today."

She glared at me.

"Nice aim though. He was impressed."

She snorted. "Guess he reminded me of Benjamin. Did he leave yet?"

"He's still tending to his wounds."

"Serves him right." She relaxed then, resting her hands on the edge of the tub. "Where were you anyway?" she said.

"I didn't want to wake you. You were so exhausted." I put my hand over hers. "Buck had an accident and we took him to the hospital. He's all right, but he's got a broken arm."

"Jesus," she said.

"I texted you to tell you we were there."

"I guess I missed it," she said. "I slept in and then took a long bath. And then I heard someone in the house, and then I had a damn heart attack."

"I'm so sorry. I feel terrible."

She shrugged, then said, "I mean, I'll never see him again, right?"

"He's Jack's best friend. Also, he's the sheriff."

She groaned. "Of course he is."

"And he's coming for Thanksgiving."

She snorted. "Of course he is."

"Why don't you get dressed and come meet him," I said. "You'll see, he's not a bad guy."

"No way," she said, cinching the robe tighter. "Forget it."

I went over to the door and said, "Come on. Get dressed, and come downstairs. This'll be funny after a beer or two."

"Easy for you to say. He didn't see you buck naked."

IN THE KITCHEN, Andre was still leaning against the cabinets, one hand resting on the expanse of white counter, as if he were holding himself up. He still held a towel to his head.

Jack, still sitting at the dining table, said to Andre, "I'd offer you a beer, but it'd probably just make you bleed faster."

"Can't believe she got the drop on me," Andre said. "Must be slipping."

"In my experience, a beautiful woman can always get the drop on you." Jack turned to me and smiled.

I took a couple of tiny butterfly bandages over to Andre and ordered him to sit. "Is that any way to welcome my guest?" I asked him, teasing. His cheeks turned pink and I said, "Are you blushing, Andre Dufresne?"

"It's the head wound."

Behind him, Jack smirked.

Outside, a cloud floated away from the sun, and the room

instantly filled with light. Jack and I had repainted it pale yellow with white cabinets, thinking it would brighten things up and compensate for having only one window by the table. Now he teased me, saying, "Every time I go to make my morning coffee, I expect to hear angels' trumpets and see Saint Peter frying up some beignets."

I'd secretly hoped the bright light would make me more of a morning person. So far, it had not.

Andre sat in one of the old wooden chairs at the table and let me dab some antiseptic on his wound. It didn't look like it needed stitches, and the bleeding had nearly stopped. I sat on the edge of the sturdy oak table, tilting his head toward the light. He flinched when I touched the cut.

"Sorry about all this," he said. "I didn't know you had company. I should go up and apologize now that she knows I'm not a criminal."

"Give her a few minutes," I said, putting the bandages on. I wiped the rest of the blood from his cheek and frowned at the cloth. "You owe me a new tea towel."

After a while, Kate came downstairs wearing jeans and a blue gingham shirt, an outfit I rarely saw her in, and one that signaled she was on vacation. From her spot in the doorway, she glared at Andre.

He stood abruptly, nearly knocking his chair over.

She looked angelic, standing in the glowing pastel of the kitchen—but she also looked like she wanted to throw something heavier than a hair dryer at Andre. He gave her a look I'd never seen from him, though, like a calf in a hailstorm, and her face softened.

"So," Kate said, "this is going to be awkward for a minute, but since Enza tells me y'all are such good friends, I figure we might as well get the uncomfortable part over as quickly as possible. She assures me our future selves will laugh about this at some point. My current self would like to hurry up and become my future self, so we can put all of this awkwardness away." She waved her hand in the space between them, in a circular motion that seemed to indicate all particles of awkwardness floating among us.

Andre stared at her slack-jawed, then glanced away as if he didn't quite know where to rest his eyes. He looked as fidgety as a kid on his first date.

She looked at me and said, "Didn't you say you had beer?"

Jack went to the fridge, trying to hide his smile as he pulled out a bottle and opened it for her.

Kate took a long drink and then raised one eyebrow at Andre and crossed her arms over her chest.

"I'm really sorry I scared you, jolie," Andre said at last. "I thought the house was empty." Right then, I'd have never taken him for a sheriff. His eyebrows had a sad little arch to them, and his big green eyes were as wide and warm as a puppy's.

"Didn't you ever hear of knocking?" she said.

"I did knock, but obviously it wasn't loud enough."

"Well," she said, taking a beer from Jack. "I'm sorry I clocked you with the hair dryer. It's salon quality."

"It's OK. I'm sorry I saw you—you know."

"Without a stitch."

He blushed all the way down past the collar of his shirt. I'd never seen Andre Dufresne this flustered. Ever.

Jack handed me a beer and gave me a look that said he was just as taken aback by all of this as I was.

"Indeed," Andre said. "If it makes any difference, though, you were kind of a blur."

A tiny smile touched her lips. "Hmm. If you say so."

He held his hand out to her and said, "Bygones, then?"

She shook his hand, and I could have sworn his face lit up from her touch.

"Bygones," she said.

"See?" I said. "That wasn't too awkward."

Andre and Kate exchanged a look, but he still couldn't hold her gaze for long.

He leaned against the counter and said to Jack, "Want to come out on the lake with me for a while, or do you go on duty tonight?"

"I just finished a week of training," Jack said. "Got a couple extra days off this rotation."

"We can just go out back," Andre said. "Ladies, if we catch anything, we'll fry it up for dinner."

"What do you mean 'if'?" Jack said.

"Great," I said. "Kate, I need to check on the floors in the house we're flipping. Want to come?"

"Absolutely." She drained the rest of her beer and gave Andre one last long look as we headed out to the car.

THE RIVER HOUSE was just a few miles from Vergie's, but the landscape was entirely different. There were fewer trees, for one thing, and more open space. The houses along the river were closer together, and this lot was only about a half an acre. There were enough trees and shrubs around to give it some privacy from neighbors, and it had a cute backyard that had a small deck and seating area—but it didn't have thick groves of trees like Vergie's did. One of its nicest features was an open kitchen and living area. The previous owners had knocked out a wall to make one big space, which I was glad of, but they had ignored the floors, leaving in place the old linoleum in the kitchen and installing a cheap-looking trim to create a boundary between the berber carpet of the living room. We'd ripped that gross carpet up immediately, and had been delighted to find hardwood floors. After trying out a new stain, I wanted to check in and see how they looked.

The new finish was a warm tone that complimented the new slate-colored linoleum of the kitchen. It looked about a thousand percent better.

"I think Andre liked you," I said. "I've never seen him get flustered like that around anybody before."

She frowned, tracing her fingers over the new marble countertop we'd installed. "Oh, please."

"He's a great guy," I said. "And he's single."

"Give me time to get over the last one, will you?"

I shrugged. "Maybe Andre's just what you need to get over him."

She swatted my shoulder. "I came here to escape drama, remember? Already I'm failing."

Benjamin was the first guy Kate had been serious enough about to marry. Men had proposed to her before, but she almost always thought it was too soon—and for her, it always was. Kate was easy to like but hard to get to know. It had taken us months to really learn about each other back in college, even though I had liked her the instant we met. I suspected she was the same way with men, slow to reveal her secrets, carefully guarding her heart. She hadn't told me a lot about her past relationships, but in the time we'd been friends, I'd only seen her date casually for the most part. It was rare for her to stay with a guy for more than three months, and it had surprised me when she'd stayed with Benjamin for so long. He wasn't the kind of guy I pictured her with—he was slick and status quo, and she was an astonishing blend of intelligence and wit. He was generic, and she was everything but.

Benjamin hadn't seemed right for her, but that wasn't my call to make. I'd breathed a little sigh of relief when she said she was finished with him, though, and hoped she'd not be so heartbroken she'd get into a funk and bury herself in her work. She did that sometimes too. She'd dive into some research project that required sixty-hour work weeks and claim she didn't have time for a relationship that consisted of more than cocktails and movie tickets.

She could be star wary of relationships, same as me.

"So are you ready for this big dinner?" she said. "The awkward moment when the worlds collide?"

"There's no awkward allowed at Thanksgiving," I said.

Kate laughed so hard she snorted. "Are you kidding? Holidays are nothing but awkward. That's what makes them holidays. You combine your dad with Jack's family, toss in this cousin and her weirdo boyfriendthat Jack despises, then add your friends who have already shared awkward nudie time together, and boom! Total combustion. Today was just the warm-up."

"I think we'll survive one dinner together."

She smirked. "Pretty sure those were Caesar's last words."

BACK AT HOME, the kitchen looked like the Pillsbury Doughboy had exploded. A fine dusting of flour covered every surface—the table, the countertops, the seats of the kitchen chairs. The contents of two frying pans popped and hissed on the stovetop, and there was a faint cloud of smoke.

Even Bella, who lay under the table, had flour on her snout.

"Look," I said to Kate. "It's Bayou Iron Chef."

Kate dusted off one of the chairs with a tea towel so she could sit.

"Hey," Jack said to me. "You're back sooner than we thought you'd be."

"Our plan," Andre said, "was to have everything cleaned up by the time y'all got back." His shirt was covered in white handprints.

"Oh my," I said, dragging my finger through the flour on the counter.

Jack walked over to me, holding his batter-covered hands out by his sides. He leaned down and kissed me, and I knew part of him was wishing Kate and Andre were long gone.

Part of me was too.

I tousled his hair, and he grinned. "You have flour in your hair," I said.

He inched his hands toward my face, and I swatted them away. "Don't you dare," I said, dodging the batter.

"Anything we can do to help?" Kate asked.

"Not a thing," Andre replied, slapping the lid back on a pot. "Potatoes are ready, veggies are done. Just waiting on the last catfish."

WE SAT OUTSIDE to eat since it had finally cooled off enough that the yard no longer felt like the surface of the sun. In the weeks before, we'd strung some lights in the oak tree closest to the house, in the limbs that curled near to the ground. The result was a cozy little alcove nestled in the trees. Near our feet, Bella looked at us with a woeful expression, hoping we'd finally break our rule and feed her from the table.

"So Kate," Andre said. "What are you planning to do while you're here?"

Spooning more potatoes onto her plate, she said, "Honestly, I don't know what to do. I just missed Enza like crazy, so when she asked me to come, I said yes. I didn't plan beyond getting here."

"We could always go into the city," I said. "I can play tour guide for a day."

"I'm happy just to unwind and read my trashy novels in the hammock," she said. "Lately I've been feeling like a spring ready to pop."

Andre raised a brow, like he had a few ideas about how to fix that.

"Holidays stress me out," she said. "Thanksgiving at my parents' has always felt like a Shakespearian tragedy." She took a big sip of her wine and said, "I just couldn't handle it this year, after the whole Benjamin disaster. My mother would love to dissect that, and it would only make me want to casually murder her for it."

Andre snorted.

"I probably shouldn't say that in front of a man who carries handcuffs and a gun," she said.

"I get it," Andre said. "I used to not like holidays either." He nudged Jack and said, "But this guy's aunt and uncle sort of adopted me, so the last few have made up for all those ugly ones."

"They do like to take in strays," Jack said.

"Lucky for me."

"Your parents are bonkers, too, huh?" Kate said to him.

Andre hesitated, taking a sip of his wine. "They're not really in the picture anymore."

"My parents are wingnuts," Kate said. "My mom's a

decorator, and a total perfectionist—I mean, she makes Stepford look like the Brady Bunch. There's just no pleasing her if you fall within even one standard deviation of the status quo. I never had a chance."

"Are you sure your mom and my dad aren't related?" I said.

"Your dad," she said, shaking her head. "Mercy. I can't believe he's coming here for Thanksgiving."

"I didn't actually think he'd take me up on it. He only said yes because he feels bad about what happened between us last summer."

"Well," Jack said. "He damn well should."

My father had always been overbearing, but it had gotten worse after my mother had left—to the point that it felt like he blamed me. The summer before, when I'd come to fix up Vergie's house, he'd bullied me through the whole process. Even though I'd worked for him for years, he couldn't seem to see that I didn't need his supervision to be successful. I was good at my job, which is why I quit working for him and started my own business.

The sense of freedom had been immediate. To say a weight had been lifted would be an understatement.

Jack had met my father when he was at his worst: angry that I'd ignored his demands and afraid of what might might happen if I succeeded without him. He'd berated me, insulted Jack, and left here in a huff—Jack though, had kept his cool the entire time.

"Is he staying here?" Kate said. She looked horrified at the idea of sharing a roof with my father.

Jack coughed.

"No way," I said. "He'll be at some B and B in the city."

Kate sighed. "Wouldn't want to have to use the hair dryer again."

"He'll be here less than 48 hours," I said. "It'll be fine. And besides, Andre can arrest him if he gets out of line."

Andre raised a brow. "Wouldn't be the first family dinner that ended with somebody in handcuffs."

Kate snorted, turning back to Andre. "This is why Enza and I became such fast friends back in college. The black hole in my heart recognized the black hole in hers right from the get-go. She thought I was a total weirdo at first, this big loud Amazon that stuck to her like glue." She poked me and said, "But I finally broke through those walls of hers, and she was like, *Yes, I have a black hole, too. My family has ensured I'll need decades of therapy, too,* and then we were totally inseparable."

Jack squinted, as if trying to picture us both in college.

"It's true," I said. "She was a total weirdo."

"You wouldn't have it any other way," she said.

"One hundred percent," I said, clinking my wine glass against hers.

Kate laughed, wrapping her arm around my shoulders.

"What'd I tell you?" I said to Jack, my voice lowered. "A couple of drinks, and they'd be all right."

"Hey," Kate said, still laughing, but clearly a little tipsy. "I'm still mortified. I was hoping that lick on the head would give him just a touch of amnesia."

Andre frowned. "You'd rob me of that memory? You standing there like Venus on the clamshell, perfectly lovely."

Kate's eyes got wide. "You said everything was a blur!"

He shrugged. "I'm sort of trained to record every little detail."

Her jaw dropped.

"Hey," he said, "Tell me how to make it up to you." He

leaned forwards, his eyes glinting in the dim light. He seemed a little tipsy too—this was a side of Andre that was new to me.

She topped off her wine glass and said, "What we have here is an imbalance in the natural order. I was in an extremely vulnerable position, and you have not been in a position of vulnerability. It's given you the upper hand."

"Are you saying you need to see me naked to make this fair?"

"It's a question of equitable more so than fair."

He stared at her and she smirked.

I looked at Jack for backup, but he just shook his head as if he'd seen this particular train wreck many times before.

Kate studied him for a minute and said, "Well?"

Andre coughed as he took a swallow of his wine. "Nobody ever actually took me up on that offer."

"This happens often, does it?" Kate said, her tone teasing.

"OK," I said, clearing their plates. "Nobody else is getting naked today. Let's just pretend that incident never happened, and we'll never speak of it again."

Andre smirked, as if he'd never forget that day for the rest of his life.

Kate grabbed the last couple of dishes and followed me up to the house, still snickering. "Did you see the look on his face?" she said. "For a second I thought he'd strip down right there at the table."

I went back to get my glass and heard Andre say to Jack, "They didn't make women like that in my neighborhood. How long's she staying?"

～

LATER, after Andre had gone home and Jack had gone to bed, Kate and I sat out on the porch, finishing the bottle of wine from dinner. The moon was high in the sky, casting a blue light across the yard. In the cypress grove, the owls called to each other in low tones.

Kate sipped her wine and said, "Did you mean what you said before, about not wanting to find your mom?

I shrugged. "Some days I just think it's better not to know. Some days I feel like I'll die if I don't."

She stared out into the darkness, twirling a lock of her hair. "I don't like to see this eating you up. I know what that feels like, to have something sink its claws into you like this." Kate had a lot of reasons for avoiding her home, and the whole town of Edenboro, where she grew up. Though she teased about us tearing each other's walls down, there were still things that she held secret. There were times that had been especially rough for her right before college, and I knew she'd lost a close friend. She'd never wanted to tell me the details, and I hadn't pressed her. But it was evident from the way she spoke about those years that something terrible had happened that had upended her world. Something about that town— about those years of her life—had been significantly dark. And whatever happened, she still carried it with her.

She teased about recognizing the dark hole in each other, but it was true—I'd seen in her a shared feeling of being broken, but somehow stronger for it. I'd seen a shared understanding that people could look perfectly put together on the surface, but have turmoil beneath that nearly tore them to pieces. But I'd also seen in her a strength and resolve to never let anyone have that power over her again—I'd wanted an anchor in my life, and I think she had too.

"Nobody around here can tell me about her," I said. "It's like she never existed."

"Maybe people just don't want to tell you."

"But why?"

She sighed. "It could be bad. Like, really bad."

"Dad won't even tell me about her. Not even now." Growing up, I'd pressed my father for details, but he always made it sound like my mother just flaked out and left him one day, for no acceptable reason. He made it sound like she never wanted to see us again and never wanted to be found.

"Would you want to see her again?" Kate said. "Do you think it would help?"

"I used to hate her for leaving." I sipped my wine. "I thought I'd never see her again, and then back at Vergie's funeral, when I saw that woman that looked like her, it felt like the whole earth had cracked in half." I'd had a full-blown panic attack that day—the woman wasn't my mother of course, but she'd looked enough like her to set me reeling.

"You need to put this behind you," Kate said. "This is the kind of thing that festers inside people for their whole lives. And they just end up miserable because of it." She put her hand on my shoulder and said, "If you think you want to find her, then you should do it now. If that's what you need to do to move on. And you know I'll help you however I can."

The thing that gnawed at me, and had ever since coming back to Bayou Sabine, was this: Vergie left her house to me. Not Martine. It made me think that they'd become estranged, and that my mother had left Vergie, too. Or could it be possible that Vergie turned my mother away?

Standing abruptly, I went inside the house and straight to the living room where I'd left the box of journals that George had sent me. Inside the roll-top desk, I'd stashed the handful of letters that Jack had given me months before, back when we were cleaning out all of Vergie's things. Before now, I hadn't wanted to read them, afraid of what they might reveal. But Kate was right—I needed to find out where my mother was, and why she had left. And then I could put this to rest.

Her reason for leaving us might be something I didn't want to hear, but anything was better than this not-knowing.

I carried the box of books and letters back onto the porch and set them down by the swing.

"What's all that?" Kate said, peering into the box. This must be how archaeologists feel right before they open a mysterious tomb that's been sealed for a thousand years. This could be nothing, or it could be everything.

"Vergie's diaries," I said. "Her boyfriend mailed them to me a few days ago. There are letters from my mom, too."

"Holy crap," she said. "Have you read them yet?"

"No. You want to help me?"

"You want me to read your mom's letters?" She held an envelope close to her face, studying the scrawled writing.

"You're right. I need to know what happened. The not-knowing is tearing me up."

She nodded and opened the first letter like it was fragile as glass. When she began reading, I dove into the books.

Vergie's journals were like scrapbooks. The softcover leather-bound books had straps you wrapped around the covers and tied to keep them closed. It was a good thing, too, because the books were filled with photographs and news clippings, recipe cards, Polaroid pictures—all kinds of ephemera had been taped to the pages. The tape had disintegrated, and some pictures had slipped out of place, her writing around them indicating where they'd been. I turned the pages carefully, not wanting the pieces to fall out of their context completely.

After skimming dates in the journals at the top of the pile, I found one dated the year my mom left us. There were postcards she'd sent Vergie from her travels—supplemental to the letters, no doubt—and Vergie occasionally wrote that she was concerned about Martine. It took a while to get used to seeing her name, Martine, written in my grandmother's gentle looping script.

"Your grandma was a badass," Kate said, chewing on her fingernail. "This one's all about this trip she took to Costa Rica with an actor."

"Like, a famous one? When?"

"A million years ago. Just uses an initial for him—B." She fanned herself as she skimmed the pages. "Damn, Vergie."

"I'll definitely read that one later." The journal I held was dated the year my mom left us in North Carolina. Postcards from Martine were intermingled with drawings of flowers Vergie was growing, recipes she'd gathered from her friends, and passages that described days she'd spent with George. One page included a drawing of a hosta leaf and a detailed description of how she and George had tried to cross-pollinate a couple of varieties they particularly liked. It was sweet, imagining the two of them with cotton swabs and bifocals, trying to create a new hybrid of their own. She called him *a nice fella with good intentions and zero practical knowledge of gardening*. I hadn't realized they'd been together so long.

A postcard from Mesa Verde was nestled in the next page, and Vergie switched from hosta drawings to one simple thought about my mother: *I hope this time away will do her good*, she wrote. *I think sometimes she wants to go back, and I think sometimes that she might be able to, and there might be hope for them yet.*

She had to be talking about going back to me and my father. I flipped through the next several pages, past more entries about George, making a mental note to study those more closely later. Part of me felt guilty reading about her with George, these intimate details she might never have told me in person, given the chance. That was the thing about diaries: They were sometimes the only way to really learn what another person was thinking, but reading them was almost certainly a kind of betrayal, because if that person wanted you to know those thoughts, he or she would have told you.

"Did you ever keep a journal?" I asked Kate.

"Hell no. I take my tawdry secrets to the grave." She grabbed another book from the pile and said, "Did you?"

"Yeah, but I tossed them all in the fireplace one day when I was in college. They all sounded whiny and ridiculous, and I couldn't stand the idea of someone who knew me reading them one day. Kinda wish I hadn't done that now, though—they'd have been good for a laugh."

"Are you afraid of what you might find in here?" she said, her tone turning serious.

"Maybe a little. But nothing's worse than what I've imagined over the years." The worst thing, in my mind, was feeling like my mother just didn't love me, and had simply wanted to cut me out of her life the way you'd trim dying branches from a tree.

Two hours later, we'd skimmed through a stack of Vergie's journals. We'd skipped the early ones and gone straight to the ones that were in the couple of years before and after my mother had left us. I'd read the letters my mother had written to Vergie, too—twice—and the last four were postmarked in Texas. In these letters, my mother described places she was visiting, like small towns and parks she'd never seen. There was plenty of detail about landmarks, as if she wanted Vergie to feel like she was visiting those places, too—but there were hardly any words about how she was feeling. There was nothing to indicate that she was sad, or anxious, or contemplating leaving my father. There was nothing about me, either.

It was as if she'd just vanished.

Vergie's words didn't give us many clues, either. There were scant lines that described places my mother was visiting, how Vergie thought Martine was just trying to find herself again. I hadn't expected to find all the answers in these pages, but I'd hoped to find more than this.

"Here's something," Kate said. "This one talks about your mom coming to stay here in the fall, living here while she— quote—*gets her bearings.*"

Vergie was never specific, usually only listing Martine's whereabouts and occasionally admitting concern about her emotional state. If there was subtext, I couldn't find it.

"You know," Kate said. "You could google her. You might find out she lives in the next parish over though."

"I tried. No luck with the name Parker. And you wouldn't believe how many women named Martine Deveraux there are in the world."

She frowned. "That's actually sort of surprising."

A letter, folded into quarters, slipped out of the journal when I turned the page. In this one, Mom was in Texas, writing about vineyards in the hill country. *I've discovered I have a taste for red wine and dry heat,* she wrote. *The sky seems so much bigger out here, and I feel free.* She wrote about going to a bar with dueling pianos in San Antonio, seeing the Riverwalk and the Alamo. She'd been to a church service in one of the oldest missions in the state, where a mariachi band played between prayers.

I continued skimming the pages until Kate sucked in a breath.

"Oh shit," she said.

"What?"

When she didn't answer, I looked up and she sat still as a stone, her mouth in a tiny O.

"What did you find?" I said.

Slowly, she handed me the diary. "You should read it."

The words blurred on the page. I had to re-read half a dozen times before it sank in.

I can't believe she's gone, Vergie had written.

My mother had simply left her, I thought—like she'd left my father and me—and I felt that familiar pain in my chest, like I'd felt when I was fifteen, and my father had told me that she didn't love us, and that she was gone.

But there was more.

There, in Vergie's tiny cursive script: *I had to drive all the way to a little Texas town to identify her.*

Chapter Four

I WASN'T GOING to find my mother.

Vergie's writing was more erratic on the next pages, where she described driving to a small town in Texas to identify Martine's body, to meet the sheriff who pulled her daughter from the river. Two hikers had spotted her in the reeds on that summer morning, when the water was still warm from soaking up the sunlight the day before. Vergie's writing, typically precise with its cursive loops, was shaky and frantic, much larger than usual, as if she could barely control the movement of the pen.

I read the page over and over, as if I might be reading it wrong, as if I was too tired to understand the words.

But I was not too tired. I was not reading it wrong.

My heart felt as if it was being squeezed like a fist. It felt wrong somehow to continue reading about what must have been Vergie's darkest days, but she didn't pour words onto the page like I expected. There was only the one page about the day she went to Texas, and on it, she wrote at the end: *They told me this was an accident, that perhaps she went swimming in the dark, slipped and went under. But my Martine swam like a mermaid, and I know as surely as I sit here that this was no accident. I thought she was happy.*

I missed something.

I failed her.

After that, there was a long break in the entries, four months until the next one. I skimmed the pages, but there was no more mention of my mother. Vergie wrote about her vegetable gardening, her visits with friends, her outings with George—but not Martine.

How had no one told me about this? Bayou Sabine was so small, people had to know. It was impossible to keep secrets in towns like this. I thought back to Vergie's funeral, to the woman with the gardenia. *You're the spitting image of Martine,* the woman had said.

Did everyone just assume I knew?

It had crossed my mind of course, all those years before, this possibility that she was dead. Years before, I'd once told Kate that my mother was dead to me, back when I was angry and hurting, and the wounds seemed raw. But now that it was truth, I felt like I'd somehow caused it. According to the date in the journal, she had died when I was twenty-four. At that time I would have been a couple years out of college, working for my father. Thinking back to that year, I tried to identify a time when I felt some disturbance in the world around me. They say often times twins have a bond so close that one knows when the other has been hurt. One simply feels the agony of the other through a connection that doesn't make sense to the rest of us, separated sometimes by thousands of miles. They say that happens with spouses, with mothers and children.

It didn't happen for me.

It was silly to think I'd have had that bond with my mother. We hadn't seen each other in nearly a decade—how could I have felt the instant she died? How could we have a connection that strong?

"I'm so sorry," Kate said, her hand on my arm. "Are you all right?"

"It doesn't say how. There aren't any details." I skimmed the rest of the journal, but there was not another instance of her name. "Why would she not say what happened?" I felt like someone had knocked the wind out of me. My head was spinning.

"I'm sorry," she said again. "What can I do?"

"I think I need to go to bed." It had been easy to be angry at my mother when I thought she'd left us and started a new life somewhere. Now, my anger felt like something I should be ashamed of. I dropped the journal back into the box with the others and went inside.

When I climbed into bed, Jack eased over and wrapped one arm tight around my hips, just as he always did. He pulled me close and nuzzled my neck, and I fought to hold back my tears.

For years, I'd been kidding myself, saying I didn't want to find her. For so long, I'd molded her into a cold, uncaring person—because what mother could leave her daughter without a trace? What if she'd intended to come back to us?

I'd been so, so wrong.

My body trembled as the tears came, and Jack stirred.

"Hey," he whispered. "What's wrong?"

When I told him, he switched on the bedside lamp and I turned to face him.

He pulled me against his chest as I told him about the

journals and the letters. He stroked my back, trying to calm me.

"I'm so sorry, chère," he said, running his fingers through my hair.

One thought nagged me—a scenario I didn't want to be true. When I couldn't tamp it down anymore, I said, "Jack, did Vergie ever mention any of this to you? Did she ever talk about my mom?"

He pulled my hand to his lips. "Of course not." His voice was gentle. "I'd never keep something like that from you, chère. Not ever."

"You mentioned my mother when we first met. Vergie never talked about her?"

"There were a few years I didn't see Vergie," he said. "And then when I moved back here, she only mentioned it one time. I'd just been chatting, asking after her family, and she got this sad look on her face and said, 'Honey, we don't see each other anymore. I guess it's what you'd call estranged.'" He sighed, sliding his hand over mine. "I never dreamed it was something this bad—I just took her at her word and thought they'd had a falling out, and that's why you weren't visiting anymore. I could see it upset her, so I just never asked again."

Of course. Jack was too considerate to pry.

He brushed a tear from my cheek as I said, "Vergie thought it wasn't an accident."

"I'm so sorry, chère," he said, his voice a murmur. "But maybe that's why no one knows. Maybe your grandmother didn't want anyone to know she might have done it on purpose."

I curled myself against him, listening to the steady thump of his heart and tried to picture anything but my mother.

But Vergie's words haunted me: *My Martine swam like a mermaid.*

In the darkness, as I drifted toward sleep, I imagined my mother out in that river, in some remote part of Texas. She walked off the bank and waded into a river as wide and lazy as the Rio Grande. She walked as I'd seen her so many times before in my dreams, with arms stretched out by her sides, fingertips stroking the surface of the water as she waded deeper, past her hips, past her waist. She ducked under the surface then, and swam out toward the middle, under the light of a full moon, her skin pale in the light that bounced off the waves. She paddled on her back, her face tilted up toward the stars, maybe naming the same constellations that Vergie had drawn out for me when I was a girl, when we lay in the backyard grass and she told me stories about heroes and queens. She moved her arms in languid strokes, slicing through the dark water, and the moon sank low like a stone. As she swam farther out toward the center of the river, she dove below the surface, her long hair swirling around her, blocking out the last of the light.

THE FACTS WERE THESE: my mother was dead, my world had tilted on its axis, but I still had a big-deal dinner to get ready for. When I'd volunteered to host everyone, Jack had insisted that he'd do the cooking—I could barely cook anyway, so he got no argument. But because of this new bombshell, a dinner party was the last thing I wanted to focus on. Everything about my mother's disappearance felt more ominous now, and Vergie's journals had dredged up more questions than answers.

When Kate came downstairs a little after seven, I was reading through another of the journals. So far there was no more mention of Martine, but I'd found another postcard stuck in this diary, seemingly at random. It was from my mother, but not addressed to Vergie.

On the left side of the postcard, only one line was written:

Enza — I love you. I miss you. I carry you with me.

On the front side of the postcard, a field of Texas bluebells. On the back side, no address.

Tears pricked my eyes and I wondered: had she tried to write me in all those months? Had my father thrown her cards and letters away? I shoved the postcard back into Vergie's journal ad pushed it aside.

"How are you?" Kate said, pouring a coffee. "Did you sleep?"

"Some," I lied. Jack had left earlier for his last shift at the station before the holiday. Usually I slept in a little after he left, but this morning I'd been wide awake.

She sat down across from me and said, "Maybe we should get out of the house today. Get out from under this for a while." She said it as if I could just shove my feelings aside like one of Vergie's diaries, but I knew she meant well. The house was starting to feel like it was closing in on me again, crowded with ghosts.

"Let's go over and see Buck and Josie," I said, closing the book. "We can take him a pie."

"Since when do you bake pies?"

"Since never. But he loves Brenda's pecan pie, and she'll have a fresh batch out soon. I'd like to make sure he's doing all right, and he'll be less surly about us checking up on him if we bribe him with pie."

"Fair enough," she said. I poured our coffees in travel mugs and when I turned to hand her one, she blocked me.

"So here's how this is going to go," Kate said. "I'm not going to bug you by asking you a million times if you're OK. I know that you're not—not really—but you need some time to absorb this. I will not ask you, because I know it's annoying. But that doesn't mean I don't care, and don't see you hurting." She put her hands on my shoulders and said, "Whenever you're ready, talk."

I nodded. "Thank you."

"You should drive. I have no idea how to navigate in a swamp, so I'll hold the pie."

Outside, she climbed into the Jeep and turned the air conditioner on as soon as I cranked it. "My God," she said. "This whole state is like an oven." She fanned herself dramatically.

"I'm really glad you're here," I said.

"I know."

WHEN WE GOT to their house, Josie was cleaning up the kitchen and had a pot of chili cooking.

"Buck's out cold with the painkillers," she said, stirring the chili. "Lucille ran to the store, but she'll be back soon."

Kate set the pie on the counter, and Josie put a kettle on.

"I was about to make some hot chocolate and pretend it's winter," Josie said. "Would you gals like some?"

Before we could answer, she was pulling out three mugs and a bottle of coffee liqueur. "I like mine with a little kick."

Kate and I smiled as she set them on the counter.

"Josie," I said, "can I ask you a question?"

"Of course." Josie's eyes looked tired, and for a split second, I thought of dropping it. But I knew I wouldn't sleep until I had some answers.

"Did you know my mother at all?"

Kate's eyes widened as Josie poured the liqueur into our mugs, an extra slosh into her own.

Josie sighed, motioning for us to sit with her at the breakfast bar. "Not really, hon. I met her once, I think, and I knew she came back several years ago to stay with your grandmother for a while, but I never got the particulars. That happened a lot around here, when women needed to go back to stay with their parents for a time. Sometimes a parent got sick, and that brought them back for a bit, but Vergie always seemed to be in good health."

I nodded, drinking the cocoa. It had a bite that wasn't entirely unpleasant.

"I'm sorry... I wish I could tell you more, but I wasn't close with your grandmother, and I didn't ask her such things. I just figured they were estranged."

"It's OK." It seemed odd there weren't at least some rumors that had circulated. Where I grew up, women who came back home to live with their parents generated all kinds of gossip. Granted, gossip wasn't terribly useful on its own, but it seemed to always contain a kernel of truth.

"Did you ever hear when my mom moved away again or where she might have gone?" I asked her.

She shook her head, taking a sip of cocoa, but she looked troubled, like this was a subject she wanted to drop as soon as possible.

There was a clatter outside at the back door and then Lucille entered, holding two paper bags of groceries against her chest.

"Hey, Enza," she said, setting the groceries on the counter. "What brings you over?"

"We brought pie for Buck," I said. "Lucille, this is my friend Kate. She's visiting this week."

Lucille nodded and said, "Nice to meet you."

"You, too," Kate said.

Lucille started putting the groceries away. Josie stood to help her, but Lucille shooed her away. "I've got this, Mom. Just rest a while, will you?"

When Buck shuffled into the kitchen, Lucille moved to help him. "Dad, what do you need? I'll bring it to you."

He huffed. "I'm not an invalid, sweetheart. I think I can manage a walk to the kitchen." He moved slow, like his ribs still ached from the fall.

"Enza and her friend Kate brought you a pecan pie," Josie said.

"Well," he said, his face brightening. "Nothing heals a man like pecan pie. Thank you, dear."

"It's from Brenda's," I said. "I like you too much to bring you something I baked myself."

"You are an angel," he said, rummaging in the drawer for a fork.

"How are you feeling?" I asked him.

"Like a damn bull knocked me over. But I'll live." he said. "Takes more than a little fall to keep me down. These two are keeping me homebound though, refusing to let me set foot outside."

"If Dad had his way, he'd be at the hardware store right now," Lucille said.

"But then you might miss out on pie," I said.

"Fair point," he said.

When the phone rang, Josie answered it and spoke quietly.

"Is that the store?" Buck said.

She waved him off and and took the phone outside onto the porch.

"Lord help me," Buck said. "These two won't let me do anything."

Lucille handed him a plate and said, "You can serve up some pie, Pop."

Toph sauntered into the kitchen, a laptop tucked under his arm. He was wearing another button-down shirt and khakis, and had aviator sunglasses pushed up into his hair.

"Hey," he said to Lucille. "Cat's brought something in the house again."

"What?" she said.

"A mouse," he said, setting up his laptop on the kitchen island. "Or maybe a chipmunk. I couldn't really tell."

Lucille groaned. "Where is it?"

"Likely eviscerated under the couch," Buck grumbled.

"Did you let her in with it?" she asked.

Toph hunched over the keyboard, staring at the screen. "She was howling at the door. You told me to let her in when she did that."

"I told you to check her mouth first," Lucille said. "Would you go get it from her please? She'll make a huge mess."

"Can't," he said. "Have to do some damage control here." He pulled up a social media account on his laptop and started typing furiously.

She sighed and stomped into the living room.

Toph ignored her, his eyes glued to the screen as he scrolled. When he caught me staring, he adjusted the laptop to the screen was angled away from me.

"Always have to check her mouth," Buck said. "Sadie likes

bringing us gifts." He cut into the pie and winced as Lucille shrieked from the living room.

"Toph!" she yelled.

The black and white tuxedo cat streaked into the kitchen in a blur, her ears flattened against her head. She skidded to a halt by the refrigerator and then began licking her front paw. She was so round it was hard to imagine her being quick enough to catch anything.

There was a groan of protest from the living room.

"Just let her eat it," Toph yelled. Sadie's ears pricked forward as if she'd located an ally.

"Gross," she called. "I'm not leaving entrails to soak into the carpet."

"Cats are self-cleaning," he said. "They destroy the evidence."

Obviously he'd never lived with a cat.

I stepped into the living room and said, "Can I help?"

"It's fine," she called. Poking her head out from the bathroom down the hall, she said, "I got it."

Buck shot Toph a look that the younger man didn't see. His eyes were still fixed on the computer screen, one hand absent-mindedly raking through his hair.

Lucille jogged into the kitchen, carrying what was presumably a dead rodent in a wad of paper towels. Her nose wrinkled as she went straight for the back door, holding the towels an arm's length in front of her. The screen door slammed behind her. The cat's tail twitched.

Toph paid us no attention, too enthralled in whatever he was reading. Cars could have crashed into the front yard and he wouldn't have blinked. He frowned as he continued typing.

Kate glanced at Toph and then gave me an exaggerated eye-roll. Lucille came back inside, frowning. The cat stared at her, her green eyes tiny crescents. She yawned and then trotted over to the kitchen island and leapt into the empty chair next to Toph. When he paid her no attention, she butted her head against his elbow. Still scrolling, he reached over and scratched her head until she purred.

"Don't let her in again without checking her mouth," Lucille said to Toph. She scrubbed her hands under the faucet, still grimacing.

Toph's phone buzzed and he looked at the screen. "Babe, I'm going out for a bit. Be back later." Lucille looked irritated, but in a way that seemed like it was a habit she'd gotten used to a long time ago. She went back into the living room with a bottle of carpet cleaner. Toph grabbed his laptop and left without another word. Outside there was the revving of an engine, then the crunch of gravel.

"Would you ladies care for pie?" Buck said.

When we declined, he sat down at the table with his slice and took a big bite. "Honestly, I don't know what she sees in that fella."

Kate shot me a look and smirked.

"He's about as useful as teats on a bull," Buck said. "But to each their own, I suppose. Josie says it's phase. Lord help us if it isn't."

I wondered what the chances were that the cat might go on another hunting spree and leave a gift of some sort on Toph's pillow as he slept.

When Lucille came back in, I said, "We should get going and let you rest."

"If I rest any harder I'll be dead," he said, finishing the pie. "A man lives longer when he feels useful."

Lucille rolled her eyes and walked us to the door. "Thanks for coming," she said. She looked exhausted and annoyed.

"Call if we can help with anything, OK?" I told her.

She nodded, offering a smile that was way too wide. "You bet."

LATE THAT AFTERNOON, while Kate went out for a jog, I dialed my father's number. Ever since we'd read Vergie's journals, there has been a question gnawing at me. It was a question that I might not like the answer to, but I needed to ask.

The phone rang three times, and I hung up before he answered. A few minutes later, I dialed again and did the same. Outside, I paced in the yard, cursing myself for still being so chicken. Bella watched me from the shade and whined.

Finally, I dialed again. When he answered, my chest tightened.

"Enza." His voice was clipped. "How are you? I'm just about to head over to a meeting."

"I need to ask you something." As long as I paced, my knees wouldn't buckle.

"I'm in a hurry," he said. "Let me call you back."

"This can't wait." Before he could argue, I said, "Did you know Mom died?"

There was silence on the end of the line. For a second, I thought he'd hung up on me.

"Dad? Are you there?"

"Yes," he said, his voice low.

"Yes, what?"

There was a heavy sigh, then more silence. "I knew about your mother."

I doubled over, like I'd been punched.

"How could you keep that from me?" My voice sounded small. "What's wrong with you?"

"Enza," he said. "How did you even find out?"

"Why did you think I wouldn't?"

There was a clatter in the background, the sound of him leaving his office and locking the squeaky door. "It wouldn't have made any difference," he said quietly.

It made me furious, the way he kept his voice so cool and even, as if this were a mild annoyance for him.

"How can you say that?" I couldn't stop my voice from rising. "It makes all the difference. I can't believe you would lie to me about that."

"Enza."

I hated to hear him speak my name.

"How could you let me believe for all those years that I might see her again?"

"You told me you never wanted to see her again," he said. "I took you at your word."

"I was an idiot teenager!" I yelled. At the edge of the yard, the lagoon was as still as a mirror. I thought of that river in Texas, in a town whose name no one chose to remember.

"Why wouldn't you tell me?" My chest ached from holding back sobs. I did not want my father to hear me cry.

"She'd already hurt us so much," he said.

"So your solution was to hurt me more?"

"Calm down," he said. "I'm not going to discuss this if you're screaming at me."

"Don't tell me to calm down. My mother died, and you lied to me. You let me think she was still alive, that I might still find her."

He sighed.

I didn't know what I wanted him to say, but nothing he said was right.

"I thought I was doing the right thing," he said. "Protecting you."

"How can you be this person?" I said.

"How would telling you that have made anything any better? It would just hurt you more."

"I hate you for this," I said, staring out at the water.

"Enza." His voice was cool, as if this was a conversation he'd already rehearsed. "Your mother was selfish and cruel to walk out on us the way she did. Have you forgotten how you felt when she left? How you hated her and wished her dead?"

My whole body trembled. My voice cracked when at last I spoke. "Was she depressed? Did she kill herself?"

"Of course not. Her death was an accident."

"Would you have known if she was?"

There was a long pause, and then he spoke slowly, his voice cold. "She was my wife. I think I would know."

"Are you sure about that?"

He didn't respond.

"I've changed my mind about Thursday," I said. "Don't come here."

"Enza, there's a lot you don't know."

"I mean it," I said. "I don't want you here." His voice droned on as I pulled the phone away from my ear and ended the call. His cool tone, his callous answers—I'd heard everything I needed to hear.

Shoving the phone into my pocket, I looked out over the lagoon, my eyes tracing the edge of its shimmering surface. Closing my eyes, I took a deep breath that made my whole chest expand.

And then I screamed.

It was one of those loud screams that rattles your chest, and sounds like it belongs in a horror movie.

I'd never made that sound before.

Bella howled. A flock of ducks burst out of the lagoon and flew up into the sky.

Collapsing on the bank by the lagoon, I lay back in the grass. Bella pressed her nose into my hair and lay down next to me with a sigh, as if she knew it was impossible to get me to move in the direction she wanted. Instead I stared up at the sky, watching the clouds drift across slowly, as if heavy with rain.

Nothing here was ever as it seemed.

"Enza!" Kate yelled. Her footsteps came closer, but I stayed on the ground.

"What happened? Are you OK?" She came to a stop right next to me, her body blocking the sunlight.

"My dad's the worst. The absolute worst."

"What now?" She planted her hands on her hips.

I told her everything he'd said, my eyes still closed. The sun was low in the sky, about to dip below the cypress trees. It was cool, but not like the winter I was accustomed to. Everything felt different down here in Bayou Sabine. Right down to the grass beneath my feet. Some days I loved that about it, but some days it made me feel like it was just another strange place where I didn't quite fit.

"Shit," she said, sounding out of breath. "I'm really sorry, Enza. I don't know what to say to make this better."

"I just can't believe he would lie to me like that. For all those years." I shook my head. "I thought I wanted to know everything that happened, but this is so much worse than I imagined."

Kate laid down next to me in the grass and we stayed silent

for a while. Deep within the cypress grove, the frogs and the birds were starting their evening chatter. Part of me hoped that if I closed my eyes, if I lay there long enough in the stillness, I'd wake from this terrible dream.

"Even when the truth is horrible," she said, "isn't it better than not knowing?"

"I used to think so."

She rested her hand on my arm.

"I'm glad you're here," I said.

"I'm sorry it ended this way."

But it didn't feel like an ending. My head was cluttered with a thousand thoughts, my heart thumping against my ribs.

Above us, the moon was beginning to brighten, already anchored high among the tallest limbs of the trees. We lay there until the owls began calling from the darkness of the canopy, until the sky turned to violet and the first stars appeared like holes in the night.

When we finally headed back to the house, I felt something large fly within a foot of my head, its feathers silent as it flapped its broad wings. It was a blur of speckled white and gray, bound for a tall dead tree at the edge of the yard.

"What was that?" Kate asked, looking behind us.

"An owl, I think."

I tracked its path as it continued toward the tree and lighted near the top. Owls were like ghosts, slipping through the darkness without making a sound, dodging you and disappearing into a dark part of the world before you ever knew they'd been there at all.

～

WHEN JACK CAME HOME, he found us on the porch, a few shots into a bottle of bourbon. If ever a day called for bourbon, it was this one. It burned in a way that wasn't entirely unpleasant, and I was grateful for the numbness that was beginning to spread all the way to my toes.

"Hey," he said. "What did you two get into today? Besides the obvious."

Kate picked up her glass and said, "I'm going to let you catch him up," and before Jack could protest, she'd gone inside the house.

He leaned down to kiss me and said, "What's that all about?"

Pouring another shot into my glass, I handed it to him and said, "You might want to sit."

He arched a brow and sat next to me in the porch swing, and I told him about the phone call with my father.

When I was finished, he said, "I was really hoping I might like your dad some day, but he's making it awfully difficult."

"Well, he's a difficult man."

"What do you want to do?" he said.

"Honestly, I want to drive to this middle of nowhere Texas town and find out what happened. But we have a house full of people coming in just a few days, and what I want most is to pretend that I can have a normal family."

"I'll go with you," he said. "After Thanksgiving. We'll dig up whatever we can find before then, and figure out where we need to go. I'll take some time off, and we'll sort this out." He draped his arm around my shoulders and tugged me towards him. In that moment, he was the only part of this town that made any sense.

I nodded, thinking of at least one phone call I could make in the meantime.

"And you *can* have a family," he said, tightening his arms around me. "You get to build your own, starting with me."

He pulled me onto his lap, wrapping his big arms around my waist. His eyes, luminous in the dim light, were fixed on mine. When he looked at me that way, it made me feel like I was exactly where I belonged.

I wanted that feeling to never end.

Chapter Five

"OH MY GOD," Kate breathed. "This coffee is better than sex."

I snorted, thinking of Jack and all the many ways he had disproven that idea without even trying. "Not possible," I said. "If so, then you're doing it wrong."

She rolled her eyes.

We were sitting at a little table at the Café du Monde, drinking coffees that were half-filled with cream.

"When are we meeting this guy?" she said, checking her phone.

"Any minute now."

Earlier that morning, I'd looked up the return address on the box full of Vergie's diaries and located George. He lived in New Orleans, and when I'd called, he'd agreed to meet me here for coffee.

All around us, Christmas lights had already been strung from the trees. Paper snowflakes hung from the roofs of the tents at the cafe, and all of the windows had been sprayed with fake snow. It was still nearly seventy degrees outside. That was likely the closest thing to actual snow that we'd get.

"Enza?" a man said. I turned and saw a tall, thin man with a full head of white hair. He had a dark tan and wore a blue button-down shirt and gray dress pants.

"You must be George," I said, standing.

He shook my hand and said, "I can see the resemblance." He smiled, and tiny wrinkles formed at the corners of his eyes.

"This is my friend, Kate," I said, and he reached for her hand.

She smiled and he sat down with his coffee.

"Thank you for coming," I said.

"Of course."

"I'm going to get us some beignets," Kate said, and strode back toward the counter. She was giving us space, but part of me wished she'd stay. My mother's story got more tangled by the day, but if I wanted to learn the whole truth, I needed to push aside my fear and hurt.

"Thank you for sending the journals," I said.

George nodded, sipping his coffee. "I thought you should have them, dear. She'd have wanted that." His accent had a different lilt to it—Creole, I'd learned.

"I need to ask you something, George." I took a deep breath. "It's something that's bothered me for a long time."

Keep it together, Enza. Don't cry in a café.

"Did she ever talk to you about her daughter, Martine?"

He sighed, his fingers tracing the rim of the coffee cup. "I figured that's why you wanted to meet today."

"So you knew my mother died?"

His eyes were sad. "I'm sorry. I didn't know if you knew, and I felt it wasn't my place to tell you if you didn't."

I nodded and said, "I understand. You're the only one left now who can tell me the truth. Could you tell me what Vergie told you about her, when she disappeared?"

He leaned back in his chair, his shoulders slumped. I'd wondered before if he'd read Vergie's journals before giving them to me. Looking at him then, I saw that he must have. He didn't seem particularly surprised by my question.

He sighed and rubbed his chin.

All around us, people were laughing and chatting about their children, their holiday plans, their most recent bad dates. The din had grown louder since we arrived, and George had to raise his voice for me to hear him.

"Vergie came to me when the police first called her," he said. "I drove her to that little town—I forget the name. It was a few hours from here, in the green part of Texas. Pretty country. Your mother had left several months before, and Vergie thought maybe she was starting over in that town. Then she got that call, though, and it just turned her whole world upside down. It was just the saddest thing."

He stared past me, and then said, "They told her it was an accidental drowning."

"What did Vergie think?"

"She was heartbroken, of course. She didn't want to believe it was an accident."

"Did you think it was an accident?"

He shook his head. "I honestly could never make up my mind. Vergie swore your mother had grown up swimming like a fish."

"Vergie said she was like a mermaid." Most memories of my mother had faded, but I did remember our summer beach trips, and how she loved to swim in the ocean.

A silence settled between us.

"We never know what anyone is capable of," he said. "Until they show us."

I nodded. That was true about my father, too.

"But people also make unwise decisions, and accidents happen that seem completely illogical."

Of all the things my father had said about my mother, he'd never once mentioned depression. He'd not been shy about pointing out her faults over the years, and he would almost certainly see depression as a weakness.

"Do you think she could have done it on purpose?" I asked him.

He frowned, staring at his coffee cup. "Vergie just told me about the divorce, how hard your mother was taking it. She hated being away from you. But your mother seemed like a basically happy person that was just going through a horrible situation. Sometimes I thought Vergie couldn't accept that it was simply an accident. Accident cometimes implies carelessness, and she didn't think of Martine as careless."

"I thought my mother wanted the divorce. She left us."

"I don't know the particulars," George said, his voice softer. "The way Vergie talked, your mother had become unmoored. She was searching for something, and she was restless. She stayed here for a while, and then she took off to travel by herself, out west somewhere. Vergie thought it would do her good, that she needed some time to heal after whatever happened with your father. Vergie knew your mother was hurting, but she thought she'd heal with enough time. Vergie tried to give her space, but then she was afraid that space became distance."

The café suddenly seemed too tiny, like it was collapsing in on us both. I'd never considered that my mother was hurting, too. In my mind, she'd made the choice to leave, and was starting a new life and doing what she wanted. It hadn't occurred to me that she might have been hurting as much as I was.

"Was my mother on any kind of treatment?" I didn't know much about mental illness, but I knew suicide didn't come on as suddenly as some people believed. She could have been depressed. She could have suffered a trauma, or been triggered by a cataclysmic event that would set her on that trajectory.

Had my father been that cataclysmic event?

"Not that Vergie ever told me about," he said. "That's not something people around here talk about, though. Vergie was so protective of your mother, she probably wouldn't have even told me such things. It's just nobody's business but your own."

It made me sick to my stomach, thinking of the kind of suffering that might have sent my mother to the river that night. It was hard for me to imagine she might have hurt herself on purpose.

"Maybe I shouldn't have given you those diaries," he said, rubbing his chin. "I thought I was doing the right thing, but maybe I wasn't. It wasn't my intention to dig up something that would hurt you."

"I needed to know," I said. "No one else would have told me."

"Vergie didn't even tell anybody she'd died." His voice was low. "I think she thought it would make it real if she told people, and she just didn't want to believe it could have happened that way. She had your mother cremated, in that little town in Texas. It was just a speck on the map, so even if the story made the news, it was a story no one out here would hear. Vergie kept that secret as long as she could. She just let people around here think Martine was off in another state, estranged."

"It was less painful that way."

"Yes," he said. "The whole thing broke her heart, but it would have killed her to have people pity her the rest of her life. She told me that much—she couldn't bear the thought of all that sympathy and judging."

"So she never had a funeral."

He shook his head. "We scattered the ashes in the creek behind her house, said some words for her. But that was all."

"Thank you for telling me."

His eyes looked glassy. "I'm sorry you had to learn about it this way. I'm sorry Vergie couldn't tell you herself. It shouldn't be a stranger telling you things like this."

"It's better to know." It hurt more, but it was better. Kate had been right about that part.

After a while, the first wave of customers left, and a new wave started coming in for the afternoon. Kate came back to the table with a plate heaped with beignets and a dusting of powdered sugar across her cheek. She looked at me and I gave her a little nod, and then she sat down again.

George sat back in his chair and sipped his coffee. His bushy white eyebrows furrowed now when he looked at me, framing kind hazel eyes. Now it was easy to picture him doing the things Vergie had described, like raising hostas and fishing out on the lake. He seemed like a good man, a good match for Vergie.

"George, do you have plans for Thanksgiving?" I said.

There was a small smile. "I'll probably stay at home and watch the parade. I like quiet holidays. Don't travel to see anyone anymore, and usually I just see my kids at Christmas."

"Would you like to come to my house?"

He shifted in his chair again, then glanced at Kate. She smiled and nudged the plate toward him. "Save us from ourselves," she said, and he plucked a beignet from the plate.

"It'll just be a few friends and family," I said. "I'd love to have you there." He'd like Josie and Buck, I thought, and I got the sense he didn't have a lot of friends left.

After a moment, his eyes shifted back to me, and he smiled. "I'd like that too. I'll bring a dessert. Your grandmother taught me how to make her prize-winning buttermilk pie."

"That sounds perfect," I said, and it did.

Chapter Six

DOWN IN THE FRENCH QUARTER, people were buzzing around like bees in a hive. It was almost as busy as the summer, when tourists seemed to outnumber locals ten to one. Music poured out of doors as they opened, the notes ricocheting across the sidewalks. Even in what would be a holiday rush anywhere else, people down here moved at a slower pace. That was something I never tired of. I'd never thought of Raleigh as being that fast-paced until I'd settled in down here, and then it seemed I'd spent far too much of my life hurrying through it.

Jack had been an excellent experiment in slowing down. I'd never known anyone like him before—he moved through life with an easy swagger, and didn't let things get under my skin the way that I did. My family had felt broken for so long that sometimes I felt like I'd learned all the wrong coping mechanisms—with my father, I'd learned to bury my fears, hide my emotions, and avoid conflict at all costs. Luckily I'd met Kate in college, and she'd been the complete opposite of me in those ways. She'd taught me that it was OK to be vulnerable (in fact, it made you human), it was OK to tell people when they'd hurt you, and there was nothing wrong with asking for what you wanted. All of those ideas seemed obvious now, but when I'd met her, she'd flipped my world upside down.

"In here," Kate said, pulling me into a kitchen store. "You need a few supplies."

She'd volunteered to help Jack with our dinner—and though he had a well-equipped kitchen, with tools I'd never even seen before, she wanted a few particular items. Since I'd learned to mash potatoes with a fork, I didn't argue with her needs.

"I can't believe you don't have a meat thermometer," she said, tossing one into the basket.

"Jack just eyeballs everything."

"That's a genetic skill," she said. "One that, sadly, you don't have."

Determined not to be sidelined, she'd told Jack that she'd handle desserts since he insisted on Andre being his sous chef. He'd agreed, even though he thought a guest shouldn't lift a finger.

She led me through the store, filling the basket with various brushes, tongs and devices that looked more surgical than culinary. She grabbed an alligator-shaped oven mitt and put it on her hand like a puppet. "Obviously," she said, and kept it on as we walked down the next aisle.

My phone buzzed in my pocket. When I pulled it out, my father's number lit up on the screen and I quickly declined the call.

"Everything OK?" she said.

"Just my dad. He keeps calling. I keep sending it to voicemail." I was still furious at him, and he hadn't even approached an apology in his numerous texts and voice messages. Typical, because he never thought he did anything wrong. To him, lying about my mother's death was just another insignificant act that I was blowing out of proportion.

Dad seemed to not understand proportions at all.

"Have I told you I'm really glad you're here?" I said.

"Yes," she said, pulling a lidded baking dish from the shelf. "Do you want red or blue?"

"Blue."

"I take it Jack doesn't mind houseguests."

"Not at all. And technically, I'm still the landlady."

She smirked. "Right. Who'd have thought that hot guy from Vergie's funeral would end up being your tenant and sharing your bed."

On that day, Jack been a stranger in a well-cut suit, offering a soothing smile on a day full of sorrow and regret. I'd never expected to see him again, but then he'd turned up on my porch, all confident and helpful and over-the-top charming, · and I was a goner.

Kate knew about most of what had happened here last summer. She knew about flipping the house, working with Jack, all of the good parts.

None of the bad.

Not at first.

I'd waited until going back to Raleigh to tell her in person · the part about the arsonist. The fires. And the part about almost dying.

It had rattled her, of course, and she'd been hurt that I'd kept those things from her—even though it was only a couple of months. She'd also been furious and wanted to come down here and murder the person who'd tried to hurt me.

Kate was like that—she was a protector, and would do

anything to defend the people she loved. Before Jack, she was the only person I could count on to stand up for me when I needed it. She was the only person I'd trusted completely.

"Are you listening?" Kate asked, holding a ceramic pie plate.

I snapped back to Aisle 6. Crock-Pots, double-boilers, Dutch ovens.

"Sorry."

"Stop fantasizing about your fella. We're talking about pie, and that's more important."

I snorted. "I was not fantasizing."

She rolled her eyes. "Please. Your walls are like cardboard. Don't even try."

I opened my mouth to protest, and she tossed the oven mitt at me. "Do you have deep pie dishes? Chocolate-bourbon pecan pie is only good if it's in a huge deep pie dish. Those little shallow ones are for amateurs."

"How deep is a deep dish?"

"How do you survive without me?" She grabbed a ceramic dish and stuck it under her arm as she led me down the next aisle.

When she was satisfied we had the tools she needed, we stashed our kitchen gear in the car and headed over to the Faubourg-Marigny district, which seldom had as much foot traffic as the Quarter. Since it was a Monday, it was even quieter than usual.

"One more errand," I said. The small shop I was looking for looked more like a house, painted yellow with white trim. It had been months since I'd come to see Duchess, but this time it was not for protection—not like before.

As I opened the door, Kate asked, "What's this place?"

"I need something for Buck."

She gave me a skeptical look. "Like magic?"

"More like holistic."

The bell above the door clanged. Duchess' big orange cat was still keeping guard, perched on the front counter by the cash register. We walked up one aisle before I heard the familiar voice. "Good afternoon. You ladies looking for anything in particular?"

Duchess drifted into the center of the aisle, a bright purple dress billowing around her. Her dark skin seemed to glow against the fabric. She had piled her hair high on her head in tight braids, and she wore one pair of reading glasses tucked into her hair, while another pair dangled from the V of her dress.

"Hi, Duchess," I said. "We're just looking for a gift."

She stared at me and then smiled. "How are you doing these days, chérie? Haven't seen you in a while, so I figured you must have chased the bad away."

At that, Kate raised her eyebrows.

"Just fine," I said. "This is my friend Kate. She's visiting for the holidays."

Duchess shook her hand, her bangle bracelets clinking together like wind chimes.

"Y'all need anything in particular?"

We'd paused by a basket full of mojo bags, not unlike the one Duchess had made up for me. She didn't cater to the tourists looking for souvenirs. These pouches, with little tags that explained what they were meant to attract, may have looked similar to what the typical tourist shops had, but I knew they were different.

These actually worked.

I picked up a blue one with a tag that read "good health."

"I just wanted a couple of things for a friend," I said. "Nothing big today."

She slipped her glasses out of her hair and onto her nose. "Your aura's looking better these days. Still looks a little pale, though."

I smiled. "What you gave me last time worked."

"No more pesky triangle, then."

"No ma'am."

She nodded, glancing at Kate, as if there was more she was tempted to say. Instead, she smiled and turned back toward her office. "Take your time. Call me when you're ready."

She sauntered back up the aisle, past the beaded curtain that led to a work table in the back room. The last time I'd been here, the table had been covered with an array of herbs, handmade dolls and small animal skulls.

"So how exactly do you know about all of this?" Kate said.

"Remember how I said the house was such a pain to fix? I started to think it might have a curse on it. I figured a little good mojo couldn't hurt, so I came here."

Kate's blue eyes widened. "You, who laughed at me for having my palm read."

"I know. Sometimes there's wisdom in the old methods. And believe me, after some of the things that happened at that house, I was willing to try anything. Now I come mostly for the tinctures. And the amazing body butters."

Kate continued down the aisle, smelling the scented candles and sliding her fingers along the fabric of the dolls. "Maybe I should get her to mix up something for me. Something to attract the right kind of man."

"She's not into love spells. Says they always go south."

"My methods don't seem to be working any more," Kate said. "I think I need a professional."

I pulled a couple of tinctures from the shelf. "Nah. You just need the sheriff."

She frowned. "You know that wouldn't work. He's hours away from Raleigh, and he's not my type. Not even close."

"Smart, kind, funny—not your type any more?"

"You know what I mean. Can you see me with a man who goes fishing and camping and wears cowboy shirts?"

I shrugged. "Actually, yeah."

She swatted my arm. "Also, it's way too soon. I think my radar is severely broken. I need to take some time away from the dating pool. Like a sabbatical."

"Or maybe you should jump right back in, while your guard is up. Sometimes the counter-intuitive move is the best one."

She sighed. "I'm just so tired of this pattern. It's like I'm doomed to pick the wrong one over and over. What if part of my brain is broken, and I'm just going to keep doing this again and again, forever?"

"Your brain's not broken. You just picked a guy that made a colossally bad decision."

She frowned, plucking a candle from the shelf. "I seem to do that a lot myself."

"Everybody makes bad decisions now and then. Sometimes it takes a long time to figure out how compatible you are with someone. That's not indicative of a problem. I think your science people call that 'trial and error.'"

She laughed. "My people?"

"Don't put so much pressure on yourself. Experiments aren't failures just because they don't turn out the way you expect. One of the smartest women I know once told me that."

"Using my own words against me, now."

I shrugged. "When you're right, you're right."

She nodded toward my armful of items. "What are you getting?"

I dangled the blue pouch. "Good health and healing, for Buck. The rest is for me. This particular tincture makes me sleep like a log."

"Definitely going to need one of those," she said.

I handed her the smal bottle along a red pouch, whose tag indicated it kept fires in the heart burning. Duchess might not concoct her own love spells, but she seemed to have no problem stocking items that one might use to plant a seed of attraction in the person she desired.

Kate turned it over in her hands and looked thoughtful. "Maybe I should get a bag full of these."

"Couldn't hurt," I said.

I didn't really think the things in this shop had any magical element, and I certainly didn't think Duchess had any supernatural ability. She was, however, a kind of healer. Some folks need different kinds of healing than others, and it seemed that sometimes people found faith in themselves by placing it in other things—even if just for a little while. If a little mojo bag could remind me to cut myself some slack and chase after what I wanted, then it wasn't so bad to have around.

After picking up a few oils and candles, I went back to the front counter. Kate wandered down the last aisle, browsing as I picked up a bar of lavender soap and added it to my pile. Duchess came out of her work room, the beaded curtain tinkling as she headed to the register.

When she reached the counter, she plucked another bar of soap from the display and handed it to me. Speckled pink and brown like granite, it smelled like cinnamon and cloves.

"This one's good for heartache," she said. "On the house."

Thanking her, I wondered exactly what she could see when

I met her gaze. I imagined she could read people the way some
folks read tea leaves, ferreting out their secrets and their shame
simply by studying the flecks of light and darkness in their
eyes.

I waited by the door as Kate checked out. She'd bought a
few tinctures, a candle, and a couple of the small pouches—a
blue one, for health, and the red one I'd handed her.

BACK AT THE HOUSE, I was surprised to see Josie's car in the
yard. Inside, Lucille and Jack were in the living room,
watching a movie and eating take-out.

"Hey you two," Jack said. "We brought a couple of plates
from Brenda's for y'all—shrimp étouffée today. I'll heat them
up." He walked over and kissed me quickly on his way into
the kitchen.

Kate smiled. "Keep feeding me like this and I'll never
leave."

I sat next to Lucille on the sofa. "Did Toph come with you?"

"Nah," she said. "He's meeting some friend of his in the
city tonight." The lilt in her voice made it sound like she
wasn't entirely unhappy with that plan. "He's already itching
to get out of here, driving me bonkers. He thinks all small
towns are boring, and full of ignorant rednecks."

"Charming," Kate muttered.

Lucille frowned. "He can be a dick about stuff like that."

Kate said, "I need something in a lowball glass. Enza, can I
bring you one?"

"Sure."

"He's just a dick in general these days," Lucille said, when
she was out of earshot. "He's rubbed everybody the wrong

way since he got here. Jack's about ready to lock me up in the basement until I come to my senses, and Mom and Dad can't stand him. They try to be civil, but I can tell." She shook her head. "Every time I look at Dad, he seems to be deciding what caliber to use."

"I know it's none of my business," I said, "but if you think he's a dick, why are you with him?"

She looked at me then, her green-brown eyes narrowed in a conspiratorial way. "He wasn't always like this. He had a certain swagger when we met—totally charming, and the life of the party. He's obviously used to getting his way and pulling strings to make things happen for himself. He also likes to win people over by making things happen for them. It's a huge ego thing, and for a while it's nice, having someone snap their fingers and talk to the right people, make a sly suggestion over cocktails and boom—your wish is my command."

She glanced into the kitchen and then continued. "I met him at a party, and he was completely insufferable—the name dropping, the bragging, the super-suave attitude. I thought he was awful. Just typical big-money Texas, all bravado and no brains." She shook her head. "He asked me out and I totally blew him off. But he was persistent. He'd come hang out at the dive bar where I worked, and I started to think this bravado was mostly an act. He was a good guy, but he'd learned that what got him farther in his business was his cocky playboy attitude. You probably think I'm nuts."

"I don't." It wasn't hard to see the seductive power of suddenly having the things you wanted. It would be hard for her to ignore, being so young and apparently unaccustomed to having men try to impress her. But the direction she was headed wasn't good. Anyone could see that. Maybe even her.

"It's selfish," she said. "I met him when everything in my life was going wrong. I was getting shitty tips from people who were as rude to me as they could get away with. I was racking up debt, and I was about to get evicted from my apartment. And then this guy shows up and wants to fix all that to win me over."

She shrugged, as if that was enough explanation. She looked far younger right then, with her cheeks a little flushed and a sad arch to her eyebrows.

"He offered to help when things were really bad, and I was desperate enough to let him. I thought he was a decent guy, and it seemed there was nothing to lose."

I nodded, wishing there was any easy way to fix this. It was easy to imagine him turning on the charm, swooping in to help her when she was most vulnerable. But it was also easy to see how manipulative that could be.

"He was really sweet," she said.

Was. As in not anymore.

She seemed to read that on my face and said, "And still is. This one time, when I was super stressed with school, he whisked me off for this spa weekend outside of Santa Fe. It was hands-down the most beautiful place I've ever been— some exclusive place that a friend of his owned, out in the middle of the desert. I'd never been to a ritzy spa before, and this one had a hiking trail and horseback riding." She smiled. "It was the perfect weekend. He used to surprise me like that all the time."

"And now?" I said gently.

She sighed. "He's just made a few bad calls lately and it's got him stressed out. And that means grumpy, and kind of an asshole. His family's got more money that God, though, so I don't get why he's so bent out of shape."

It sounded like one of those red flags everyone pointed to after violent events came out in the newspapers. I'd been around plenty of guys like him in Raleigh, clients of my father's, who thought their money entitled them to do anything they wanted. They'd use it to impress others of course, when it suited their needs, but just as easily they'd shift gears and use their means as license to treat people as badly as they wanted in order to get their way. My father had several clients, also investors, who thought of people just as they thought of their investment properties: a means to an end, and a loss you cut when the time came to take your next leap forward.

"We're just going through a rough patch," she said.

"Do your parents know any of this?"

"God, no!" she said. Glancing toward the kitchen she lowered her voice. "And they're not going to, either. I didn't want them paying for anything for me anymore. They put me through undergrad, and I know they had to take out loans. If Toph wanted to help me, and feel like he was coming in on his big white horse, I figured what harm could it do?"

A lot, I thought, but kept that to myself.

"What about Jack? Have you told him any of this?"

She frowned. "He's worse than my parents. He wouldn't understand."

"He might surprise you."

She arched a brow. "I've tried to tell him about all the good things Toph's done to help me, but it doesn't matter. He thinks he's taking advantage."

"Is he?"

She frowned. "I used to think we were good for each other. Now I'm not so sure. But I can't just leave him. Not now."

"You can if that's the best thing for you," I said.

"The thing is, he can be better. He was fine before—supportive, funny, sweet. Now he just expects me to do everything he tells me to." She shrugged. "I think work is stressing him out and he's just lashing out at the nearest person."

When I didn't reply, she said, "Plus, he got me this amazing job at the theater. He knew somebody, pulled some strings. I'd never have gotten it on my own, and if I stay with them, it could launch my career."

I wondered what he wanted in return but knew that was too crude to ask. No doubt Jack was wondering the same thing.

"It was a nice thing for him to do," she said. "He wanted to help me, and yeah, show off a little too. But deep down, I still think he's an all right guy. He's just going through a really hard time and he doesn't know how to deal." She shrugged. "Maybe this is how I can help him, you know? Help him learn some actual coping skills."

"OK," I said, but I still thought this was pretty far from OK. She seemed to be speaking in code, and I couldn't quite decide if she meant for me to decipher it.

"Isn't that what love's all about?" she said, "Sticking with your partner when things get hard?"

"Not if you're being hurt."

"It's not like that. He's—"

She stopped when Kate came back in with two drinks. Jack was right behind her, carrying two trays of steaming étouffée on proper plates.

"I heated it in the oven," Jack said, handing me one. "Brenda's is too good to murder it in the microwave."

Kate handed me a glass and clinked hers against it. "Cheers," she said, glancing at Lucille.

Jack sat next to me on the sofa and kissed me on the cheek. "Did y'all stay out of trouble today?"

"Mostly," I said.

Lucille finished her beer as Kate teased Jack about all the kitchen utensils he was missing, and how she'd decided to take me shopping to fill in the gaps. While she kidded him about meat thermometers, I considered Lucille's words, and wondered what she'd left out.

After Lucille had left and Kate had gone upstairs to bed, I ran a hot bath and climbed in with a paperback and two fingers of bourbon, trying not to think about Lucille and Toph anymore. Despite her assurances that everything was fine, I felt like I should say something to Jack. She was like his little sister, and he was fiercely protective of her. But two things were clear: Lucille still had feelings for Toph, and she genuinely wanted to help him through a hard time. It was absolutely none of my business, and I was hardly a relationship expert. Though I was concerned, it would be a betrayal of her trust to tell Jack anything she'd shared with me.

But he already despised the guy, and I didn't want to fan those flames.

When I'd read only a few pages, the door squeaked open, and Jack said, "Can I come in?"

"Of course."

His eyes drifted over my body as he knelt by the tub. "Hi there."

"Hi yourself."

He slid his hand along my shin. "I miss you."

I smiled. "But I'm right here."

"Yeah, but I want you all to myself again." He lifted my hand to his lips, kissed my palm as he laced his fingers in mine. His eyes were smoldering. "Kate's here, my family's here, I feel like a teenager trying to kiss you behind the bleachers."

"I hope you want to do more than kiss me."

He grinned. "Let's take off tomorrow. We can spend the night in a bed and breakfast in the middle of nowhere."

"What about Kate?"

"I'm sure she can entertain herself." He slid his hand beneath the water, tracing the curve of my thigh. A shiver ran along my skin. He leaned over, bracing one arm on the tub, and kissed me like he wanted to climb right into the tub with me. I ran my fingers through his hair, wondering if maybe he might, and then stopped when a ringing filled the air.

He pulled back. "Is that your phone?"

"It's on the counter," I said. "I keep it close because of Buck."

He picked it up and said, "It's your dad."

"Leave it." He'd called twice already today, and I refused to answer. He'd only tell me more lies, give me more excuses. I was tired of both.

Jack silenced the ringer and placed the phone back on the counter.

"See?" he said. "One more reason to escape for a day." He knelt beside the tub again, sliding his fingers along my ribs, down to my hips, creating the most delightful tingling sensation.

"Why don't you get in here with me," I said. When I shifted my knee, a little wave of water sloshed over the edge of the tub and onto his jeans. "Oops. You're all wet now. Might as well."

He grinned, his eyes darker in the dim light. "I'm dying to," he said, "but I don't think I could keep quiet. And I know you couldn't." He teased me with his fingers until my breath caught in my throat.

I splashed him again, and he caught my hand and brought it to his lips. He traced his tongue along my fingers, giving them a tiny pinch with his teeth, and I wanted to feel his tongue and teeth everywhere.

"Tell me more about this escape plan," I said.

"What if I said I wanted to surprise you?" he said, his lips moving along my knuckles. He was awfully good with surprises.

"Fair enough. Surprise me."

He leaned down to kiss me, catching my lip in his teeth. "You got yourself a date, chère. I'll arrange everything. We can leave after breakfast."

He kissed me harder as I tugged at his shirt. His hands slipped beneath the water, squeezing my hips, and all I wanted was to feel his hands slide over every inch of me. When my fingers slid to his belt, he stood abruptly and flashed his crooked grin.

"Hey," I said. "Where do you think you're going?"

"I have a few things to plan. And your water's going to get cold."

"Shame on you, getting me all worked up."

"You're going to love the way I make that up to you, darlin'." He winked in that way that meant he was already planning wicked things to do to me—and I couldn't wait to be alone with him so he could tick every one of those ideas off his list. Slowly.

Chapter Seven

"OH, I see. You need some sexy time." Kate stared at me over the rim of her coffee cup.

I swatted her on the shoulder. We were at the kitchen table, which had become the war room for our dinner planning—Kate had dubbed it Operation Turkey Trot. Jack was out on a recon mission for groceries, his last errand before we went to the bed and breakfast he'd found.

"I get it. You're in the honeymoon phase. I'll just stay here with the dog, and watch goofy rom-coms and drink all your bourbon. It's cool."

"He asked me very nicely. And it's impossible to say no to him when he—"

"Got it," she interrupted. "The executive summary was just fine."

"You should ask Andre to come keep you company."

She arched a brow. "You are merciless."

"You'd do the same for me."

She rolled her eyes.

"Admit it. You think he's hot."

She snorted. "Of course he's hot. I'm not blind."

"Call him," I said.

"Isn't that breaking some cardinal rule? Fun naked times with your boyfriend's BFF?"

"Please." I pulled my phone from my pocket and dialed Andre's number.

"What are you doing?" she said, narrowing her eyes.

"Hey, Andre," I said. "What are you doing tonight?"

"I'm going to murder you," Kate said. "I'm going to hide your body out in the swamp, and not even this dog with the super sniffer will find you."

"If you want him to slap cuffs on you, you could probably just ask," I told her. Then to Andre, I said, "I had an idea you might like."

THE BED AND BREAKFAST, to my surprise, had one room left. Most places were likely booked this whole week, but Jack had found a nice remote place that had one night open. The inn was an old colonial-style house with a wraparound porch and wood shutters. Hundred-year-old oak trees lined the path to the front of the house, one of them braced with a system of two-by-fours meant to stop the tree from splitting under the weight of its limbs.

We were only thirty miles from Bayou Sabine, but it felt like we were days away. Jack had taken back roads, on purpose I thought, to make me feel like we were farther away from the parts of our life we wanted to escape. Here in the delta country southwest of New Orleans, the land felt almost primordial, like it had just emerged from the Gulf through a violent act of nature. Verdant and lush, the trees wavered in the ocean breeze. The air was salty, filled with the twittering of birds hidden in the brush. There was something eerie about being right at sea level, knowing you could dig a hole with your boot heel and watch as ocean water filled the void. The breeze lifted my hair, and I had a flash of memory from a college architecture course, a professor who droned on about Grecian temples at Delphi, the navel of the world. Delphi was where the oracle lived, at the center of Zeus' "Grandmother Earth." It was a sanctuary, where you went to find wisdom and peace. Standing in the spongy soil, it wasn't much of a stretch to imagine this delta as that same hallowed ground, the point tying us to whatever force had pushed this land up from the crust of the earth.

Out here, you could drive for five full minutes without seeing a house. The bayou was bigger, wilder, with taller grasses and louder birds. Cypress roots tangled like the tentacles of giant sea creatures, tumbling over each other in the dark water.

After taking a walk around the grounds, Jack said, "So your next surprise is a massage over in the spa building. There's a steam room there, too, and there's a little wine and cheese tasting that starts at five."

"I can't even remember the last massage I had."

"Correct. So we're rectifying that today." He smiled and said, "I'll have some wine waiting for you when you're all done. You can meet me in main building."

"OK, you were right. This was exactly what I needed."

He smiled his crooked smile and laced his fingers in mine. "I thought you could stand to get away for a minute.

～

AFTER HAVE the best massage of my life and a couple of glasses of wine on the porch with Jack, I felt like I was approaching normal again. My body had been a tangle of tension and frayed nerves, but now I felt like I could breathe again.

"It's nearly seven," Jack said. "I should probably make myself presentable for dinner." The inn's owner, Maggie, had told us when we arrived that she served a candlelight dinner in the formal dining room. Thankfully, I'd listened to the part of my brain that insisted I bring something nice to wear and take this rare opportunity to dress like a woman—and not look out of place doing so.

When we went up to our room, I said, "I'm going to take a quick shower."

Jack stepped close to me, slipping his hand around my waist. "Would you like some company?"

"That would make us very late to dinner."

"Definitely." He bit his lip, sliding both hands over my hips. "What if we skipped dinner?"

I slid my hands under his shirt and said, "How about you spend the next hour thinking of all the things you could do to me that would constitute dessert."

"That'll be a mighty long list, chère."

"It better be." I tousled his hair as I stepped into the bathroom.

I showered quickly, and when I emerged, wrapped in a towel, Jack kissed me quickly on the cheek. "My turn."

"It's quarter till."

He smirked. "I'll be fast." The water was already running.

"I'll meet you downstairs, OK?"

"Sure," he called out, and I heard his belt buckle clatter against the floor.

If I hurried, I could be downstairs before he finished his shower.

Quickly, I unzipped my suitcase and pulled out the purple halter-top dress I'd bought with Kate back in the spring. She'd insisted I buy it, though it cost more than I ever spent on clothes. I didn't even spend that kind of money on my favorite cowboy boots. But Kate had said I'd soon have a reason to wear this "va-voom" dress as she called it, and this was that special occasion. Jack needed a surprise, too.

I slipped the dress on and zipped the side zipper, then leaned over and ran my fingers through my hair, trying to encourage more bounce into it. I thought briefly of those commercials I'd seen as a teenager, as women bent their heads and tried to fluff their hair up after work before a night out, as they stepped off the subway, or in the ladies' room on a date. I hadn't had many occasions to do such a thing, and it made me laugh doing it then.

After spritzing my hair with some magical tonic that tamed my curls into beach waves, I put on a little mascara and lipstick. The shower turned off just as I stepped into my heels. After a couple more fluffs and squeezes, I slipped out the door and went downstairs, trying to remember how to walk gracefully in shoes that were not cowboy boots.

The dining room was like something out of a movie. The owner, Maggie, was a petite woman who looked about fifty. She wore a sleek black pencil skirt and black polka-dot blouse, and had her blonde hair piled in a messy bun. She'd told us earlier that the house had been in her family for five generations. Her mother had turned it into an inn, and Maggie had taken over a dozen years before. She smiled as I sat down at a table set for two in the back of the dining room by the windows. From there, I'd see Jack when he entered the room.

Maggie came by and filled two water glasses. "That's a great color for you," she said. "Would you two care for wine this evening?"

"Thanks—and yes, we'd love some."

She nodded and disappeared into the kitchen. The room buzzed with the chatter of the other guests, mostly couples.

After a while, a movement in the hallway caught my eye. When I looked up, I saw Jack paused in the doorway. When his eyes met mine and he walked toward me with his slow swagger, I couldn't stop the grin from spreading over my face.

He was wearing the gray suit. The one he'd had on when I first saw him, when I'd had no idea how he was about to transform my life. He'd joked about wearing that suit again, after he'd learned how I'd admired the way it clung to my favorite parts of him. It was just snug enough in the shoulders and the hips for me to notice those parts now and think fondly of what I'd do with them later. He'd made it slightly more casual tonight, skipping the tie and leaving his light blue shirt unbuttoned at the collar.

"Well, hi there," he said, pausing by the chair. "Mind if I join you?"

"Nice suit."

He sat across from me. "And that, darlin', is one incredible dress." His eyes drifted over the lines of the halter top.

"I was saving it for a special occasion."

"Is that right?" He grinned his wolfish grin, and I felt my cheeks burn.

"Why, Miss Parker. You're blushing."

"Just thinking of you, Mr. Mayronne, and the cut of that lovely suit."

Before I could say more, Maggie was back with a bottle of

red and two glasses. "I knew he wouldn't be too long," she said with a wink. "Good evening, Mr. Mayronne."

"Good evening," he said, and I fought back a chuckle, thinking of the times I'd called him by his full name, back before we'd become so delightfully entangled.

"I told you I'd find an occasion to wear it again," he said, clinking his glass against mine. "If for no other reason than to let you separate me from it one button at a time."

He slid his knee against mine under the table, and I felt the warmth spread through my entire body. Part of me wanted to march right back up to that room and skip dinner altogether.

"You're staring," I said.

"I'm admiring. That's not at all the same thing." He smiled and sipped his wine. When he set the glass down, he looked serious. The color of the suit made his eyes look a deeper shade of blue.

"What is it?" I asked him.

"I'm just awfully glad you walked up onto my porch that hot and muggy day."

"That was *my* porch." I took a sip of wine to hide my smile.

"Details, details." He slid his hand over mine. "I never expected someone like you to wander into my life. I just wanted to make sure you knew how happy I am that you stayed."

"I'm glad *I* stayed—and I'm glad you were too stubborn to leave."

"And people talk like stubbornness is a bad quality."

Maggie came over and set two plates in front of us. "Lamb chops with mango salsa," she said. "Fresh greens and roasted potatoes. Enjoy."

There was a little tower of lamb and vegetables on each plate, sauces drizzled across the white of the dish.

"Best inn ever," I said, and Jack grinned.

"Glad you like it."

"I love it. Thanks for taking me out for the day."

"My pleasure."

We ate in silence for long enough that it started to make me nervous. I knew Jack had something on his mind, but I couldn't figure out why he was being so secretive about it. He usually had no problem telling me what was bothering him. It wasn't until Maggie cleared our plates away that I spoke.

"What's going on with you?" I asked.

"What do you mean?"

"You seem distracted."

He sighed, laying his napkin on the table. "I'm sorry. I don't mean to be."

"Maybe it was you who needed to get away for a day." I was only half-joking, but he gave me a sweet smile that said I wasn't entirely wrong.

Maggie reappeared with two crème brûlées in tiny saucers.

"Jack."

He raked his hands through his hair. He was nervous. "I need to ask you something."

Quick as a cat, Maggie slid two flutes of Champagne in front of us without asking.

Shit. I swallowed hard. We'd barely talked about marriage, and suddenly he was nervous, and twitchy, and there was Champagne and a fancy dinner.

"Thank you," Jack said to her, and every part of my body seemed to go numb. I glanced around the room, trying to determine just how big of a scene this was going to be. My throat tightened, and I hoped I'd be able to choke out a few words without sounding like a fool, without crushing him into pieces. The room spun like a carousel, and I took a deep breath. I was not ready for this. I didn't like big scenes, surprise proposals in front of strangers. I didn't like to be the center of attention, and he knew all of these things.

His eyes leveled on mine.

I thought of bolting, running to the restroom to give him some hint that I wasn't ready, to spare him hurt feelings, but I felt cemented to the chair.

"I didn't want to do this here," he said, shaking his head. "This was supposed to be just about you and me."

Downing half my Champagne with a complete lack of grace, I glanced toward the doorway again.

"But I can't shake this thought," he said. "I can't think about anything else, no matter how hard I try."

I took another swig from my glass and willed my body to stop shaking. I loved him. What we had was exactly what I needed. I didn't want to hurt him. Not here, not tonight. Not ever.

He leaned forward. "Did Lucille say anything to you about Toph?"

"What?" I said.

"I know she's not telling me everything. I know something messed up is going on."

As I looked at him, I willed my heart to get back into its normal rhythm. "That's what you wanted to ask me?"

"I'm sorry," he said. "I wanted to take you away and have you all to myself and make some time for just us. But I just can't get this out of my head."

I opened my mouth to speak, but no words came out.

"I'm worried about her," he said. "I didn't want to ruin our night. But I have a seriously bad feeling about that guy." He reached across the table and took my hand, his fingers sliding over my palm.

I let out a heavy sigh, heavier than I'd intended. He gave me a quizzical look.

It wasn't my place to tell Lucille's secrets. I knew that. But I also knew that Jack thought of her as his sister, and he was fiercely protective.

"She didn't tell me much," I said. "Just that he was a jerk to people sometimes, but not to her. She asid he's been really stressed out lately."

Jack watched me as I picked at the crème brûlée.

"She's a smart girl," I said. "She won't take any shit from him." That was mostly true, I suspected.

"I'm not sure I believe that entirely." He took a sip of the Champagne and eased back in his chair. "Something's not right with him. There's something going on that she's not saying."

I wanted to tell him the rest of it, right there. About Lucille, about Toph, about this debt she thought she owed him. I wanted to tell Jack everything she told me, but when I opened my mouth, I saw her face, felt the tug of her hand on my arm, the way she'd dug her fingers into my skin and begged me not to tell.

It was not my secret to tell. But I couldn't say nothing.

"It's her decision," I said, placing my hand over his. "You have to trust her to figure this out and do what's right for her."

He said nothing, but I knew he was thinking of my bad decision. The one that had put me in the path of a dangerous man. He wouldn't say that to me directly because he was too kind. But I knew what he was thinking. I was thinking it myself: one careless move had put me into a situation that I was lucky to get out of. It wouldn't have ended that way for everyone.

And I'd had people to help me.

"You should ask her," I said. "But you have to let her know you're not judging her, and that you have her back. She won't talk to you if she thinks you're going to pull a caveman move and tell her what to do."

He was quiet for a long moment and then said, "I don't want us to keep things from each other. I don't like secrets." He leaned close to me then, a brushed a lock of hair behind my ear. "I mean, I'm sure there's a world of things I don't know about you, but I don't want us to hide things from each other intentionally. Can we have that agreement?"

"I don't like secrets, either," I said. And I didn't. They ate me up inside.

His eyes were steady on mine, that cool piercing gaze. I couldn't look away. If I did, he'd know I was still hiding something. But if I stared at him too long, he'd see it in my eyes.

"Would you talk to her? See if she'll tell you anything more?" There was a hint of pleading in his voice.

"I really don't want to be in the middle, Jack. It's not fair to her."

"I think she's scared to tell me," he said, sipping his water.

"You just need to be straight with her. And don't be scary."

He nodded. "Less scary. I can do that." He topped off our glasses and said, "But if she tells you anything else, you'll let me know, right? You'll tell me if there's something bad going on."

"Of course," I said and the words tasted bitter. I hoped to whatever higher power was in the universe that Lucille would talk to him first.

∾

LATER THAT NIGHT, when all the other guests were back in their rooms, Jack and I sat on the wraparound porch under a string of white lights that blinked like fireflies. The empty wine bottle from dinner sat on the floor between us, and I was back to feeling pleasantly tipsy and relaxed.

"I think there's a maze out back in the garden," he said. "Want to come and get lost with me?"

"Absolutely."

He took my hand and led me through the backyard, past the oaks with their curling limbs. The moon was high, full as a plate. My heels wobbled in the soft earth, and when I paused to slip them off, I leaned against his shoulder and felt his hand against the small of my back. "Here," he said, and slipped his jacket off his shoulders and onto mine. He kissed me quick, right below my earlobe, and then led me into the maze.

The air was beginning to cool but was still oddly warm for November. The farther we went into the maze, the warmer it felt, as if the walls of foliage had blocked the chill. The walls were made of boxwoods, nearly eight feet tall and dense from years of growth. They were manicured to look like real walls, with only a few rogue sprouts breaking the smoothness of the surface. I dragged my free hand along the stubbly leaves as Jack led me toward the center, winding to the left, then the right, as if he knew exactly where we were headed. The leaves were stiff and waxy, not soft as I'd imagined they'd feel beneath my fingers.

He pulled me deeper along the corridors, and soon we came to a small space with a bench and an arbor covered in vines that likely bloomed in the summer. The only sound was the rusting of leaves in the breeze, and the occasional call from a distant bird. As he pulled me against him, sliding his hands down my back, he said, "Finally, I get you to myself again."

His lips moved against my neck as he told me all the things he was planning to do to me, and I ran my fingers through his hair, tugging him closer. He pulled me toward the bench and sat, his fingers laced in mine. When I climbed onto his lap; straddling him, he slid his hands under the skirt of my dress.

"Are you cold?" he said.

"Not anymore."

He watched as I slipped his jacket from my shoulders and laid it next to him on the back of the bench.

His eyes were luminous in the dim light, wide and full of longing. His hands were warm against my back, pulling me against his chest. I rested my hands on his shoulders as he slid his fingers along my cheek and kissed me, gently at first. He still tasted faintly of wine.

"I miss this," he said, and then his fingers were in my hair, gently tugging in that way he knew made me wild. "I miss having you all to myself."

He sighed as I unbuttoned his shirt, my hands sliding along his chest. "Do you think everyone in that big old house has gone to bed?" I said.

"Probably." His hands slipped under my dress again and squeezed my hips.

"That bed upstairs is awfully creaky." I caught his earlobe in my teeth and I felt his body tense beneath mine. "I bet we'd knock every single slat out and wake the whole place."

"We'd be blacklisted forever." His hands drifted over my thighs, his fingers drawing a slow, deliberate line. "And this is such a nice place. I think I'd like to come back some day."

When I leaned down to kiss him, I slid my hand down his chest, inside his pants, and found him already hard. "We should probably just stay out here," I said, my lips moving against his ear.

"But you'll ruin that lovely dress."

"Not if you take it off."

His grin was wicked. I tugged at the zipper, and he pulled the dress over my head in one fluid motion, then folded it in half and draped it on the bench on top of his jacket. His eyes were dark and wide in the dim light. His hands roamed over my skin, warming me.

"Nice lace," he mumbled, tracing his fingers along the top of my bra. He kissed a line along my neck, his stubbled jaw tickling me in that way he knew made me shiver down to my toes. My squirming made him chuckle and hold me tighter in place. He was merciless in his teasing, his rough hands moving me exactly where he wanted me.

Frustrated by the limitations of this bench, I wriggled off his lap and got to my feet.

"Where do you think you're going?" he said, his eyes fixed on me.

"Come here," I said, tugging on his belt.

He stood then, and let me pull him against me as I slowly peeled his shirt from his shoulders.

He sighed as I eased the shirt down his arms, letting my palms linger over the taut muscles of his forearms. His breaths quickened as I unfastened his belt and pants. As soon as he's stepped out of them, he moved toward me, quick as a cat, and his body was hard against mine, one arm tight against my hips, his other hand tangled in my hair. He kissed me fiercely as he nudged us toward one of the boxwoods. My hands clawed at his shoulders. My heart banged against my ribs. His teeth pinched my lip as he kissed me with an urgency I hadn't felt in weeks. He groaned my name as I tugged at his hair and then he eased me onto the grass. The ground was cool, the grass prickly, but I forgot that as soon as I felt the warmth of his body pressing into mine.

One of his hands slid along my cheek. The other he trailed along my side, over my hip, and slid into the fabric of my panties.

"What are these still doing on?" he said. "Such bothersome things, these undergarments."

I laughed as he slid them down to my ankles, shivering in the chilly air. Before I could complain, he was back on top of me, teasing me with his fingers. I gasped as he traced tiny circles, and I caught myself before I cried out.

He grinned, fixing me with his eyes. "I'd love to make you howl out here in the dark, Miz Parker. But we're not so far from the main building, and I'd hate for someone to interrupt us."

"Right," I breathed. "Quiet."

"So let's play a game, shall we?"

His lips moved along my skin as he spoke, teasing one breast with light kisses before he caught my nipple in his teeth.

I gasped and he grinned a devilish grin.

"See, I did my homework. I made this list like you asked." His lips brushed my ribs, down to my navel, across to my hip. "I'll do every naughty thing you asked me to think of, but only if you can keep quiet." His lips brushed the top of my thigh, and my whole body tensed. Already, I couldn't get enough of him.

"One loud noise, and you'll make me stop," he said, his thumb sliding up the inside of my thigh.

My body arched toward him, aching to feel his hands and lips everywhere.

"Those are the rules," he said. "Agreed?"

"Yes," I whispered, grabbing a handful of his hair.

He smirked as he kissed the inside of my thigh. One swipe of his tongue and I gasped, clawing at his shoulders. He made a contended sound and then there was only his expert tongue, his nimble fingers, and his big hand pinning my hip down as if it were the only thing holding me to the earth.

I writhed beneath him, but he took his time—he took such delight in working me into a frenzy, and I wanted to live here, pinned by his hands and his piercing gaze forever. There was a tiny pinch of his teeth—damn him—and I stifled a cry.

He paused and whispered, "Careful, chère," his voice like gravel, and I tugged at his hair until he started again. My heart hammered in my chest and when I felt myself start to come apart, he brought his face back up to mine. "You make me crazy," he whispered, his lips moving against my ear as he moved inside me, one quick motion that made my entire body arch beneath him. He traced his lips along the curve of my neck, his words falling as softly on my skin as his tongue. Above us, the sky was as black, the stars scattered like pinholes of light.

"Jack," I whispered, and heard the ragged edge to my voice. I struggled to keep my breathing even as he moved faster, his hips keeping a circular motion that would certainly unravel me. I tightened my legs around his waist, and he groaned, a rough sound that sent a shiver along my arms. He pinned my hands into the grass, his fingers laced in mine, and gazed down at me as he slowed his movements.

My head still buzzed from the wine, my chest tingled from the cool night air. I squeezed my thighs tighter around him, and he gasped, tilting his head toward the stars. When he looked back at me, his eyes were wide, a crooked smile on his face.

"I'll never get enough of you," he whispered.

I bit my lip, trying not to call his name into the night. He only grinned as he watched me struggle, my body shuddering under his. Then he leaned down, his forearms resting by my ears. He kissed me lightly on the lips, and I felt his heart pounding against my skin.

He tangled his fingers in mine again, then brought them to his lips. After a minute, he said, "Do you have any idea how much you mean to me?"

"An inkling," I said.

He smiled so wrinkles formed at the corners of his eyes. "Surely it's more than an inkling." He slid over to my side, wrapping his arm over my chest, draping his leg over mine. We lay like that for a while, staring up at the moon, and I thought of the prickly grass, the dappled light, the cluster of stars directly above: If I thought of those things, I didn't think of Lucille and the words I'd said that I hoped were true.

HE STOOD SLOWLY, then pulled me to my feet, brushing the grass from my backside.

I slipped my panties back on as he stepped into his boxers and then the suit pants. He buttoned his shirt, smiling as I struggled to get my dress on the right way in the dark. He draped his jacket over my shoulders and then retrieved my shoes. When we were convinced we weren't leaving any traces of us behind, we wound our way back to the outside of the maze, where the air was crisper, the light brighter.

Late in the night, when we lay with our limbs tangled in the big four-poster bed, he traced his fingers from my shoulder to my hip, over and over, lulling me to sleep. "I'm glad you came away with me," he said.

"So am I." I laughed then, still a bit giddy from the wine.

"What is it?"

"Nothing."

I giggled again, and he slid his fingers along my ribs, making me squirm.

"Tell me," he said. "Or I'll be forced to tickle it out of you."

"It's just the Champagne," I said. "Do you even like Champagne? Did you order it tonight?"

"No," he said. "She surprised me when she brought it out."

"I thought you had it sent over. It scared me for a second."

"Champagne scared you?"

"I thought you were about to propose," I blurted out before my brain had time to filter the thought. I immediately regretted it and wished I could snatch those words out of the air and stuff them right back in my head where they belonged.

I turned to face him, and his eyebrows shot up.

"Oh," he said.

I stared at him, trying to think of anything I might say to fix this.

After a long pause, he said, "And that scared you?"

"Scared is the wrong word. Startled."

"Why would that be startling?"

"Startlingly romantic, but sort of sudden." I bit my lip, wishing I'd just rolled over and gone to sleep without another word.

"I see."

"I'm just saying, six months is a little fast. You wouldn't move that fast."

He shrugged. There was a hint of a smile. "So if I'd asked you, you would have said no?"

"No. I mean yes. I mean—never mind." I sighed, sliding a

pillow over my head. "Can we just forget the last five minutes happened?"

"You don't want to get married," he said. "Like, not ever?"

"It wrecked my parents. Sometimes I'm afraid it would wreck us too." I studied his face, but whatever he was feeling, he was hiding it well.

"I see."

"I love you, Jack. I love being with you, and I love what's happening between us. But marriage terrifies me."

He pulled me against him and kissed my forehead. "I get it."

"Why are we talking about this? You didn't even ask. We had a perfect day."

He chuckled, and I relaxed a little. For an instant, I was afraid I'd hurt his feelings, but he squeezed me tighter and said, "You've thought about it. I'll take that."

"Well, of course I've thought about it."

He smiled. "I wouldn't do it like that. I know you hate big scenes."

"But you've thought about it, too."

"I'd marry you tomorrow if you'd let me." He tightened his arms around me, and kissed me on the forehead. "But I'll wait."

My body relaxed as he folded his arms over my chest, and I fell asleep before I could think of anything else to say.

Chapter Eight

I KNEW something was wrong the second we set foot in the house. Kate was in the kitchen, whisking something in a bowl with all the fury she could muster. An open bottle of George Dickel No 12 sat on the counter next to a shot glass and one of Jack's dog-eared cookbooks. It looked like a bakery had exploded.

"I'll just be...somewhere else," Jack said, and squeezed my shoulder before going down the hall to the bedroom.

"Kate?" I asked. "What's going on?"

"I'm making a sponge cake," she said. The kitchen window was open, but it still felt like it was ninety degrees inside. Kate had stripped down to a tank top and jogging shorts. Her hair was piled high on her head, a dusting of flour in her bangs.

"So I see."

She dumped the contents of the bowl into a cake pan, slapped the last dollop in with a spatula, and shoved it into the oven.

"I thought sponge cakes were delicate," I said.

"They are!" She slammed the door to the oven.

I cringed. "Is this about Andre? What did he do?"

She brushed her hair out of her eyes and grabbed another mixing bowl from the cabinet. "No. Andre was charming, and delightful, and completely wonderful." The bowl clattered against the counter—it was one of Vergie's old ceramic ones that I loved. She rummaged through a utensil drawer and the sound was like a car being compacted.

"Kate," I said calmly. "Could you stop ravaging my kitchen for a minute and tell me what happened?"

Her whole body heaved as she let out a heavy sigh. "Benjamin," she said, as if that one word could convey everything that was causing this mini tornado.

"He called me. The nerve of that guy. Honestly."

I sat down at the table. "And?"

"He kept calling and texting while Andre was here. We had a nice dinner, opened a bottle of wine—and then my phone rang—three times! And then blew up with texts. I checked to make sure it wasn't you, and then saw it was him."

"Oh, no."

She rolled her eyes. "I didn't answer of course, just tried to put it out of my mind for the rest of the night. But I saw his stupid texts. And now Andre thinks I'm a hot mess because I did the whole angry cry while we were watching a movie."

"Did you tell him what happened?"

"I had to! Otherwise, he'd think I was having a meltdown over nothing—or worse, just over a goofy Colin Firth movie." She grabbed the hand mixer and cranked the beaters up as high as they'd go. Wincing, I quickly unplugged it and pried it from her hands. Kate's stress baking almost always ended up with something getting broken: a mixing bowl, a spatula, an index finger.

"How about you sit and tell me the rest," I said, putting the mixer aside.

She poured herself a shot of whiskey and collapsed in a chair. "When Andre left, I listened to the messages, and almost threw my phone against the wall. That little doucheweasel told me he wanted to get back together. That he *forgave me* for invading his privacy and that he thought we should try again."

"His new girlfriend must have dumped him. Because he's a doucheweasel."

"Probably." She tossed the shot back and banged the empty glass down. "You'd have been proud of me, though. I sent him one text, telling him to never call again, and then blocked his number. That's all he gets."

She went back to the counter for the Dickel and a plate of cookies, then sat down again.

"Are those gingerbread?" I reached for one and then paused. "You snapped all their heads off."

"They started to remind me of Benjamin. He was always a little too bronzed."

I popped one in my mouth. "Not bad. Spicy."

"Andre and I made them last night. We thought we'd get a jump on the desserts for tomorrow." The cookies were piped with white icing sweaters, and ties, and even little pants.

"Sort of thought you might have jumped on something else." I grinned and she tossed a tea towel at me.

"So did I until those stupid texts."

I WAS SHOCKED that her famous sponge cake didn't cave in completely, with Kate slamming it around the way she did.

But it came out fluffy and tall, because of "tough love" she said.

At noon, Andre arrived. After knocking—loudly—he came into the living room and set up a whiteboard on an easel. Then he opened an expandable folder and pulled out a stack of papers and dry erase markers. He moved swiftly, like he had a plan. He wore a close-fitting tee shirt and snug dark-wash jeans, and had styled his hair to look like it was tousled by the wind. There was the faint hint of cologne.

"What's all that for?" I asked him.

"Our operational agenda." Very methodically, he took the stack of papers, which I saw were recipes with photos, and began taping them to the board in a precise order.

"Hey," Jack said. He brought his own stack of papers over to the board, like this was a completely normal exercise. This is what I'd expect in a high-end restaurant on their opening night —not in my living room.

"I made a timeline for us," Andre said, sounding excited. He'd begun writing times under the photos with a red marker. "I set up everything outside for the turkey. If we let it thaw today and prep it tonight, then we can drop it in the fryer around noon. Then it's on the table by thirteen-hundred."

"Perfect," Jack said. "I already cleaned out the fridge, so we can prep side dishes today and cook them two, maybe three at a time starting in the morning."

"Kate's on dessert detail?" Andre said.

Jack nodded. "She'll have the oven most of today, but she should be done around five."

Andre wrote that time in green, under the dessert quadrant of his board.

"I'm just going to leave y'all to it and see if I can help Kate," I said. This level of detail seemed more appropriate for a manhunt than a buffet, but it was certainly intriguing to watch.

They hardly noticed when I left, still writing on the board and calculating times. This was not going to be like any family dinner I'd ever had—that much was clear.

"Make yourself useful," Kate said, "and taste this glaze." She shoved a spatula at me before I could protest, and then there was the most delightful lemon-lime zing on my tongue.

"Wow," I said.

She nodded, checking her own list. "Cake's done, glaze goes on later. Brownies are in the oven. I still need the chocolate pecan pies and the sweet potato pies. Let's start peeling." She grabbed what looked like thirty pounds of sweet potatoes and handed me a peeler. "You ever use one of these before?"

"Very funny." I took the peeler and sat down at the table.

She grinned and handed me a bowl for the potatoes. "I'll make the crusts," she said, and tightened her apron, as if things were about to get serious.

There were four pie plates lined up on the counter, along with every mixing bowl I owned. My kitchen had never seen this much action. Not where food was concerned, anyway.

When she was kneading the dough, she stopped and said, "Oh crap."

"What is it?" I'd made it through exactly six of her potatoes.

"Pecans." She turned to me, her eyes wide. "I forgot to tell Jack I needed some. Do you have any? Like in the freezer?"

I dug through the bags of frozen vegetables and meats, but there was not much else. "Sorry," I said.

"What house in the south doesn't have ten pounds of pecans in the freezer?" she yelped.

I laughed. "Do we look like the kind of people who hoard nuts?"

She rolled her eyes and then yelled, "Jack!" stretching his name into three syllables. "Jaaaaaaack, SOS!"

When he came to the door, his eyes were wide. "What's the problem?"

"Pecans," she said. "Do you have any?"

He frowned, like he'd been bested. "Sorry. No."

"Oh my God," she said, exasperated. "How."

"Josie does, though," he said. "They put a bunch up every fall."

"Perfect!" I said, dying to get out of that kitchen and away from these people who were letting a little nut drive them straight to DEFCON 1. "I'll go see if I can borrow some." When I stood, I plucked a few stray potato peels from my shirt.

"Three pounds, please!" Kate yelled as I left. "And don't dawdle!"

"Yes ma'am," I said, and grabbed my keys. By the time I got to the front door, Jack and Andre were on the potatoes, peeling and chopping.

Once in the car, I felt my cell phone buzz in my back pocket. Thinking it was Kate, I slipped it out to see what she'd forgotten. My father's name popped up on the screen, and I quickly sent the call to voicemail. He'd called half a dozen times since our argument in the days before, and had left me two voice messages that I hadn't listened to.

This time, the call was followed by a string of texts.

Enza, we need to talk.

As usual, you only have part of the information. There is more I need to tell you.

Please call me back asap.

Enza, this is your father. Call me.

Shoving the phone into the cup holder, I started the Jeep and tried to tamp down those feelings of shame, and hurt, and regret—the same ones that gnawed at me as I slept and were at the forefront of my mind each morning. The nightmares about my mother had gotten worse. I hated her for leaving us, and I hated her for dying because it meant she'd never know how much hurt she'd caused.

And my father. I hated him for keeping this secret from me, for acting like he'd done some noble thing by hiding me from the truth.

"WELL, HEY," Josie said, opening the door. "What brings you over today?" She looked more rested than before, but her eyes still looked tired.

"Cooking emergency," I said. "Do you happen to have any pecans?"

She smiled. "Only about fifty pounds. Come on in."

"Kate's baking like she's on one of those contest shows, and she's elbows-deep in pie crust."

Josie led me into the kitchen and said, "Are you sure I can't make more than stuffing?"

"It's under control," I said, and told her about the guys and their whiteboard, and how they'd turned the living room into command central.

"Those boys get serious about their food," she said.

"It's a little intimidating. I can barely peel potatoes."

She laughed. "Nuts are in the deep freeze. I'll be right back."

While she went to get the pecans, I went into the living

room to say hi to Buck. I'd brought the little mojo bag from Duchess' shop and fished it out of the pocket of my jeans.

Buck was stretched out in his recliner, watching TV.

"Hey, I said. "How are you feeling?"

"Well hey, kid," he said, turning the volume down. "I'm a little achy still, but not bad. Josie's still fussing over me, though, and won't let me out of her sight." He shifted in his chair, wincing as he did so. He reminded me of my father then, pretending that everything was fine, even when the pain was obvious.

"I brought you something," I said.

"Is it pie?"

"That's tomorrow," I said. "Thanks to a few pounds of your pecans."

"Oh, good," he said. "I'd hate to think we shelled a thousand pounds for nothing."

"Kate makes a killer chocolate bourbon pecan pie."

He sighed, wistful. "I knew I liked that lady."

"I saw this and thought of you." I dropped the little blue mojo bag into his hand, and he examined it, his brow furrowed.

"What's this for?"

"Good health," I said. "A speedy recovery."

He looked at me like I'd just placed a bullfrog in his hand. "I thought you didn't believe in this stuff."

"I think it's good luck," I said, kissing him on the cheek.

He sighed and placed it on the table next to his chair. "Then maybe it is," he said. "I'll take what I can get."

"Here we go," Josie said. She walked in cradling a plastic bag of shelled pecans. "Is this enough?"

"Oh sure," I said. "You just saved Thanksgiving."

She smiled, handing me the big. "Well, you just holler if you need anything else, hon."

"I'm on strict orders to get back ASAP," I said. "But y'all come by whenever you like tomorrow. We'll eat around one."

When I walked outside and onto the porch, I heard muffled voices coming from the backyard. Thinking it was Lucille, I walked around the side of the house to say hello. But as I approached, the other voice lowered and then there was Lucille's voice, agitated. I kept to the grass, straining to hear what the argument was about, but could only catch a few words. Stepping back on the gravel driveway, I rounded the back corner and saw them just a few yards away. Toph grabbed Lucille's arm and yanked her towards him. She yelped and tried to pull her arm free, but Toph gripped her harder, pulling her off balance so she stumbled and crashed into him. His voice was a low rumble.

When she saw me, she froze, her eyes wide. Toph followed her gaze and dropped her arm. He said something to her, then put his hand on the side of her head—the gesture would look gentle if I hadn't seen them just moments before. Giving me a hard stare, he stalked toward the back door and shut it quietly behind him as he went inside.

"Hey, Enza," she said, walking over. "Sorry—that was nothing."

"It didn't look like nothing. Are you all right?" Blood pounded in my ears. It wasn't so long ago that I'd been in a position very similar to hers, and I remembered how trapped I'd felt. So helpless.

It wasn't a feeling I wished on anyone.

She nodded. "Please don't make a big deal out of this."

"Has he been violent with you before?"

"Not really," she said with a shrug.

My head felt hot. "This is unacceptable. He can't treat you that way."

She straightened her blouse and said, "I can handle him."

"You need to tell your parents. Get him out of here."

Her eyes hardened in an instant. "This is not your problem," she said, walking back towards the house.

"Lucille," I said, and she turned to face me. "You have to stop this. Now."

She came back toward me and lowered her voice. "I can't leave him. I'll lose everything." She glanced at the house and then fixed me with a stare. "And I've worked too hard and been through too much to lose it all. Don't make this worse."

I sighed, thinking of what she'd told me that night at my house. The apartment, the new job. Toph had bailed her out, she'd said, and loaned her a lot of money. What else had he done? The way that she said *too much* filled me with dread.

"Whatever you need, your parents will help you. Jack and I will help you."

Her eyes widened. "They can't know about this. You can't say a word to Jack. Promise me."

When I didn't answer, she stepped closer. "Jack will lose it." Her jaw tensed, and she inhaled sharply. "And he'll make all of this worse."

Lowering my voice, I said, "He just wants you to be safe. He'd want to help you—you know that."

Her eyes filled with tears. "Please," she said. "Don't tell him. This will blow over, like it always does."

"You can't stay with him. Men like him don't change. You know that right? He's showing you who he is. This is a part of him that doesn't go away."

She sat down in the grass and stared straight ahead. Tears fell down her cheeks. "I don't know how to get out."

"You just leave." Sitting next to her, I shoved the bag of pecans aside.

"He'll ruin me. I'll lose my job."

"Does that job matter so much?"

"Yes. It's the only thing that's going well right now. I can't just throw it away."

"No job is worth what he's doing to you. I think you know that."

She shook her head, avoiding my eyes. "You don't understand."

"These situations always end badly. Always. But I think you know that too. "

"Just a few more months," she said. "Until I save up enough. I'll have been at the theater long enough that they'll know me, and know how good I am. Right now, they barely know me—one word from Toph could end it."

"Lucille," I said. "Look at me." When she finally did, I continued, "You can't keep this from Jack. If you don't tell him what's happening, I will." He'd been so worried the night before, so desperate to know what was going on. I didn't want to keep this from him, but I knew it should be Lucille who told him.

She held her face in her hands. I sat next to her and draped my arm over her shoulders.

After a while, she said, "I'll talk to Jack this weekend. Not today. I don't want to be the one who ruins Thanksgiving."

"*You* wouldn't be ruining anything." I hoped she understood the emphasis, but she just shook her head, her eyes reddening.

She grasped my hand and squeezed so hard I jumped. "Please," she said. "Promise me you won't say anything to Jack."

It hurt to see her so desperate, and while I couldn't understand why she would put up with that jerk for ten seconds, I said, "OK. But Friday you have to tell him."

She looked like she wanted to argue again.

"Friday," I said. "Or I tell Jack myself."

She nodded, combing the grass with her fingers. "OK."

When I stood, I saw movement at the back window. Toph was staring at us, his lips in a tight line. The way he stood glaring at us filled me with anger and dread. I wanted to take Lucille from there, back to my house, and tell Jack everything. If Jack knew what was happening, he'd find a way to make sure Toph never touched Lucille again.

They had to be on the same page, though: Lucille had to want to leave Toph, too. There was only so much that Jack—or I—could do to protect her. She had to save herself, and sometimes that was the hardest lesson to learn.

Driving home, I felt like I'd made a devil's bargain. Lucille was right that it was none of my business, but the thought of Toph mistreating her burned me up inside. And the thought of keeping this from Jack, pretending that everything was business as usual, was just as bad.

Chapter Nine

BACK AT MY HOUSE, Kate had Andre smashing sweet potatoes while Jack was melting chocolate over the stove. Kate looked up from glazing her sponge cake and said, "Oh, your timing's perfect. I'm going to put the potato pies in and then an hour later the pecan pies go in, and then the second string comes in to start all the savory dishes."

"Second string?" Andre said with a smirk.

"You can put us to work dicing and whatnot," Kate said. Somehow, she seemed energized by cooking. The mere thought of preparing an entire meal made me feel exhausted, and watching the three of them buzz around the kitchen did, too.

"Absolutely not," Jack told her. "You ladies have done plenty, and we'll take it from here."

"Seriously?" she said, giving her potato mixture a final stir. "You're going to do all the rest?"

"We got this," Andre said. "We've got plenty of time, and we'll take care of dinner tonight, too."

"I won't argue with that," she said, placing the two potato

pies into the oven. "I'll never say no when a guy wants to cook for me."

She turned quickly and nearly collided into Andre. He smiled and she scooted around him, motioning for me to give her the pecans.

"Want to help me with the bourbon pie?" she asked me. She raised a brow, like she knew something was up. It was impossible to hide anything from Kate.

"OK, fellas," she said, corralling Andre and Jack. "Y'all give us a few to mix up the last pies, and then the kitchen's all yours." Jack grabbed the plate of gingerbread cookies from the counter as she ushered them out.

"Hey," he said, looking puzzled. "Why don't they have heads?"

As soon as they were out of earshot, Kate said, "Spill it. What's the matter?"

"Nothing. It's just my dad. He's calling and texting nonstop, and I just can't with him right now."

She arched a brow, whisking the pie filling on the stovetop. "So don't. You're a grown-ass woman and you decide who you talk to and when."

"I know. But I can't avoid him forever."

"That's debatable." She poured two shots of Dickel into the pie filling and after a quick stir, held a spoonful out for me to taste.

"That's amazing," I said.

She nodded. When the two pecan pies were inside the oven along with the others, she set a second timer on her phone, grabbed two glasses, and handed me the Dickel. "Tell me the rest outside," she said, leading me onto the porch.

From the hallway, she hollered, "OK, sheriff, you're up! Come get us if you want backup!"

Outside, we sat in the porch swing and she said, "Now tell me what the real problem is. And don't say *nothing*, because you look like somebody set your favorite boots on fire."

The whiskey stung as I downed the shot. "I'm worried about Lucille."

She nodded. "That guy's a jerk. What happened?"

I told her about them arguing in the yard, how he'd put his hands on her. And everything else that Lucille had told me.

"If I tell Jack, he'll blow a gasket. He already hates the guy."

"She feels indebted to him," Kate said. "Like she owes him something."

"And we're supposed to have him over here for dinner and pretend everything's fine." I sipped my drink and said, "She promised she'd talk to Jack on Friday. I feel like I should keep my mouth shut and give her time."

Kate sighed, leaning back in the swing. "It's better if she tells Jack and her parents. She'll feel betrayed if you tell them behind her back."

"I know. I just hate keeping this from him."

She frowned. "Don't make her feel like she has to choose sides. She needs to know we're all on her side, and she won't feel that way if you go back on your word. And if Jack goes charging over there like a caveman, she'll be terrified and think we're all judging her."

"I'm afraid she won't tell him, though. Or her parents. What if she just goes back to Austin with him?"

"Give her a day," Kate said. "Then you've kept your word. And then if she doesn't tell Jack, you'll have to. We need to help her, but we need to not betray her trust."

~

WHEN JACK and Andre had the fridge full of curried potato salad and six kinds of casseroles, they stopped prepping for the night. The whiteboard had been updated with check marks and cook times for tomorrow, and the status of each dish was marked. The whole house smelled like onions and bacon, and the kitchen was so hot we were sweating through our shirts again. Since the living room was the coolest spot in the house, the four of us had landed there after tidying up the kitchen.

"What this evening needs is some Scrabble," Kate said. "Where's your board?"

"What makes you think we have a Scrabble board?" I said, teasing.

"Um, because I know it's your favorite. And you're a sucker for nostalgia."

Jack shot me a questioning look and I said, "Some people in our dorm played quarters. We made all of our favorite nerd games into drinking games. Scrabble was the best."

"Obviously," Kate said. She stared at me until I laughed and went across the room to dig through the bottom of the book case. She was clearly trying to keep me occupied with thoughts that didn't center on Lucille, my father, or my mother. I'd been trying to shake off the last few days, but Kate could always see right through my facade. She knew when something was eating at me, and she knew how to help me relax. It was goofy, but it would work.

At least for a little while.

"Jack," she said, "go get us some booze, will you?"

"I just learn more about you every day," he said to me, striding into the kitchen.

"He's about to learn how cutthroat she is when it comes to triple word scores," Kate said. While Jack rummaged in the kitchen, the rest of us sat down on the floor. Kate arranged the board and mixed the tiles together in their velvet pouch.

An hour later, my brain had a pleasant fuzzy feeling to it, and my body had finally started to relax. This would be fine, I thought, watching the three of them laughing together. Jack was right: dinner wasn't just a favor to Josie—it was a way to mark a clear beginning here, with this new life I was building with a family I chose myself. Kate was one of my oldest friends, and now I had Jack, who I now couldn't imagine my life without. His friends were becoming my friends, and his family had taken me in as one of their own. I hadn't felt love quite like this in a long, long time.

I hadn't even realized I'd been missing it.

"You used all seven letters," Kate said to Jack. "Take a shot."

Andre poured a half shot of whiskey into a glass and passed it over to Jack.

"You're penalizing me for being good?" Jack said. "I thought the point was to use all the letters."

"We're leveling the playing field," Kate said. "You also have to take a shot if you use stupid slang words or try to use something not in the dictionary."

"Don't you just challenge?" Andre asked.

"Yes," Kate said. "And then whoever is wrong takes a shot."

"I should warn you fellas," I said, "Kate reads the OED for fun."

Andre leaned toward her. "Bring it on. I do my crosswords in pen."

Kate's lip curled in that way that meant she was amused. And dead set on winning.

Andre went next, dropping each tile into place with a deliberate *plink*, laying down *harlot*.

"Really?" Kate said.

Andre shrugged, smirking so his dimples showed. "That's thirty-seven points," he drawled. He leaned over her shoulder as she scribbled down the score, checking her math.

Kate didn't stand a chance against those dimples.

The tiles clicked as she spelled *twerk*.

"Slang," I said. "Shot."

"It's in the dictionary," she said.

"I'm sure it's not," I countered.

"Want to challenge?" she said. "It's a shot of the cheap stuff if you're wrong."

I thought for a minute. "No way that's in the dictionary. You're bluffing."

"Pour her a shot," Kate said, tapping on the screen of her phone.

Jack did as she said, despite my frown. Kate held her phone out to Jack. "Would you care to read the entry from the esteemed Mr. Oxford?"

Jack looked at the screen. "I'll be damned. It was first recorded in 1802."

"No way," I said. "Let me see that."

"Twerk," he said, adopting a professorial tone, "first spelled with an i, later with an e. Believed to be a combination of 'twist' and 'jerk.' Common usage describes a provocative dance that involves thrusting the hips and bottom while in a low squatting stance."

"Thank you, Dr. English," I said. "Do we get a demonstration with that?"

"I'd throw my back out," Jack said.

"Drink up," Kate said with a grin.

I slammed the shot and coughed. The cheap stuff burned all the way down.

Kate had invented Drunken Scrabble in graduate school. She'd been bored by cups and quarters and the other typical drinking games people fell into during their college enlightenment. Kate had decided the game should be challenging in the beginning and become harder after taking a couple of penalty shots. She considered it a kind of brain exercise, so didn't feel as guilty as she would playing something as inane as quarters.

Also, Scrabble was her game. And Kate liked to win.

After a couple of hours, we were doing well to eke out three and four letter words. Kate was lying on the sofa, her feet pressed up against Andre's side. For warmth, she'd said, but I knew better.

"I'm going to put the turkey up," I said, and dragged myself to the kitchen. My whole body felt like it was made of lead, and the hardest thing I'd done all day was peel potatoes.

Well, that, and tamp down all the rage I was feeling towards Toph, and all the worry I felt for Lucille.

Kate was still wide awake, laughing with Andre.

"I'm off to bed," Jack said. "Got to rest up for round two in the morning."

"Me too," I said. "Y'all going to stay up a while?"

Andre glanced at Kate, then dropped his hand on top of her feet. He was rearranging the tiles in his trough, but I didn't miss the faint tapping of his fingers along her ankle.

"We'll just finish this game," Kate said. Andre had whispered something to her, making her shake with laughter.

"How about sudden death to the end," Andre said. "I have five tiles left."

"OK," Kate said, sitting up straight. "Sudden death."

As I followed Jack into the bedroom, I could still hear their laughter through the wall.

"They seem to be getting along well," he said, stripping out of his clothes. When I climbed into bed, he pulled me against his chest, folding his arms around me. "You OK?" he said. "You've seemed a million miles away all night."

"Yeah, just tired." And trying not to think of Lucille stuck in her house with Toph, trying not to imagine what else he might have done to hurt her or what he might do when she broke things off with him.

Had my mother felt the same? Was that why she'd left us? My father could be cold, but I'd never known him to be violent. It hurt to think of him doing something to hurt my mother so badly that she left and never came back.

As I drifted off to sleep, the image of her swimming in the dark Texas river came creeping back. Her body was almost translucent against the deep green of the water as she raised one arm over her head and then the other in swift strokes, her hands cutting the surface like fins as she paddled on her back. She dove below the surface, and then I was in the water with her, sinking to the bottom, but unafraid. We sank down deep to where the light was dim and the weeds brushed against my legs. The water turned cold, and the weeds tangled around my feet, tightening like ropes. My chest burned as I tried to pull myself free and swim back to the surface, but my legs were stuck. My mother was next to me, but she'd stopped trying to break free and swim away. Her dark hair was swept across her face, and when the current pulled it aside, I saw her face clearly, and saw that it was not my mother sinking to the bottom, but Lucille.

Chapter Ten

JACK'S ALARM startled me awake. His arms were wound tight around me, but I managed to free one arm long enough to turn off the alarm. Grumbling, he pulled me against him and nuzzled my neck.

"Come on, Romeo," I said. "Phase Two of Operation Turkey Trot is underway."

He snorted as his hands slid down to my hips. "Lets' play the quiet game again."

"Those casseroles aren't going to cook themselves, mister." I wriggled out of his grip, laughing when he tickled me.

As I reached for a clean tee shirt and jeans, he lay back on the pillows, staring at me like he wanted to eat me up.

"You can give me that smoldering look all you want," I said. "But your cute dimples and your hot bed head are just going to have to wait."

He smirked, raking his eyes over me as I shimmied into jeans. "The things you do to me, chère."

"T-minus 6 hours," I said, tossing a shirt at him. "Andre will be here soon."

He muttered something about payback as I pulled my hair back into a ponytail and shut the bedroom door behind me. Kate was likely still sleeping, but I wanted to make a quick breakfast for us before the guys commandeered the oven to finish up the cooking.

As I made my way down the hall toward the kitchen, something in the living room caught my eye. The Scrabble board was still spread out on the floor, along with my lowball glasses and a nearly empty bottle of whiskey. A giant comforter was piled on the sofa, two feet sticking out from under it, propped on the arm of the couch. An arm stuck out from the other end of the pile of fabric, a hand nearly touching the floor.

Andre.

I chuckled to myself as I continued into the kitchen and started the coffee. It wasn't all that surprising he'd ended up on my couch.

By the time I had coffee going, there were footsteps above me. Kate was downstairs a few minutes later, wearing a blouse and jeans. Her hair was piled up in a messy bun, and she looked as put together as she always did.

"I thought you'd sleep in a little," I said.

She poured a cup of coffee. "I can't sleep late anymore these days. Plus, the vent in my room seems to be situated right over the coffee maker. Since when do you make breakfast?"

"I've been learning." I sprinkled cheese over the breakfast scramble of eggs and sausage. Jack was an excellent teacher.

"Have a nice night?" I asked, setting a plate in front of her.

She arched a brow, sipping her coffee.

"You must have," I said, "judging by the fact there's a sheriff out cold on my sofa."

She grinned.

"Something you want to tell me?"

She sipped her coffee. "He's pretty good at drunken Scrabble. He almost beat me."

I raised an eyebrow, expecting she might tell me something else he was good at.

"I thought he was going to leave early," she said, "before anybody got up. Since he's so stealthy and all."

I shrugged. "You must have worn him out. With the Scrabble and whatnot."

"There was no whatnot. It was late when we finished, and we were both a bit hammered."

"Uh-huh."

She winced, taking a gulp of coffee. "This isn't awkward, is it?"

"Nope."

"Liar."

I smirked. "It's not awkward for me."

Jack came around the corner, his hair standing straight up.

"Hey, Kate," he said, heading for the coffee. "I think you left something in the living room."

Kate turned pink down to the collar of her shirt. She hardly ever blushed.

"Your porch is amazing," she said, "I'll finish my breakfast out there."

Jack grinned as he sat next to me. "I'll give him thirty more minutes."

AN HOUR LATER, the four of us were going full speed in the tiny kitchen. We'd put a green bean casserole in to bake and started rice, cornbread pudding, and five kinds of casseroles that Jack assured me were somehow different from one another. Andre made gravy from the turkey stock, his great-grandmother's spicy recipe, and Kate was buzzing around like a hummingbird as she set up a "tablescape" outside. We'd pulled the two picnic tables together in the backyard, since the weather was still warm, and so far Kate had gathered a couple of old lanterns of Vergie's, some brightly colored scarves from a closet, and camellias that had been tricked into blooming early by the heat wave.

All morning, Kate and Andre kept bumping into each other like dancers just a half beat off-rhythm. They stammered apologies and shared furtive glances between the chopping of tomatoes and frying of sausage.

It was really pretty cute to see her all flustered over a man again. Kate didn't usually get flustered—this was a sure sign that she liked Andre more than just a little.

Just before noon, Josie came by with Buck and Lucille. She'd insisted on coming early to help since I wouldn't let her host the whole dinner at her house. Buck was doing better, but she still didn't want to leave him for long periods of time. He could get around the house all right, but he grimaced with pain when he lifted anything, including himself.

Today, Buck shuffled slowly into the backyard, Andre at his side, asking, "You ever deep fry a turkey?"

"Where's Toph?" Jack asked Lucille. His tone was bristly.

She took a covered dish into the kitchen and placed it on the counter. "He's coming a little later. He needed to pick up something."

He gave her a hard look. "What's he going to pick up on Thanksgiving?"

She lowered her voice. "You know, like something to bring

you for having us over. He just wanted to do something nice for y'all." She glanced at me and said, "You know, like a nice bottle of wine?"

Jack stared after her, as if he wanted to say more but didn't know how.

"Can I help with something?" she asked me.

"Kate could probably use a hand outside," I said.

She nodded, looking grateful. "You got it."

Once she was outside, I put my hand on Jack's shoulder. "Go easy on her," I said. "It'll be OK."

"Will it?" he said, his jaw tense.

WHILE THE GUYS fried the turkey out in the backyard—with Katie on standby with a fire extinguisher—Josie and I prepped the last few things in the kitchen. She was rolling out a pan of her famous biscuits, and I was trying to commit the steps to memory. I'd never been able to make biscuits that weren't like rocks.

At a quarter to one, the doorbell rang. Bella barked from her spot in the living room and inched toward the hallway, her head cocked. When I got to the door, I realized I still had my apron on.

George stood on the doorstep, holding a covered pie.

"Hi, George," I said. "Happy Thanksgiving."

"I brought that prize-winning pie," he said, with a hint of a smile.

He looked like he was going to church, dressed now in pressed slacks, a sweater vest and a button-down shirt with sleeves rolled to the elbows.

I led him to the kitchen and introduced him to everyone,

then took him outside to meet the guys and Buck. Andre was standing guard over the turkey, and Jack was counting down on the timer. George commented on the Adirondack-style chairs in the yard, a couple that Buck had made out of reclaimed wood. Buck started telling him how they were made, and I knew they'd be fast friends.

Andre and Lucille followed me into the kitchen to grab the last of the side dishes while Kate went out with a tea pitcher.

"That's everything," I said, grabbing the bowl of potato salad. "We're good."

"Is this everybody?" Andre asked.

I nudged Lucille and said, "Is he coming?"

"I don't know what's taking him so long," she said, avoiding Andre's stare. "But don't wait for him."

It wasn't until we all sat down at the picnic table that I thought about Vergie. I'd never been one to throw parties, but as I sat there in warm sunlight, watching everyone chat as they passed dishes of potatoes and cranberries, I thought, *This is what family is supposed to be like. This is what it's like when they don't leave you.* I couldn't remember the last time I'd had that many people in my home, but it was a feeling I didn't want to forget.

I sat at one end of the table, with Jack next to me. He winked at me, and my heart swelled. I liked the sight of him there, holding things together.

NOT LONG AFTER we started eating, Bella barked from under the table and ran to the front yard. There was the crunch of tires on gravel, then the slam of a car door.

A few moments later, Toph appeared at the side of the

house, making his way toward us. His face was was stern, but as he came past the camellia bushes and saw us all seated, he slowed his pace to an easy stride and smiled like he was the guest of honor.

When I moved to stand, Lucille said, "Let me." She intercepted him ten yards from us, and I heard Toph's voice, low and clipped, and then hers, nearly a whisper. It was impossible to make out the words, but she sounded irritated. They stepped a few yards closer to the house, which put them right behind a butterfly bush that was nearly as tall as they were.

Next to me, Jack bristled as he watched them, but now it was impossible to see more than Toph's hand moving in the air by his side.

When I glanced at Kate, she gave me a tiny shrug.

The conversation at the table continued as I rose and walked toward Lucille and Toph. Lucille was speaking in a hushed tone. Toph frowned at her and reached for her wrist. Because of the way they were positioned, with his back to everyone, no one at the table could see.

"Hey there," I said, my voice chipper. "Glad you made it." I forced a smile, wishing he'd just get back in his car and keep driving until he hit the ocean.

Toph quickly withdrew his hand and turned to me, smiling a little too wide. Lucille crossed her arms over her chest.

"Enza, so sorry I'm late." He handed me a small brown shopping bag with a handle. "I brought you these. I had to find just the right ones, and almost every shop I tried was closed."

I took the bag and looked inside.

"Belgian truffles," he said. "And a couple bottles of my favorite port."

"Thank you, Toph. Come join us. There's plenty of room." Lucille led him towards the table while I followed a few steps behind. When I sat back down by Jack, he gave me a curious look. Lucille introduced him to everyone and George asked him what he did for work in Austin.

He started talking about investments, and a couple of clubs he was part-owner of. "I like to back dark horses," he said. "They're usually desperate, and hungry. And when they win they have the biggest returns."

"Toph's into lots of entertainment venues," she said. "Music, theater, the film festival circuit."

"I like the indie scene," he said. "There's a lot of creative people out there who just need a little cash and the right connections to get them noticed. I felt the same way when I met Lucille. She was hiding in a little no-name theater, a total waste of her time and talent. She's going to make big waves one day." He reached over and gave Lucille's thigh a squeeze.

Jack glared at Toph from across the table, gripping his fork so tightly it made me flinch. When I nudged his thigh under the table, he arched a brow at me.

Toph politely answered everyone's questions, complimenting Josie on her biscuits and telling Kate he could get her a meeting with a talent scout if she got tired of working in a lab.

"You could be a voice actor," he told her. "People go nuts for your kind of accent, with that subtle lilt. You could make a boatload and retire young."

"I'll keep that in mind as a Plan B," Kate said, her voice cool.

"I'm telling you," he said, offering a megawatt smile. "You'd make a killing."

It was easy to see why Lucille found him charming. He

knew all the right words to say, and knew how to flash a smile and a wink to make people feel special. But it seemed that this was a well-crafted facade—one that he was no doubt used to using in his business partnerships and his investments.

It was hard to shake the idea that he thought of Lucille as an investment, too, and I cringed as I considered what he expected as a return on that investment.

"I'm starving," Toph said, reaching for the nearest casserole. "I didn't realize it was so late." He heaped a spoonful onto his plate. As we passed him each dish, he did the same, a graceless *thwack* echoing down the table. "And I thought Luce lived in the middle of nowhere," he said. "I almost never found this place."

Lucille sighed. "Well, you tracked us down," she said, looking annoyed.

Toph guffawed, like that was immensely funny. Then he pulled his napkin from the table and draped it in his lap with a flourish.

"This looks like a picture in a magazine," he said to me. He'd leaned close, like he intended to whisper, but his voice boomed in my ear.

"Thank you," I said. The nearness of him made me uneasy.

He winked at me, the way a car salesman does when he thinks he has you just moments from signing on the line. That kind of look always made me feel like I was being underestimated and manipulated, and I hated feeling that way. Toph was trying hard to win everyone over.

I wondered why.

Jack stood, and a chill rippled along my arms. For a moment I imagined him dragging Toph out into the swamp by his collar. Instead, he held up his glass and said, "I just want to make a toast," and glanced over at me. "To Vergie, for bringing us all together today. She's still looking out for us, and still bringing us the people we need most in our lives." He looked at me and smiled so his dimples showed, and I saw then that I loved him more than I'd ever loved anyone.

"To Vergie," I said, and everyone raised their glasses in turn.

At the other end of the table, Kate mouthed *Oh my God*, with her hand placed firmly on her chest.

I grinned at her and mouthed, *Right?*

When Jack sat back down, he said, "So, Luce, how long are y'all staying in town?"

"We've got to leave tomorrow," she said. "Toph has a meeting back home."

Across from her, Josie's lips formed a tiny frown at the word *home*.

"That's too bad," Jack said. "I was hoping we'd have more time to catch up. I never get to see you anymore."

"We knew it'd be a quick trip this time," Toph said. "This meeting's a big deal for me."

"Well, it's not so long until Christmas," Josie said, smiling faintly. "We'll get to see more of you then."

Lucille started to answer, but Toph cut her off. "Oh babe, didn't you tell them?" He turned back to Josie and said, "I'm sorry, but we'll be in Tahoe for Christmas."

Josie's face fell. Jack's eyes narrowed.

"Well that's not definite," Lucille said quietly, staring at her plate.

"Of course it is," Toph said, matter-of-factly. "The house is already rented. My family is expecting us, and some very important people will be there."

"Some very important people will be here, too," she said, glancing up at Jack.

Jack's lip curved upward with a hint of a smile.

"We can talk about it later," Lucille said, her voice low. "We can find a way to split our time."

Toph stared at her and said, "You already agreed. We've discussed this." His voice was as smooth as honey.

Lucille looked like she wanted to crawl under the table.

"Who's ready for dessert?" Kate said. "We have five kinds of pie." She stood from the table, taking Josie and Buck's empty plates. "I'm happy to take orders, or y'all can come help yourselves to a dessert buffet in the kitchen."

I grabbed a few plates and followed Kate back into the house.

"I want to slap that guy into next week," she said. "What the hell?"

"Too bad we can't feed him to the gators." I arranged the desserts onto the table while Kate stuck pie servers into the pies and used a 10-inch chef's knife to slash into her sponge cake.

"Who says we can't," she said.

"Hopefully she'll end this tomorrow. We just have to make it through this dinner without shedding any blood."

She laughed. "It's not a family holiday until someone throws a punch." With her brothers, that was accurate.

"We should try. Lucille's already mortified and I'd like to stay on Jack's family's good side."

"Sounds like you plan to keep him around for a while." She swiped a bit of icing from the cake and popped it into her mouth just as Andre walked in through the back door. His eyes went straight to Kate's lips.

"I came for pie," he said, apparently frozen in his tracks.

"I promised Buck a tiny piece of everything," I said, handing him a plate. He took it without breaking his gaze and Kate grinned, cutting a small slice of buttermilk pie.

"What kind of trouble are you two getting into in here?" he said. "You get a certain glint in your eye when you're thinking of something devious." He looked at me and I shrugged. He'd seen me make some questionable decisions in the last few months, and at least one had ended up with me bleeding on the floor.

"We're discussing what a shame it would be if Toph were devoured by alligators," Kate said.

Andre took a bite of the pie and said, "That would be a shame. And a lot of paperwork that would ruin my otherwise lovely day off."

When the doorbell rang, Kate said, "Someone else coming?"

"Could be another of Jack's friends," I said. "There were a couple of guys from the station that said they might stop by after their shift."

Kate went back to adding slivers of pie to Buck's plate while Andre asked if she'd share her recipes. Josie and Jack came in the back door just as I went out to the front. The doorbell rang again and Bella barked from outside, near the porch.

When I opened the door, I felt all of the blood drop from my head to my feet.

My father was standing on the porch, holding a bottle of wine.

Chapter Eleven

MY INSTINCT WAS to slam the door and go back to my dinner. Instead, I squeezed the doorknob and said, "Dad, what are you doing here?"

As usual, he looked impeccable, wearing a dark blue button-up shirt and crisp wrinkle-free khaki pants. His shoes alone probably cost more than the set of tires on my Jeep.

"You never answered your phone," he said.

I glared at him, considering slamming the door.

"I know you're upset," he said.

My stomach twisted into a knot. "That's an understatement."

He stared at the space between his feet. After a long moment he said, "There are things we need to talk about. I'd like you to hear me out."

"I have people over." Bella sniffed his shoes, a low growl rumbling in her throat.

"I figured." His eyes looked sad. His typical bravado was gone. After another long pause, he said, "Please, dear. I've come all this way."

I couldn't remember the last time he'd called me "dear." It felt like a full minute before I said, "Come in, I guess." I didn't want to talk to him, and I didn't want to hear excuses. But it felt cruel to turn him away, and there had already been so much cruelty in my family.

He followed me into the kitchen, where Jack and Josie were heaping desserts onto their plates. Kate and Andre were leaning against the counter, Andre halfway through another slice of pie.

The whole room seemed to freeze, like in a tableau, and all eyes were on my father, forks hanging in mid-air. A lump formed in my throat, and it felt like it would surely choke me.

"Dad, you know Kate, and you remember Jack." I nodded at them, taking in their stunned expressions, and said, "Josie is Jack's aunt, and this is our friend Andre."

Josie smiled and shook his hand. It was easy for her to smile, I supposed, because she hadn't heard me talk about my father.

"Mr. Parker," Jack said, shaking hands. "We weren't expecting you."

Kate's eyes narrowed. I'd told her plenty, and she took her grudges to the grave.

"We should probably go share these," Kate said, pulling Andre by the arm. Jack and Josie took their plates and followed.

Dad looked at me, his brows furrowed. "Always could clear a room," he said.

"That is one of your superpowers, yes."

He set the wine on the table. "The house looks good," he said, taking in the cabinets, the new paint, the new floor. The last time he'd seen it, one room was a heap of cinder and ash. He'd stormed out, furious with me for not doing the renovations his way. He hadn't even stayed long enough to see all the improvements Jack and I had made.

"Thank you," I said cooly.

My father looked awkward and uncomfortable, and I took momentary delight in being the root cause. He crossed and uncrossed his arms, finally shoving his hands into his pockets as he studied the room.

"Why did you come here?" I said.

"I needed to talk to you. In person."

"I have guests," I repeated.

"So I see."

My father, the man who bulldozed his way through all parts of life, seemed to be waiting for a cue. He looked shorter now, and I wondered if it was because he wasn't wearing a suit. Suits had always made him look like a giant—stern and intimidating, towering over me.

At least, I'd always thought it was the suits.

To save myself from more awkward non-talking, I pulled another plate from the cabinet and grabbed some silverware from the drawer. "Dinner's still on the table outside," I said. "Come eat, and we'll talk later."

He didn't argue. He followed me outside and into the yard, his loafers making a dull thump against the floorboards.

At the table, the din quieted as we approached. I introduced him to everyone else and noticed that Toph was several yards away, talking into his cell phone.

I set a place for my father and he sat down by my side for the first time in years. I was accustomed to him sitting across from me, staring at me over a desk or a restaurant table. Or gazing down at me as he sat on the corner of his desk while I slunk in the chair front of him.

But here, sitting elbow-to-elbow, it felt like we were almost equals, like we were on the same side, and it felt completely alien to me, like trying to write with my left hand.

Seated on my other side, Jack looked like I could have knocked him over with a feather. He whispered, "You OK?" and I nodded, though I was pretty damned far from OK. My heart felt like it would hammer a hole in my chest.

I was seeing my father for the first time in months. For the first time since he'd admitted he knew my mother had died.

And he was being civil. Friendly, even. But all I felt was fury and disappointment—especially because he was acting like everything was normal.

Everyone resumed their chatter, passing him dishes as if I'd been expecting him. Josie asked him where he was staying while he was here, but George eyed him carefully, his gaze stern. Vergie had likely told George some things about my father, but I wondered how much. What exactly had she felt towards him? Rage? Resentment? Maybe nothing at all.

As my father spooned rice and turkey and potatoes onto his plate, I felt the blood rising in my head. His elbow brushed against mine as he unfolded his napkin, and I felt like I'd been touched with a live wire.

"Excuse me a minute," I said, and went back to the kitchen.

When Jack came in he found me struggling with the corkscrew, attacking the bottle of wine my father had brought —Shiraz, which he knew I liked, but a label that was far too expensive for me to buy myself.

"Whoa," Jack said, taking both in his hands. "Let me help." He popped the cork, and I handed him a glass.

He poured a bit and said, "What's he doing here? I thought he said he wasn't coming."

"Keep pouring," I said.

He handed me the glass, three-quarters full, and I took a long swallow.

"I told him not to come. And yet, here he is," I said.

Jack poured himself a little wine, then slid his hand along my shoulder. "Maybe he's trying to set things right."

"What if I'm not ready to set things right? What if I need to rage at him for a few more years? I mean really, how can he ever make this right?"

Jack pulled me against his chest and kissed me on the forehead.

"All I wanted was a peaceful dinner with your family," I told him. But beneath this facade was the ugly secret I was keeping for Lucille, and now my father and the lie he'd carried for so long. I was unravelling, and just wanted everyone to cut the bullshit and tell each other the truth.

Me included. I hated keeping things from Jack, and hated feeling like telling him the truth would hurt Lucille. Secrets had torn my family apart, and I did not want to start down that path with Jack and his family. But here I was, already feeling like my loyalty to him and Lucille was being tested. And no matter what I did, I'd fail one of them.

"I feel like I'll explode if I talk to him," I said. "I'll rip his head right off."

"He probably deserves that." He stood back and put his big hands on my shoulders. "But people pretend to not hate each other at every holiday. You can handle this."

Jack gave me a slow wink and finished his wine. "Come on," he said. "I'm your backup now." I followed him back outside, wondering what in the world I could say to my father that might pass as polite familial conversation at that table full of people.

GEORGE WAS the first to leave, shortly after my father finished his dinner.

"We should get going, too," Josie said, helping Buck up from the table. "This one could probably use a nap after all that pie."

"I had to give them all a fair sampling," Buck said, patting his rounded belly.

As Josie hugged me, she said, "Thanks so much for this, dear. I just don't think I could have done it this time."

The three of them walked around to the front of the house, Buck and George chatting the whole way about who was going to win the football game that afternoon.

As Jack and I cleared the plates away, Kate and Andre wrapped up leftovers in the kitchen, trying to wedge all the dishes back into the refrigerator. Lucille and Toph had disappeared. Outside, my father sat at the picnic table, staring out over the yard, sipping his coffee.

It was hard to imagine how to mend what was broken between us, but I knew it was wrong to keep avoiding him. He was one of the only people left who could tell me anything about my mother, though he never wanted to discuss her. He'd avoided my questions for years, and the idea that he'd hidden her death from me felt like the ultimate betrayal. He'd let me wonder about her for years, and let me have this hope that I might see her again. It was unforgivable.

What else had he been hiding from me?

When I went back outside, the table was empty. I walked around the side of the house to check for his car and found him standing near the back corner of the house, near Vergie's old bottle tree. It was an old oak that held a couple dozen bottles of all sizes, mostly clear glass and green. They seemed to float in between the limbs, held by invisible fishing line. When the breeze caught them, a series of calming notes filled the air.

"I came here a few times with your mother," he said, "back when you were just a little squib. Vergie had this tree full of bottles then too."

"She said it trapped bad spirits."

"Not all of them. But I wish it had." He slid his hand along the trunk of the old oak. "I should have waited to come later. I didn't intend to interrupt your dinner."

"It's all right," I said.

"You never answer your phone. I left you a lot of messages."

"I didn't know what to say."

"I figured this was the only way to talk to you." He glanced over at me, then back at the tree. He looked so out of place, standing there in the weeds with his tailored pants, his expensive shoes. "I should tell you some things."

I crossed my arms, staring past my father and out at the backyard. Lucille and Toph had appeared, and were standing close to the lagoon, thirty yards away. They were several feet apart, and Lucille was pacing.

"Now's not a great time," I said. My heart was hammering again, and the thought of hearing more excuses, more lies—it was too much.

He was quiet, his eyes drifting over the limbs of the tree, as if the words he needed were trapped in the bottles. At last he spoke. "I wasn't always the bad guy. Your mother did some things too."

"Dad," I started, feeling my face start to burn.

"It takes two people to wreck a marriage, Enza. I didn't do

it all by myself." He looked genuinely sad, for the first time in a long while. "There's a lot you don't know."

Down near the lagoon, Toph had begun shouting. He waved his hands in the air, stepping closer to Lucille. She'd stopped pacing and looked to be staring him down, her hands on her hips. Dad, with his back to them, had no idea they were there.

"I know I should have told you about your mother," my father said. "I just didn't know how."

"I don't think I can talk about this now, Dad."

He shook his head, frustrated. "There will never be a good time to talk about these things."

It was impossible to hear the words between Lucille and Toph, but they both were clearly agitated. Toph stepped closer, looming over Lucille, and I felt my jaw tighten. Worried, I glanced back toward the house, but there was no sign of anyone else. Kate, Andre, and Jack were probably inside, giving us space.

"Listen," my father said, his voice low. "I never wanted to tell you the whole story, because I figured you'd think I was lying, just trying to be mean and vilify your mother. But she made the choice to leave, Enza. She left us because she cheated on me, and I couldn't forgive her."

I stared at my father, slack-jawed. It was hard to determine if he was telling the truth. His eyes were sad, and when he looked at me, he looked like he might cry.

He had never cried in front of me. Not even when his own mother died.

"I suppose I drove her away," he said. "She had an affair a year or so before she finally left us. She said she was sorry, that she knew it was wrong, that it meant nothing. She said all the things you'd expect someone to when they're caught, and I think part of her did want to try again. Part of her was remorseful. I knew what a divorce would do to you, and part of me wanted to just find a way to get over it, for your sake." He stared past me and wrapped his arms around his middle, as if he were struggling to keep some part of him in place. "But I just couldn't go on living with her. She was the only woman I ever truly loved, and she broke my heart like I never imagined she could. There are some things you just can't forgive."

My father looked smaller then, standing there in my yard, deflated like a balloon that gets away before you tie off the knot. He shoved his hands into his pockets and stared at the dirt between his feet.

"I don't know what to say, Dad."

"I don't expect you to. I don't know that it's possible for you to know the whole story, but you should have more than the pieces you have now."

I imagined none of us would ever know the whole story. My mother had taken that with her into the deep waters of the river, but it would help to know what my father had been keeping from me all these years. Even if he thought keeping secrets would spare me heartache or anger, I hated that he had made that decision for me. I deserved to know what he knew.

"I already lost her," he said, and his voice had the tiniest crack that made me think he'd been faking his bravado for all these years. "I really don't want to lose you too."

"None of this makes what you did OK," I said.

He sighed. "When it comes down to it, kid, some things hurt you so bad you never want to speak about them to anyone. Telling people about it makes it hurt that much worse, over and over, like a nightmare that eats you up every night."

His eyes were sad, his lips in a taut line. My chest tightened, but I willed myself not to cry. He'd never told me this much about my mother—not ever. I couldn't even remember the last time he'd mentioned her, and now hearing him speak the words made all of this feel so much more real.

For all those years, I'd assumed he wasn't hurting because he didn't tell me that he was. He'd always seemed full of anger when he talked about her, and I'd taken that to mean that he hated her, resented her, and blamed her. I'd been too naive to understand he was angry because he was in pain.

And I'd despised him for it. Hearing him now made me think that perhaps he'd missed her as much as I had.

"When I heard she died," he said, "I felt tremendous guilt. I knew she would still be alive if she had stayed with us, and she would have stayed if I'd been able to forgive her. But I couldn't. I've thought about that for a lot of years, wondering why I couldn't get over it. People cheat and get back together all the time, but I couldn't. I just—"

Lucille yelped in the distance. Dad didn't hear her, and went on talking. Toph had grabbed her by the arm and yanked her towards him. She struggled to get free, and he grabbed both of her wrists in one hand and then slapped her hard across the cheek. The blow knocked her off balance and she fell to her knees. It happened in a blink, but Toph stood looming above her.

"Shit," I said, moving towards them.

"Enza," Dad said. "Please, let me finish."

"Wait right there," I said over my shoulder. I half expected him to follow me, but he didn't.

Toph dropped his hands and Lucille stared at me, her eyes wide. Then she clambered back to her feet and ran back towards the house. For a second I nearly turned to go after her, but I went to Toph instead. He watched me as I stalked toward him, resting his hands on his hips.

"What the fuck?" I said to Toph.

He stood still, raking a hand through his hair, as if collecting himself. Then he tried to walk past me.

"Hey," I said. "You don't get to do this."

"Back off," he said, his voice a low rumble. "This doesn't concern you."

"Bullshit," I said. Blood pounded in my ears. "This stops right now. You're going to break up with her, and you're going to drive away from this place, and you're never going to see her again."

He smirked. "That's not really your call, is it?" His eyes were cold like a shark's. He straightened his shirt, and slowly rolled his sleeves to his elbows. "If you're half as smart as you think you are, you'll stay out of this." His voice was cool and even. I wanted to knock that smug grin right off his face.

Movement at the back of the house caught me eye and Toph followed my gaze. Andre's big frame filled the doorway as he turned in our direction. When I glanced toward the bottle tree, there was no sign of my father. He probably thought I'd just stormed off, angry at him.

Toph took a step back and held his hands out to his sides in a *who, me?* sort of gesture. His eyes belied his calm body language. "Lucille and I have an arrangement," he said. "It works for us." He shrugged and stared at the ground, no doubt trying to look as non-threatening as possible to Andre. "But one word from me, and her life will be ruined." He shrugged again, and then shoved his hands into his pockets.

My face felt hot with rage. From thirty yards away, he probably looked like he was apologizing, and not delivering ultimatums.

"Lucille owes me a lot," he said, his voice gravelly and low. He cocked his head sideways, but his eyes remained cold. "She got herself into a shitload of trouble, and I got her out." He smiled then, and it chilled me to the core. "And I can just as easily undo all of that with one phone call, and she can suffer the consequences. Is that what you want? For her to get kicked out of school? Lose her job? Embarrass her family? Did she tell you anything about what she's done?"

When I didn't answer, he smirked and said, "Yeah, I didn't think so."

My jaw tightened. I couldn't imagine what she might have done that was so bad that she'd turn to someone like Toph. He was more clever than I'd given him credit for, and more calculating. He wasn't going to do anything that looked remotely threatening, especially with Andre here.

He was even more of a threat than I'd first believed. The thought of Lucille being with him one more minute, feeling controlled by him—it made me sick to my stomach and hot with rage. The last time I'd felt that way, I'd been certain I was going to die, the target of a man not so different from Toph.

The idea of Lucille going through that same thing was unbearable. When I glanced back toward the house, Andre was gone.

"Leave her," I said.

He chewed his lip, squinting up at the sky. Then he snapped his head back to me. "Sorry. No." And the he leaned closer, so close that I could see flecks of green in his eyes. "And if you say one word about any of this, I'll make that phone call." He grinned, and I balled my fist at my side, and then next thing I knew, it was colliding with his mouth and there was a burst of main in my knuckles that felt like fire.

He staggered backward, that stupid grin still on his face. He touched his fingers to his split lip and said, "You're going to regret that."

"Hey there," Andre said from behind me, and my heart felt like it twisted into a knot. "Everything all right out here?" His tone was friendly, as if he'd walked up on two normal people having a chat. He'd snuck right up along the edge of the cypress and popped out a few feet from where we stood. His body seemed relaxed, but he'd zeroed in on Toph and had probably already calculated precisely how to take him down if necessary.

"Sure," Toph said. He slipped his sunglasses from his hair down onto his nose and tapped his fingers against his lip, as if he might hide the cut. "I was just saying what a lovely afternoon we had, but that we've got to hit the road." He turned toward the house and said, "We'll see you next time. Nice to meet you, sheriff."

Toph gave a little wave and walked back toward the house, as calmly as if he was walking along a beach.

Andre arched a brow and said, "Care to tell me what that was about?"

"Not particularly."

He nodded, his eyes still on Toph. "You probably should, though."

I breathed a heavy sigh, trying to calm my pounding heart. Toph glanced over his shoulder as he opened the back door.

"How's your hand?" he said, still watching Toph.

"Hurts like hell."

He nudged my arm. "Let's get you some ice, then. And you can tell me what he's done."

"How much of that did you see?"

"Enough," he said. "I came out here when your dad left. I assume there's some pertinent details you can give me to fill in the gaps."

I sighed. "Lucille's going to need our help."

He nodded, his jaw tightening.

By the time we got inside the back door, Lucille was coming down the stairs. Toph was standing by the front door, with Jack and Kate in the hallway giving him quizzical looks. His lip was still beaded with blood.

"OK," Lucille called from the stairs. "I'm coming. What's the rush?"

"Long drive tomorrow," he said calmly. "I'm beat."

She stopped on the last step and stared at him. "What happened to your lip?"

Kate looked at me and I swallowed hard, shaking my head just the slightest bit. Her eyes narrowed at Toph. Jack followed her gaze and caught sight of my hand and my bleeding knuckles. His brow furrowed as I crossed my arms over my chest to cover my hand. I shook my head and his jaw tensed.

"What's going on here?" Jack said, his voice like a growl. He stalked towards Toph and said, "If you laid a finger on her, I will bury you."

Toph smirked, leaning closer. "Take your shot, tough guy. And I'll press charges against you both. And believe me, my lawyers will find ways to sue you until you don't have a dime."

"What the hell is happening?" Lucille said. She narrowed her eyes at me and then looked back at Toph.

Andre tensed next to me, placing his hand on my arm when I stepped forward. He was watching them carefully, his body rigid, no doubt watching for any excuse to arrest him.

Toph's gaze shifted to Lucille and he said cooly, "I'll start the car. Ten seconds and I'm out of here." His glare dared her to refuse.

The screen door banged shut behind him and Lucille rushed at me. "What is wrong with you?" She got right in my face, her eyes blazing. "You promised me you'd stay out of this."

"Lucille," Jack said, reaching for her arm. "Just stay here. Tell me what's going on."

"I can't," she said, and shot me a look that could cut glass.

"You can," he said, taking her arm. "Whatever this is, let me help."

Kate stared at me, her mouth open. *What the fuck?* she mouthed.

Outside, Toph revved the engine.

"I've got to go," Lucille said to Jack. "I have to fix this."

He reached for her again, but she slipped away and ran out the door, the screen slamming behind her. The car door shut and the tires squealed as Toph pealed out of the yard and down the gravel drive.

Jack was by my side in a flash, checking my hand. "Are you all right?" he said. "What did he do?" His brow was furrowed, his lips a tight line.

"I'm fine," I said. "He was just talking shit."

"Did he hurt you?"

I shook my head, fighting back the angry tears. I was furious—at Toph, at Lucille, at myself. I'd made a stupid move, and now there was no going back.

He looked at Andre. "What are y'all not telling me?"

Andre arched a brow. "It seems he's worn out his welcome, as they say."

"Please go over to Buck and Josie's," I said to Andre. "They won't leave without all of their stuff. Maybe you can get her to stay." I hoped that was true, that Lucille might end this right now, and let Toph leave her.

He nodded, but we both knew the chances of that happening were slim. Right now, they were likely speeding toward Josie's house, where they'd gather up their belongings and head straight for Austin. I couldn't imagine them staying the night, and as hard as I hoped that Lucille would stay and let Toph drive back to Texas alone, I knew that was not going to happen.

Whatever was going on between them, I had just made it so much worse.

Kate rushed into the kitchen, and then came out with a half-empty pie plate. "Take this," she said to Andre. "Tell them you came to bring leftovers. Then you can stay a while and it won't worry them."

He nodded.

My whole body felt like it was turning inside out. Even if I told Andre what had happened between them, Lucille wouldn't admit it. He couldn't arrest Toph, and it would only make this worse.

Jack followed Andre to the door and said, "I'm going with you. You can explain on the way." Jack shot me another questioning look.

"It's better if you don't," Andre said. "I'll call you once I'm over there and this has settled down." With that, he'd shifted back into sheriff mode, and he was out the door.

Kate and Jack turned to me at the same time, and I leaned against the wall, feeling like I'd collapse if I didn't.

"Enza," Jack said, laying his hand on my arm. "Tell me what happened."

Next to him, Kate nodded, her eyes filled with worry.

Chapter Twelve

IN THE KITCHEN, Jack wrapped some ice cubes in a towel and placed it on my hand, sitting me down at the small dining table. My knuckles still throbbed from connecting with Toph's jaw, and his teeth had left a couple of cuts.

Kate sat next to me and Jack was on my other side. The kitchen was mostly tidy, with just a few desserts left out on the table and the counter.

Jack placed his hand on my shoulder and the words came pouring out. I told them about what Lucille had said to me that night she was here, about how Toph had loaned her so much money and gotten her this job that she loved. Fighting back tears, I told them how Toph had grabbed her, both times, and how she'd begged me not to tell Jack. With every word, I was unraveling more and more, and Jack was becoming more agitated. He stood and paced across the kitchen as I told him about what Toph had said to me just today, and Kate leaned forward, held her face in her hands.

"I don't see why she's putting up with this," he said. "Josie taught her to stand up for herself."

"That's the complicated bit," I said. "She still loves a part of him. She's thinking of the guy she fell in love with."

"She told you that?"

"She didn't have to."

He stared at me for a long moment, and his voice lowered. "You've know about this for days."

"I didn't know what to do," I told him. "I wanted to tell you, but I didn't want to betray her trust."

"But you were OK with betraying mine?" he said. He was thinking of our talk at the inn—it was written all over his face. He'd asked me if I knew details about what was going on between Lucille and Toph, and I'd said no.

Kate looked at Jack, then at me. "I'm just going to be upstairs," she said.

Jack stared straight ahead, refusing to look at me as her footsteps filled the silence.

"That's not fair," I said. "This put me in an impossible situation. You have to know that I wanted to do what was best for her."

He snorted, and began pacing again. "What was best for her was to get her away from that asshole as soon as possible. What was best was for you to tell me what was happening so I could do something."

"And what would you have done? You hated the guy from the minute you met him. You think she didn't know that? If you'd gone charging in and pulled some caveman move, then she'd freeze you out and side with him."

"You mean some caveman move like punching him in the face?"

My cheeks burned. "That wasn't my smartest move. You're right about that."

He raked his hands through his hair in that way that meant he was trying to hold himself together.

"She asked me not to tell you the details, Jack. I know how protective you are of her, and I knew if I told you, you'd run over there and yell at her for staying with him, and it would scare her. I thought if I told you, she'd feel like we were ganging up on her."

"You don't always know what I'm going to do."

"This one was pretty easy to predict. You're not exactly subtle when you're in protective mode."

His eyes darkened. "She's my family. I deserve to know what's going on, and I need to know when she's in trouble."

He hurled the word like a stone. *Family.*

"I made her promise to tell you everything after today, or I would. But I knew it needed to come from her."

"Oh that makes it all better," he snapped. "You were *going* to tell me."

"Jack, she was so afraid you'd be mad at her—and disappointed."

"You're damn right I am. But I'm more disappointed in you."

I'd only seen him this angry one other time—back when he was trying to protect me from a dangerous man. This was so much worse, being the cause of his hurt and anger.

He was right about one thing: I shouldn't have hit Toph. But his smug face had reminded me of every man who'd bullied me, hurt me, and tried to control me—and then I'd thought of him hurting Lucille in those same ways, and I'd lost it.

That was precisely what he'd wanted.

"Jack, I feel terrible that it all happened this way. Tell me what I can do to fix it."

"I don't know," he said, his voice low. He gripped the back of the empty chair, his knuckles white. After a moment, he said, "I should be over there. I have to make her stay."

"You can't make her," I said. "As badly as you want to. I screwed this up—I know that. Now she's angry, and feels betrayed, and probably terrified. But don't go over there and make her feel like she has to choose between him and her family. Don't put *her* in an impossible situation." I lay my hand on his arm, but he quickly pulled it away.

His glare chilled me. "Don't tell me what's best for my family," he said.

I sighed as he stalked toward the door, and then turned to face me. "Did it ever occur to you that you've put *me* in an impossible situation?"

"I'm sorry," I said. "I didn't want this. You have to know that."

He shook his head. "I can't believe you kept this from me. This—we—will never work if you lie to me."

"Jack, I—"

"I can't even stand to look at you right now." He stalked into the hallway and grabbed his keys from the table by the door.

"Please wait," I said, following him to the door. "Don't leave like this."

He paused at the door and turned to me. "I can't be here right now. Not with you. I need a break." He started to say something more, and then shook his head and slammed the door behind him.

And then the tears finally came. As I sank down to the floor, my back against the wall, I heard Kate's footsteps on the stairs. She sat down next to me and wrapped her arm around my shoulders, leaning her head against mine.

"This is the worst feeling in the world," I said.

"I'm so sorry," she said.

"This is all my fault."

"That's not entirely true."

I snorted.

"Did you keep things from him? Yes. Was it in order to hurt him or someone else? No."

"He doesn't see it that way."

"Not now," she said, her voice calm. "Maybe when he cools off and thinks about it."

We sat there for several minutes, until my hands stopped shaking, and my heart stopped pounding. My head hurt and my hand throbbed, and whenever I looked at the cuts on my knuckles, I saw Toph's stupid smug face and it reminded me of how I'd wrecked everything in one careless move.

"I should text Andre," I said. "Tell him Jack's probably headed over there."

Kate pulled her cell phone from her jeans pocket and started tapping out a text. "On it," she said. "I texted him a few minutes ago, but he hasn't answered."

We stared at the screen.

Three dots.

Nothing.

"What if something's happened?" I said. The lump was back in my throat.

Three dots again.

Toph just left, Andre wrote. **Lucille's staying. I'm going to wait here a while, just in case.**

"Thank God," I said.

Kate let out a deep breath.

How's Lucille? She wrote, holding the screen so I could see.

Upset, but OK. She's talking to her folks.

And Toph? Kate typed.

Left without incident.

Text me if Jack comes over?

Sure.

"Jack's going to lose his mind," I said.

"I was hoping Toph would do something stupid and Andre could arrest him."

"He's too smart for that," I said. "I'm the only one being stupid today."

"Stop," she said, turning to face me. "I can't say I'd have done anything different. Except I might have kicked him in the balls first."

I snorted.

"Too soon?" she said.

"I don't want to be here right now. I can't be here when he gets back." My heart felt like it was being squeezed in a vise. Thinking of Lucille, feeling trapped and afraid, made me sick with regret. Buck and Josie would be so worried when Jack told them everything that had happened here—and he most certainly wouldn't hold anything back.

He'd tell them about me, too, and how I'd kept this from him. They'd be hurt. Furious. And now Toph would still be out there, probably working himself up into a rage. Men like him hated to feel like something had been taken away from them, and they'd do anything to get back those things they wanted because they felt entitled to have them.

Even if what they wanted was another person who only wanted to be away from them.

Men like Toph felt the world owed them something. They felt that people like Lucille owed them everything. When strong women like Lucille told them no, that made them feel weak—and feeling weak made them think they needed to prove they could break them.

If anything happened to Lucille because of what I'd done, I'd never forgive myself.

Neither would Buck and Josie.

And neither would Jack.

We'd be over, if we weren't already.

If Lucille stayed here, she'd be surrounded by people who could protect her, but she'd have to save herself—and cut herself free.

"I can't stay in this house another minute," I said. Jack was livid, and I hated the idea of being here when he got back—if he came back at all. But more than that, there was something I had to do to cut myself free, too.

I'd been avoiding it too long, and it was time to face it.

"What do you want to do?" Kate said.

"Put something to rest," I said. "And bury it."

Chapter Thirteen

IN TWENTY MINUTES, Kate and I both had a bag packed and were out the door. Bella whined from the porch as we hurried down the steps. Even she seemed disappointed in me.

"I'll drive," Kate said. "You're too worked up." She opened the trunk of her car and tossed our bags inside.

"Yes, and I had two fingers of bourbon while you were packing."

She arched a brow. "How's the hand?"

"Pleasantly numb." Now that the adrenaline had worn off, my whole body felt tired and sore, but the bourbon had calmed me down and stopped my heart from fluttering like a bird. It had stopped the swirling of thoughts in my head, and narrowed my focus down to one task: the one I'd been avoiding for so long. The one thing that I hadn't lost control over.

Once we were on the highway, headed toward the interstate, Kate said, "What's the GPS say?"

"Five hours to Green Bluff." If we were lucky, we'd make it there before midnight.

Kate nodded, her jaw tense. "Are you sure you want to do this? We could just go to that little inn we stayed at in Algiers," she said. "Let you cool off, visit the city, get hammered in our room. Avoid dudes for a while."

"This isn't about him," I said. "This is about finding out what really happened to my mother. I'm tired of the secrets. I want to see this place for myself."

She bit her fingernail, a sure sign she was worried.

"Relax," I said. "I just want to see where she spent her last days. I'm not going to drown myself in the river."

"Of course you're not," she said, turning the radio on. "We are not women who drown ourselves in rivers. I just think you should be prepared for this dredging up even more hurt."

Green Bluff was a tiny Texas town, just a speck on the map. I'd never heard of it until Vergie's diary, and after a little internet sleuthing, I couldn't see why my mother would have spent any time in such a place. We might not find anything there, but I hoped that being in the same spot that my mother was in might be a way to let this part of my life go. She'd become a dark cloud hanging over me, and learning that she'd died had made it seem even heavier, more ominous. If nothing else, this could be a way to say goodbye. Once and for all.

After a few miles, Kate said, "You ready to talk about this yet?"

"My mother?"

She frowned. "Jack."

"Nope."

The last thing I wanted to think about right now was Jack Mayronne. He'd talked to me so coldly, blaming me for everything that had happened with Lucille. How could he think of me as reckless? How could he think I was doing anything but helping her? I'd never thought he could turn on me so quickly, but the way he'd said *family* when he talked about Lucille made me think he'd placed me in some other category entirely—one that would never hold the same bond of loyalty. The worst part was that he didn't even seem to think hard about that insult: He didn't pause and consciously choose the word to hurt me.

It just came out that way. On instinct.

Because that's the way he thought of me, deep down. Not family. Something less than. Other.

Even worse, he'd said he wanted a break. Like he wanted to give up on me and leave me—the same as the people I loved most had done before.

I rolled the window down enough to feel the breeze. The rain had let up, but a mist still wafted into the car, a stray droplet stinging my cheek now and again. Beyond the breaking storm clouds, stars blinked in the spaces between tree limbs, tiny holes pierced in the night. I tried to forget the look on Jack's face, the way he'd so easily dismissed me, how he'd left the house without another word.

I can't even stand to look at you, he'd said.

The GPS bellowed its directions, telling us to pick up I-10. Kate made the turn and I said, "Why do you have an Australian man doing the voice of your GPS?"

"Why wouldn't I?"

"Can you understand him? I think he just said *by-yow*."

"I find him soothing," she said. "Especially in rush hour traffic and in trying emotional times. It makes me think of Hugh Jackman, and I find him delightfully calming."

She stepped on the gas as we merged onto the interstate. I leaned back, trying to forget about Jack's angry words, and how he'd made all of this my fault.

"For what it's worth," Kate said, "You are not careless with other people."

"You heard all that, huh?"

She shrugged. "The walls are thinner than you think."

"He obviously didn't feel about me the way I thought he did."

"I don't know if I'd go that far, but that was really an impossible situation for everyone."

"Still not ready," I said.

"I know, but until you are, you need to have that thought in your head too. I know you well enough to know what muck is rolling around in there right now. I also know you were trying to do the right thing."

"Noted."

Kate was quiet for a while, staring at the road ahead. It was so dark that the whole world seemed to run together, the ground blending into the water and the sky. That darkness had unnerved me when I'd first moved here, but now it was comforting somehow, like things weren't as divided as they had been before. There was more fluidity, more overlapping. Lines weren't so clearly drawn.

"What do you know about Green Bluff?" she said.

"It's north of Beaumont, still down in the bayou country." It had probably reminded my mother of her home—maybe that's why she landed there after her travels. There would have been a comforting similarity, but not that overwhelming feeling of everyone in town knowing your business.

"The place I'd like to see is a wildlife refuge. It's where they found her." My internet search had led me to an article in the *Green Bluff Gazette* that detailed a tragic drowning in the refuge. It was the only mention I could find of the incident.

Kate let out a heavy sigh.

"We can stop if you get tired," I said.

"I don't mind," she said. "I'm wired now."

Pulling my phone from my pocket, I checked for any missed calls or text messages from Jack.

There were none.

Part of me had hoped there might be something—an apology for being so hard on me, an indication that he'd given this some thought and realized I wasn't trying to be hurtful. But there were neither. He was still angry, still blaming me. He'd said he wanted a break, so I'd give him one.

How could I be with him if he thought I was so reckless and thoughtless? If that was how he felt, I didn't see a way for us to stay together. This is how we would end: he'd vanish the way my mother did, the way Vergie did. Jack would slip out of my life as quickly as he had slipped into it. This would be just another broken thing I didn't know how to fix.

"TALK TO ME," Kate said. "I'm tired. And you never told me if you got to talk to your dad."

We'd stopped for terrible gas station coffee an hour before, when we'd crossed the Sabine River into Texas. According to the GPS, Green Bluff was another hour and a half away. There was almost no traffic, aside from semis, and hardly any lights along the road. It felt like we were hurtling toward the edge of the earth.

"He told me that Mom cheated on him. That's why she left."

"Wow. Bombshell. You believe him?"

"I think he was telling me truth. He looked genuinely sad."

But it was more than that—he'd looked remorseful, and that was not something I'd seen in him before.

After I told her the rest of what he'd said out in the yard, she stayed silent for a long moment.

"You know we might not find anything out here," she said quietly.

"Yeah. I know. But at least we'll have tried."

Ahead, there were signs for a hotel at the next exit. According to the app on my phone, there weren't any others until Green Bluff.

"Why don't we stop?" I said. "We can go the last hour tomorrow."

"Yeah, whatever you want," she said.

She took the next exit and we followed the signs onto a two-lane highway. After a mile or so, we came to the hotel. It was a small two-story with a kidney-shaped pool that had been drained for the winter. The safety lights in the parking lot cast an eerie green glow on the bricks, making them look like the thick hide of a reptile. A vacancy sign glowed in the window.

Inside the lobby, the night clerk was watching TV. He looked about eighteen, with shaggy blond hair that almost touched his shoulders. He didn't move until Kate rang the bell at the front counter.

"Oh, hey," he said, jumping up from his chair. "Sorry, they were showing highlights from the bowl game."

"You have any rooms left?"

"Oh sure."

He went behind the front desk and started typing on the computer, eyeing the car in the lot as I gave him my information. "Breakfast is served from six to ten," he said, handing me a receipt to sign. "Your room's upstairs to the left of the elevator."

"Thanks."

"Yes, ma'am. Y'll have a good night."

Kate and I carried our bags to our room and collapsed onto the beds. Light from the parking lot poured into the tiny space from the gaps around the edges of the curtains. The room had been remodeled recently, but was sparsely decorated. Two brightly colored paintings of longhorn steers hung above both headboards.

"How very Texas," Kate said, peering at the first one.

"As long as it has decent beds and a hot shower, they can put cows all over everything." I checked my phone again for messages, but there were none.

Kate stepped inside the bathroom and said, "Yes, this will do just fine."

When she came back out, she said, "Any word from Jack?"

"Nope. Any word from Andre?"

"No." She pulled her phone from her pocket and said, "I should tell him where we are. And you should probably tell Jack so he doesn't worry." She started typing.

I snorted. "Jack won't be worried about me tonight."

"You know that's not true. You had a fight. That doesn't mean he stopped loving you."

"I think I pretty well wrecked everything."

She sighed. "Don't be so sure. Text him. I'm going to take a shower and wash off the road dirt."

First I sent my father a text: **I won't be able to meet you tomorrow. I'm sorry. I'll explain later.**

I didn't expect an answer. It was nearly one in the morning in North Carolina.

Then I texted Jack: **Kate and I went to Green Bluff. We'll be back in a couple of days.**

Three dots appeared.

Then nothing.

I waited, but he never responded.

"Copy that," I said.

Chapter Fourteen

"MAYBE THIS TOWN of yours will have a nice coffee shop where they know how to make lattes," Kate said. She scowled as she sipped the coffee from the hotel lobby and reached for a container of cream. "One more cup like this is going to give me an ulcer." She bit into a biscuit from the continental breakfast and scowled.

Outside, it looked like rain was coming. Dark clouds rolled overhead, and the air felt heavy.

"How is it you look so put together?" I said. "I feel like I've been run over by a bicycle."

Kate always looked chic, even when traveling with only her toothbrush. She could sweep her hair back into a ponytail, splash cold water on her face, and look like a model trying to travel incognito. In her fitted shirt, black pants, and knee-length rain jacket, she looked like she'd stepped out of a trendy outdoorsy clothing catalog.

I, however, always had pillow hair, puffy eyes, and a few imprints of the sheets pressed into my cheek. This morning was no different—plus, my brain felt fuzzy, like the last twenty-four hours had just been a bad dream. My blouse was wrinkled and my jeans had a nickel-sized hole in the knee. Luckily I had grabbed my brown motorcycle jacket on the way out of the house, and it could make anything look purposefully edgy.

"Come on," she said. "Let's hit it."

"What's got such a fire lit under you?"

She fixed me with her eyes, which were entirely too bright and alert for this hour. This is how she looked at me when she was fiercely set on an idea.

"We have an objective," she said, gesturing toward me with her coffee cup. "I'm here to hold the pedal down. You want to find out what happened and put this to bed, and I'm going to help you."

I took another swallow of the awful coffee and we took our bags out to the car. I didn't know what it was like to have a sister, but if I'd had one, I'd have wanted her to be Kate.

WE PULLED BACK onto the state highway and followed it north through the rolling hills. This part of Texas looked just like northern Louisiana, with its blend of pine trees and farmland. It was chilly, but pleasant enough to drive with the windows cracked.

Still, there was a niggling feeling of dread.

After turning onto another two-lane road, we slowed to twenty miles an hour and pulled into the incorporated community of Green Bluff. It looked like an ordinary small Southern town, with one main street that had a post office, a gas station, and a diner. Small businesses dominated the main street, and there were a few abandoned buildings dotted in between. We drove around for a few minutes, looking for any government buildings that might be useful. A couple of streets had nice historic houses, and a few had clapboards and single-wides. It was like any other small town, really, with clear demarcations of the well-off and the not so. After driving past the post office three times, Kate parallel parked on the main street in front of what appeared to be the town's only restaurant. The Frogtown Diner was clearly a remnant of the 1960s, complete with a J-shaped sign that was an arrow directing us inside.

"What do you say to a real breakfast?" Kate said. "That biscuit was like a stone."

"Sure. Maybe we can get some directions."

The diner was smaller than it looked from outside. Red vinyl barstools lined the counter, each of them occupied. There were ten or so booths, also red vinyl, and a couple of tables that looked like they'd been there since the very beginning. Ceramic frogs sat like sentinels on the bar, along the window sills, and by the cash register. We chose a booth in the back, and I tried to ignore the fact that everyone watched us as we walked past.

We ordered two breakfast specials. Our waitress—Tanya, her name tag read, though she never introduced herself—was friendly enough, but she knew we didn't belong there. As she flitted from table to table, she chatted with everyone else like she'd known them her whole life, asking about their kids and parents as she refilled their coffees. I wondered if my mother had sat in this very diner, pushing eggs around a plate like I did.

When Tanya came back to check on us, Kate picked up our frog-shaped salt shaker and asked, "Why's it called Frogtown?"

Tanya smiled. "They call this part of town Frogtown because it's right on the creek. You know, frog level."

"Ah," Kate said.

"What brings y'all to our neck of the woods?" Tanya asked.

"Just a road trip," I said. "My mom stayed here for a while."

She nodded, refilling my coffee.

"You get many tourists around here?" Kate said.

"No," Tanya said, not unkindly. "Can't say we're really on the way to anything."

"Where's the police station?" I asked.

Tanya wrinkled her brow. "The sheriff's office is next to the library. Back on Greene Street." She pointed in the direction of the post office. "Two streets over."

"Thanks," I said. "And the wildlife refuge?"

"Take highway eighty east. It's about six miles from here, right on the river."

"Thank you."

She smiled and went to refill coffee cups at the table next to us.

"Why do you need the police department?" Kate asked, stabbing her pancakes.

"I need the police report from when they found my mother."

She studied me for a long moment. "Why would you want that?"

"Vergie thought it wasn't an accident. I'd like to see what the official report said."

She swallowed hard and reached for her coffee. "And you think they're just going to hand that over to you?"

"It's worth asking. I'm her last kin."

She drizzled more syrup on the pancakes. "Don't you have a death certificate?"

"No."

"That might be easier to get."

"I looked online, which was an endless rabbit hole—but I can send a request to the register of deeds in the county where she died."

She nodded, sipping her coffee. "You think your dad has a copy?"

"It's possible."

Tanya came by and slipped the check on the table. "Thanks," she said. "Y'all have a great day."

"Hey," I said. "One more question. Where would the county courthouse be?"

"Liberty. About an hour west of here. They're probably closed today, though." She turned and walked over to a table where two middle-aged women had just sat down.

Kate pulled her phone from her pocket and said, "Let's find out."

My phone buzzed next to us on the table. It was a text from my father saying he was flying back this afternoon, that he'd call me later.

Kate turned to me, nodding toward the phone. "Jack?"

I snorted. "No."

"Courthouse is closed," Kate said. "Open again Monday."

"So let's try the next best thing."

THE GREEN BLUFF sheriff's office wasn't very different from the one in Bayou Sabine—except for all the cowboy hats. When Kate and I walked into the station, the first thing I noticed was a stern-looking blonde woman sitting at the front desk, behind a Plexiglas window. A tiny Christmas tree sat on the far corner of her desk, draped in tinsel and twinkling lights.

"Could I speak to the sheriff?" I asked.

"Do you have an appointment?" The sharpness of her chiseled cheekbones and pointed chin matched her tone.

"No ma'am," I said.

"What's this regarding?"

"I was hoping to get some information about an old police report. My mother's case."

She glared at me.

"It'll only take a minute," I said. "And actually, I might have some new information about her case. It was a suspicious death." It was stretching the truth, but I had to get past this gatekeeper and talk to someone who could tell me more about how my mother was found. I couldn't leave Texas without answers.

The officer picked up her phone and dialed, then took a couple of steps away from her desk. After a few hushed sentences, she hung up and moved closer to the glass. "Have a seat out there," she said, pointing toward a plastic chair that looked like it belonged in a high school cafeteria.

After a few minutes, a lock buzzed and the metal door across the room opened. A dark-haired man in a tan and brown uniform stepped into the waiting room. "Miss Parker?"

"Yes," I said, extending my hand as he approached.

He shook my hand a little too hard and said, "I'm Deputy Chavez. We can chat in my office." He was tall and broad-shouldered, with hair cropped in a military-style cut. His jaw was rigid, but his eyes were warm.

I followed him down the hall into a tiny office with another uncomfortable plastic chair. He leaned against the corner of his desk as if to hide the heap of files that covered it.

"What can I do for you?" he asked.

I quickly explained about my mother, how she'd been missing and turned up in the river, how we'd been estranged, how I'd just recently learned about it all. He looked like he was in his late forties, which meant he could have been on the squad when my mother was found.

At last he nodded. "I remember that case. I'm sorry for your loss."

"Did you work on the case?"

"Not exactly," he said.

I waited for him to explain. He didn't.

"The thing is," I said, "I need to know how my mother died."

He crossed his arms over his chest, and his sleeves strained over his shoulders. "Next of kin should be able to get a death certificate," he said. I caught myself staring at the crisp lines in his shirt, the brass nameplate that said *D. Chavez*, resting just above the shirt's pocket, centered exactly on the vertical seam. I wondered what the D stood for. Daniel. David. Damian.

"It's kind of a complicated situation," I said, and his quiet stare told me he'd heard those words about ten thousand times before. "The thing is, I just learned that my mother died all those years ago. I can't get answers anywhere else but here. I just need to know if it really was an accident." I paused, thinking of how Kate could turn on the charm in her big gray-blue eyes and put the whammy on men without even trying. She'd probably eke out a tear or two if she were in my position.

"Right before my grandmother died," I continued, "she told me she thought it might not be an accident, and I just want to know what really happened. Put this all behind us." I stuttered a little at that last part, the lie catching in my throat. "Please. I drove three hundred miles. Isn't there something you can tell me?"

I felt real tears filling my eyes and thought, for once, they might actually come on command and work in my favor. Or this man might grab me by the elbow and usher me right out the door.

Deputy Chavez pulled a pair of reading glasses from his chest pocket and slipped them on. He walked behind his desk and typed something quickly into his computer, his fingers striking the keys so hard the keyboard rattled.

He looked at the screen as he typed, then shifted his gaze back to me. I swiped a finger over my eyes and sniffed.

"May I see your license?" he asked. His voice had softened, but just barely.

I dug it out of my purse and handed it to him.

He looked at the photo, then looked at me, and resumed typing. After reading the screen, he handed the license back to me.

"Typically we can't give out information like this," he said. "But sometimes things make their way into the wide, wide world and become public record." His eyes narrowed as he said, "In a manner of speaking."

He reminded me of Andre, the way his voice was gruff but not unkind.

"Thank you," I said.

He turned back to the screen, but it was difficult to read his expression. Like Andre, he seemed to have mastered the stone-faced give-nothing-away façade that appeared to be standard issue for anyone working in civil service. His eyes darted across the screen as he read, scrolling slowly. After a few minutes he typed something else and began reading again.

At last he said, reading from the screen, "The local paper reported that a woman, at that time unidentified, was pulled from the Trinity River. Found on the refuge side. A later report says it was ruled an accidental drowning."

I waited for more.

"The later report says she was Martine Devereaux of Bayou Sabine, Louisiana."

"That's her. So it was accidental?"

"I believe the article to be accurate," he said, his eyes resting on mine. He was choosing his words carefully.

"Is that what's in the coroner's report?"

He turned back to the screen, and I fought the urge to run around the desk and read over his shoulder. "I don't see inconsistencies," he said. He pushed his glasses up into his hair and rested his elbows on the desk. "I'm afraid that's all I can say, Miss Parker. You can fill out some paperwork and fax us your birth certificate if you want a copy of the full report."

I nodded and stood up. I shook his hand again. "Thank you, Deputy. I appreciate your help."

KATE SLAPPED me on the shoulder when I told her. "I knew you had it in you," she said. "You just had to learn how to set your gaze to 'smolder.'"

"Whatever."

"Was he cute?"

"Stop."

She grinned. "I knew I should have gone in too. I do love a man in uniform."

"Yes, I've learned that about you recently."

She started the car and cleared her throat. "So what did he tell you about your mom?"

"Accidental. No evidence of suicide or foul play. I'll get a death certificate, but I don't expect it to say anything different." Deputy Chavez had given me a lot—he'd mentioned the name of the local paper, and I'd search that later to see if I could find the same news articles. A death certificate would confirm cause of death, but it would be impossible to know if it was suicide. That seemed unlikely, given what I remembered about my mother, and what Vergie wrote about her—but that piece of the story had vanished with my mother.

"You still want to go to the refuge?" Kate said.

"Yes. I need to see it." Some parts of this puzzle would never be revealed, but I needed to see the place where she was found. I couldn't explain why, but I felt a pull to go there and feel like I was standing in her footprints for one moment.

We followed the two-lane highway west, threading through the bayous. This part of Texas looked very similar to Bayou Sabine. It was lush and verdant near Green Bluff, and as we came out of the town limits and approached the refuge, the manicured trees gave way to a thicket that was eerie even in daylight. The closer we came to the river, the denser the vegetation became. The dark greens of the cypress trees began to look black.

My phone rang, and I hesitated before finally silencing the call.

"Is that Jack?" Kate asked.

I waited to see if he left a voice message. He didn't.

"Maybe you should call him back," she said. "Maybe he wants to apologize for being an ass."

"Maybe I'll call him tonight. But honestly, I think it might be over."

"Do you want it to be?"

Placing the phone in the cup holder between our seats, I turned it so the screen was visible.

"You heard what he said to me. If that's how he feels, then yes."

"People say stupid things when they're mad." She turned and gave me a hard look. "You included."

"Can't I deal with one crisis at a time?"

She snorted. "Yeah, because *that's* how life works."

Up ahead, there was a sign for the refuge tucked into the trees. The pavement abruptly ended and turned to packed gravel. "I'll call him back and hear him out. But not right now." We'd been through too much for me to not give him one opportunity to apologize. If he could stop blaming me and try to understand why I did what I did, we might be able to start over.

The phone's screen lit up with a text message.

Where are you? he wrote.

Kate glanced at me, but I pretended to ignore the text, staring out the window, listening to the splatter of rain on the windshield. Everything outside was gray, and a light rain was falling.

The phone lit up again. **I need to talk to you. Please just let me know you're OK.**

I picked it up, and Kate said, "Yep. Do it."

"Stop," I said.

I finally texted back, **I'm fine. With Kate.**

When are you coming back?

Talk later, I typed. **We're driving now.**

That was it. No apology.

When the road ended at what seemed like a parking area, Kate stopped the car. An error message popped up on my phone: *message not delivered.* After trying twice more, my last text still didn't go through. We'd driven into a dead spot, and the phone showed no service.

The rain was barely a drizzle now, but the air was still heavy. We got out of the car and walked along a path toward a trail head. With very few markers around, this was like many national forests I'd visited: there were occasional USGS markers, but very little signage to help you navigate.

The trail quickly turned into a boardwalk. The ground beneath us was pluff mud, holding a tangle of marsh grasses. A flash of memory struck me, from being a kid and walking into the marsh grass deep in the woods behind Vergie's house. She'd warned me about it, but I went anyway, and quickly sank to my knees in the mud. The ground would deceive you that way around here. It looked like solid earth, but as soon as you put your weight on it, you sank like your whole body was made of cast iron.

The boardwalk creaked and groaned as we followed it across the swamp. It was wide enough for two people to walk abreast, but it still felt like the swamp was too close, like it could reach up over the boardwalk in a wave and drag us down to the depths of the mire.

"This is all kinds of spooky," Kate said at last. "Why would anyone want to come out here?"

"To be alone."

"This is where they found your mom?"

"So far, I can't imagine why she would come out here to go swimming."

Our shoes clapped on the boards and seemed to reverberate across the water. After another thirty yards, the trees opened up, and we could see sky again. The boardwalk turned into a pier as we reached the banks of the river. The pier was an elaborate structure with chest-high wooden rails that extended into the water in a T-shape, ending in a square deck about twenty feet across. Plaques posted near each corner displayed drawings of fish and birds native to the river. The river stretched wider than I'd expected, looking more like a lake. The very middle reflected the crisp blue of the sky, but the water darkened toward the banks, with small waves lapping at the shore.

Close to the pier, the water was an odd shade of dark turquoise. I could barely see the sandy bottom at the bank's edge, extending a couple of feet into the water. Then there was only darkness. I leaned against the rail, and a couple of plovers shrieked from the bank, bursting from the brush and rattling the branches.

"It looks deep," Kate said. "You think she'd really go swimming out here?"

"Maybe it's more inviting in the summer." Looking at the shoreline, the way the marsh abruptly gave way to the river, I couldn't imagine my mother making it to the bank easily. I thought of how I'd thrashed through the marsh behind Vergie's house in the summer, how I'd become more tangled in the trees' roots with every step, ripped apart by briars and thorns. "I don't know exactly where they found her," I said. "One of the newspaper articles said it was here in the refuge, near a popular trail."

"What else did the article say?"

After I'd first talked to George, I'd done some digging on the Internet and found one article in the local paper that discussed the woman who'd drowned in the Trinity River. She wasn't local, so the details were scant. It had been the only mention of my mother I could find.

"Woman drowns in wildlife refuge," I said. "A cautionary tale for people not to swim in the Trinity. That was about the extent of it."

She sighed, leaning against the rail. "I'm sorry."

We walked back down the boardwalk to the parking lot. There was a small building, a visitors' center, but it was still closed for the holidays. Kate held her hands up to her face and peeked in the windows while I studied a map of the refuge posted at a kiosk. The refuge boasted thirty miles of walking trails, most of them ending near the water.

"You want to check out another trail?" Kate suggested.

"Sure."

We picked up another path that started much the same as the one before. All along the way were more signs with drawings of plants and animals common to the marsh. The trail would have been dappled with wildflowers in the spring and summer, but this time of year it was mostly scrub brush. I tried to picture what it would have looked like when my mother was here, imagining the last living things she would have seen as she walked toward the water. Had she been alone? Had someone been with her? In all of my digging, I hadn't found any indication that someone else might have harmed my mother that day, but I couldn't rule out the possibility. She was traveling, maybe lonely. She could have met someone in Green Bluff, in the very diner where Kate and I had eaten. That person could have invited her out here for a walk, saying he wanted to ease her loneliness. My stomach twisted into a knot at the thought of someone hurting my mother, causing her to drown—or even just being here with her and panicking, running to get help and leaving her to be overtaken by the swift waves in the river.

There was no evidence to suggest any of that, but that's the problem with knowing so few details. Your imagination fills in the gaps, and sometimes that's far worse than any facts you might unearth.

We soon came to another boardwalk and followed it to the water's edge. This walkway opened into a structure more like a dock. There were no boats around, and there was only a thigh-high rail around the structure. It would be easy to jump into the water here, easy to slip under the rail. Off to our right, a clearing led to a sandy area, almost a beach, that was easy enough to access from where we stood. It made me wonder if locals came to swim here. The water in this part would be cooler and probably have fewer alligators lurking under the surface.

It would be an oasis in the spring and summer, touched by sunlight and tucked away from the rest of the world.

Kate sat on the railing, holding a hand up to shade her eyes from the sun.

"This could have been the place," I said.

Kate just nodded, her brow furrowed. She buttoned up her rain jacket and cinched the belt at her waist. The wind had picked up, and it was drizzling rain again.

A flock of ducks chattered in the distance, growing louder as they cut a path across the clouds and splashed down near the sandbar.

I sat there for a long while, staring at the water. I could understand why my mother might have liked it here. One of the few things I remembered clearly was how much she enjoyed sitting outside to paint. She would never call herself a painter, and certainly not an artist, but as a kid I thought it was magical the way she brushed paint onto canvas and captured what it felt like to be outside, seeing what she saw. She loved the water and loved to swim. As Vergie had written in her diary, she was like a mermaid.

It wasn't hard to picture my mother here, walking out on that sandbar barefoot when the river was quiet, listening to the chatter of the birds, watching the ducks bob up and down as they fished in the water. Had she come out here in the daytime, or at night when the gates were closed and you had to sneak in to reach the trails?

"Vergie seemed to think my mother took her own life," I said at last. "She didn't want to believe it was true, but she thought it couldn't have been an accident, either."

Kate was quiet, then said, "But the sheriff told you it was accidental. Right?"

"He did."

"You don't believe him."

"It just seems so unlikely."

Kate slid over and draped her arm around my shoulders. "Honey, a lot of accidents seem very unlikely. That's what makes them so heartbreaking."

Then she continued, "You read all those letters from your mother. Did she sound depressed?"

"No."

"Did Vergie say anything in her diary about her leaving a note? Did she say what made her think it was suicide?"

I shook my head. Now I wanted to re-read every word. But I knew I wouldn't find anything different from before. "There was no note, and Vergie didn't say anything specific. I think she just found accidental drowning to be unlikely too."

Kate plucked a piece of grass and twirled it in her fingers. "Seems to me most people say goodbye in some way, if they're going to do that," she said. "My dad's uncle Carson did that. Went to see my dad—he was twelve or so—and gave him his old Army rucksack. He said, 'I took this on all of my adventures, son. Thought you might need it for yours.' Then he went home and shot himself in the barn."

"Jesus," I said. "You never told me all that."

She shrugged. "Nobody saw that one coming. Or at least that's what they said. But it was the sixties. People didn't diagnose depression so much back then." She tossed the grass into the water. "Dad told me once he felt strange that day, almost like Uncle Carson was telling him goodbye."

"Vergie didn't say anything like that in her diary." And I felt sure she would have, since she made her other thoughts known.

"I don't know why I can't let this go," I said.

"How would you feel about her if it were true? If it hadn't been an accident?"

"I think I'd hate her. It'd be like she found a way to leave me a second time."

Kate locked her arms around me and rested her chin on my shoulder, her eyes still fixed on the water.

"You think that's it," I said. "That I want to make her the bad guy." I felt the tears then, streaking down my cheeks.

"I don't think that."

"Maybe I do."

"You never got to say goodbye," Kate said. "That's more important than you realize, sometimes."

"I told my father, back when she first left us, that I wished she were dead."

Kate was quiet for a while, and then gave my shoulder a squeeze.

"Then I had a panic attack at Vergie's funeral when I

thought I saw her. I couldn't stand the idea of running into her after all that time."

"And both were perfectly natural reactions," Kate said.

"I love you for saying that, but it doesn't make me feel any better. I don't know what I expected to find here."

She sighed and stared over the water. "Sometimes we don't get all the answers. You just have to make peace with what you have."

I nodded, although that didn't seem one bit fair. "How'd you get so goddamned wise?" I said.

"It took me way too long to make peace with some things that happened," she said. "And I wasted a hell of a lot of time agonizing over things I imagined to be true, but weren't. You'll drive yourself nuts that way."

"I know."

"You can't let this consume you, Enza. This will eat away at you the rest of your life if you let it."

I nodded.

"I'm serious," she said. "I'm going to need you to promise me, right now, that you won't let it eat you up. You have to find a way to let this go."

"I know."

"I need to hear you say the words."

"OK," I said. "I promise. I will find a way to let this go."

When I turned to look at her, she gave me a serious look, then nodded.

"I may need you to help me though," I said.

"You know where to find me."

We sat like that for a while, shoulder to shoulder, as the clouds drifted over the sun and veiled us in shade. Toward the middle of the river, the water was still. The current was swift near our feet, but the surface was smooth out near the horizon.

The sunlight didn't bounce off it in the same way, and I pictured my mother paddling on her back, drifting out to the center toward the calm, tilting her head back toward the first rising stars of evening, swimming toward the horizon, to that point where the shimmering water dissolves into sky.

Chapter Fifteen

"THAT MOON IS WINKING," Kate said. "It's kind of creepy."

Green Bluff had one hotel—a mom-and-pop kind of a place that had a big vintage sign out front with a grinning crescent moon. It was so overcast that the neon had come on, flickering as it outlined the moon's face and caused one eye to blink open and closed. After paying for a room, we went inside to get cleaned up. My boots were muddy from the trail, and my hair was frizzy from the rain. The heat of the shower was enough to wash away the brine smell of the swamp and coax some of the tension out of my shoulders, but my heart still felt heavy with grief.

The grief, I understood then, was what I'd been refusing to feel. It had been easier to pore over the diaries and letters, to try to piece together the portions of my mother's life that felt like a mystery. It was far harder to be still and feel the loss. If there was a mystery to unravel, then I could tamp those feelings down and focus on facts and reports—but once those were all exhausted, I was left only with hurt.

After having dinner back at the Frogtown diner, we found

a grocery store to buy some snacks and wine. We walked a few blocks of the town, and I pictured my mother walking that same street, visiting the diner, the post office, the library. She could have stayed here for just a few days, or weeks on end. She could have had friends here, or no one. This town felt haunted by her, and no one knew it but me.

Back in our hotel room, we popped open a six-dollar bottle of red wine and sat on the balcony drinking out of plastic cups. It was after nine by then, and even though I was exhausted from the walking all day and the not-sleeping the night before, I wasn't ready to try for sleep again.

"Thanks for coming with me," I said. "I didn't want to do this part alone."

Kate tapped her cup against mine. "I wouldn't want you to do this alone."

"It's better to know. You were right about that part." It was still difficult to believe these details I'd learned about my mother—especially because Vergie had had her doubts, too. But the deputy had seemed like he was telling the truth, and really, why would he lie? These non-answers were all that I'd get. They would have to be enough.

"You think you'll come back to Raleigh?" Kate said.

I sipped my wine, thinking of Jack. As angry and hurt as I was by his words, I didn't want things to be over between us. "This feels like home now. Is that weird?"

She smiled. "No. But I miss you."

"You big softie."

She punched me in the shoulder. "You know I only have like three friends in the whole world."

"Move down here," I said, topping off our cups.

She scoffed. "I'm a city girl. You're a thousand miles from

everything. And this humidity is going to permanently wreck my hair."

I laughed. "You'd get used to it." From the balcony, we had a view of the downtown area. The streetlights had come on now that it was dark, along with the snowflake lights that were attached to the lamp posts. "If Jack and I are over, then our business arrangement is over too. I couldn't work with Buck and Josie any more. I hadn't thought of all that until now."

She sighed. "Don't say the town's not big enough for both of you."

I frowned. "It kind of isn't."

"You'll figure it out. You'll do what's best for you, and you'll forge ahead. This is what we do."

She said that matter-of-factly, but I thought about it the rest of the night. I'd just gotten settled in Bayou Sabine and my life had finally started to take a shape that felt right. Jack and his family had started to feel like my family. I'd finally found a way to work on my own, out from under my father's thumb. I'd started a business there, found the courage to go our on my own and build the life I wanted, and now it was all slipping away.

We sat out there until a train came past, rattling the walls so hard the picture frames clanged against the plaster. The horn blared, and the whole building seemed to vibrate.

"Well," Kate said. "That explains why it's only seventy bucks a night."

When she went inside to go to bed, I stayed out on the balcony and called Jack. He hadn't texted me again since earlier in the day, and it was nearly eleven o'clock.

After three rings, it went to his voicemail.

I ended the call without leaving a message and finished the

last bit of wine, thinking that he might text me back. After another half an hour, I went back inside and changed into a tee shirt, and climbed into bed.

"No answer?" Kate said.

It was impossible to hide anything from her.

"Nope."

The train rumbled past us again and I said, "Kate, I want you to promise me something."

"What?" she said.

"No matter what happens, what stupid things we might do to each other, promise you won't ever leave."

"Hate to tell you, but you're stuck with me until the grave. Maybe even past that."

"You swear?"

"If I go first," she said, "I'll totally haunt your ass. You can count on that."

"You better."

I crawled under the covers and set the alarm on my phone, checking once more for any texts.

There were none. Jack must have given up on saying whatever he wanted to say to me.

As I drifted off to sleep, I saw the Trinity again, the way the light bounced off the waves near the shore. In my dream, I was floating on my back, relishing the warmth of the sun on my skin, the feeling that everything around me was golden. I could understand then why my mother might like to swim there, in the calmness. My arms moved in lazy arcs as I skimmed the water.

Then, in the length of one stroke, the day was gone, and I was in darkness with not even the moon above me. The water turned suddenly cold, the waves slapping my face as I tried to swim, knocking the breath from my lungs. My body felt heavy.

The current moved faster and faster, pulling me below the surface. I struggled to keep my head up, but soon the darkness was everywhere, and I could no longer tell when I was under the water or above it. The current dragged me down, deeper into darkness, and my chest ached as I tried to breathe. When I inhaled, it burned, and when I exhaled, there were bubbles. I panicked, trying to kick my way back to the surface, but which way was it? I couldn't see anything in the black that had swallowed me.

Then something twined around my ankles, tickling like weeds. My arms thrashed, but I couldn't pull away from what was holding me. There was movement next to me, then a shaft of dim light, and my mother was there, looking as she did when I was fifteen. She was suspended in the dark water, her hair floating around her face like a cloud. Still I struggled to free my tangled legs, and she stared at me with a hint of a smile, her tight lips still holding a secret. My body went numb, cold as ice, and the darkness covered her again.

Clutching my chest, I sat up in bed, gasping and shivering. My skin still felt like it was burning from the cold water of the Trinity. I took deep breaths, willing my heart to stop hammering in my chest, not wanting to wake Kate. Tears stung my eyes as I thought of the cold pull of the water, how it had separated us so completely.

I knew then what I had to do, to stop myself from being pulled down into the darkness with her.

Chapter Sixteen

LEAVING Texas felt like leaving a house behind unfinished. There were still questions surrounding my mother, but I knew that Kate was right. In this case, all the details didn't matter so much. Even if I had the answers to my questions, I wasn't convinced I'd feel any differently about how things had ended. There was nothing I could change about any of this: the reasons my mother left, the way that she spent her last days, the way that she died—my mother had made her decisions, and they had their repercussions. I could either tangle myself in the *what ifs*, or I could find a way to say goodbye to her and move forward.

It was nearly ten when Kate and I left Green Bluff. For a Saturday, there wasn't much traffic on the roads. The storm had passed by overnight, and the sky was that crisp blue that only comes in autumn—the kind of sky that feels like everything in your sight is in sharper focus.

"You should find a way to say goodbye," Kate said. "Even if it's just you, in your backyard."

"We could do it tomorrow," I said. "Will you stay long enough to help me?"

"Sure," she said. "I've got more vacation days. I'll email work and tell them I'm taking a couple more. Family emergency."

"I can't imagine this was the vacation you had in mind. Things went sideways the minute you got here."

"You might have outdone my family drama this time." She smiled. "But it's OK. I'll take you over my brothers any day."

"Someday we'll take a real vacation. We'll go someplace tropical where every drink has a little umbrella."

"I wouldn't know what to do with myself," she said. "Tranquility is so very boring."

She had her giant Jackie O. sunglasses on, so it was impossible to tell if she was one hundred percent serious. I couldn't quite see the laugh lines at her eyes.

"I was getting used to it," I said. "I was OK with a little boring."

A smile touched the corner of her lips as she said, "You and I weren't cut out for boring."

WHEN WE GOT BACK to the house, it was empty. Jack's truck was gone, but I walked through every room of the house anyway, thinking he somehow might still be there. The dishes we'd used at Thanksgiving dinner were all washed and put away, some leftovers still in the refrigerator. It was a little after three o'clock, and he wasn't scheduled to be at the station.

In the bedroom, one of Jack's shirts lay on the rocking chair in the corner. I opened the dresser drawers and found most of his clothes still folded neatly inside. His boots were still in the closet, but a few of his shirts were missing, and his travel bag was gone. The bed was made, just as it had been when I left. Somehow the room seemed emptier and bigger already. I hated the feeling of him not being there.

Bella wasn't in the house, either. She was usually on the porch at this hour, pretending she wasn't waiting to be fed. But she was gone, too. *That's it*, I thought. *He's really left.*

Without another word between us, Jack was gone. I blinked back tears, imagining him coming back to pack up his things and driving away. I couldn't be here when he did that. I couldn't stand to watch him leave me.

Kate took her bag upstairs, and I lay back on the bed, holding a pillow close to my face, but it didn't smell like Jack. It didn't smell like anything.

My thoughts shifted to Lucille and I wondered what had happened after I left, wondered if she was all right. I thought briefly of calling Josie, but she almost certainly wouldn't want to talk to me. Jack would have told her everything, and she'd likely never want to hear from me again. I hated the thought of her and Buck being angry at me. They'd become my family, too, in these short months, and it had never occurred to me that I might lose them so quickly. Kate might be right. As much as I loved it here, I might need to leave this town all together and start over again in Raleigh. For a moment, I wondered if this was what my mother had felt all those years ago. Was a feeling like this one what made her leave?

The thought made me sick to my stomach. I didn't want to leave Bayou Sabine. I didn't want to leave this house, this lake, this yard, these people. Despite all of the holes in my memories of Vergie and my mother, this place felt more like home to me than any other place ever had.

This couldn't be over. It couldn't end this way.

~

"Hey," Kate said, stepping into the bedroom. She flopped down onto the bed next to me.

"He left," I said. "It's over."

Jack hadn't retuned my call from the night before. He hadn't sent any texts since we'd been at the refuge.

"Call him again," she said.

"I don't think I can stand to hear his voice right now." Or more accurately, I couldn't stand to hear him tell me he was leaving me.

Kate sighed, pulling her phone from her pocket. "I'll text Andre," she said, and then huffed, pushing the button. "Phone's dead. Let me have yours."

When I gave it to her, she texted Andre.

Hey, it's Kate. Do you know where Jack is? She held the phone between us so I could see, too.

The phone rang with a call from Andre. She answered and put it on speaker.

"Hey," she said. "You're on speaker and Enza's here."

"Kate, why haven't you answered my texts?" He sounded out of breath.

"I've been driving all day," she said. "I didn't notice my phone had died. What's wrong?"

There was a heavy sigh, and then he said, "There was a car accident. Lucille's in the hospital. Toph, too."

"What happened?" I said, grabbing Kate's arm. "I thought he left."

"He did. And then he came back."

My heart sank. When we'd left on Thursday night, Andre said she'd been at Buck and Josie's. She'd told Toph she wasn't going back with him. We'd thought she was safe—but that's always the mistake we make. We think we're safe right up until the moment that we aren't.

"Lucille's all right," he said. "She's got minor injuries. His are worse."

"Good," Kate grumbled.

"They want to keep Lucille one more night just as a precaution. She was lucky."

"Which hospital?" I said.

"Tulane," he said.

"We're heading over now," Kate said.

"Jack's there now too," he said. "I'll text you the room number."

THE TULANE MEDICAL Center was in the heart of downtown New Orleans. We went in through the main entrance and were greeted by a stout security guard who looked to be in his sixties. After he pointed us in the direction of the wing where Lucille was, we hurried down the hall to the nearest elevator. My heart pounded in my chest. Kate reached for my hand and said, "It's going to be all right."

"This is my fault. I never should have cornered him."

"Don't," she said, squeezing my hand. "Whatever happened, it's not your fault."

When the doors opened, we exited and turned down a hallway and past a nurses' station. Kate checked her phone and said, "This is it."

The door was closed.

"I can't," I said, thinking of Jack, and Buck, and Josie, all on the other side. They'd all blame me, and they had every right to.

Kate knocked. A voice from inside said, "Come in."

She opened the door and nudged me forward. Inside, Lucille was sitting up in the bed, propped up on pillows. Josie and Buck sat in two chairs along the far wall by the windows. Lucille pressed a button on the remote and muted the TV. My throat tightened as I studied their faces, expecting to see anger and hurt.

Josie stood and hurried over.

Then she wrapped her arms around us, and said, "I'm so glad you're here, hon. We were worried about you, too." Something in her eyes told me that Jack had told her at least part of what had happened between us, but maybe not all of it.

"Lucille," I said, "how are you feeling?" The monitor next to her beeped steadily. She looked annoyed. Her right arm was in a cast and sling, partially covered by a blanket. A bandage covered the right half of her forehead, and her face and bare arm were covered in tiny cuts and scratches.

"I'm ready to get out of here," she said. "I'm bored out of my mind."

Buck snorted. "Next time we'll arrange for better entertainment."

Lucille rolled her eyes.

"They said she has a slight concussion and a broken arm," Josie said. "She has to take it easy for a couple of months."

Behind us, the door opened with a loud click. Jack stood in the doorway, carrying a coffee. As soon as he saw me, his eyes darkened and his jaw tightened. Without a word, he turned and walked out, letting the door slam behind him.

Kate frowned. "I'll go talk to him." Before I could protest, she was out the door.

Lucille turned to Josie. "Could y'all give us a minute?"

Josie nodded. "We should really get going anyway. We'll

see you in the morning, OK?" She leaned down and kissed Lucille on the forehead.

"Goodnight, Mom," Lucille said to her. "Don't worry. I'm fine."

Josie patted her shoulder, frowning like she didn't believe that for a second. "We'll see you in the morning," she said.

Buck eased out of the chair, still sore from his fall it seemed. He lay his hand on Lucille's foot as he shuffled by and said, "Get some rest, kid."

"Love you," she said as they left.

The door clicked shut behind them. Lucille lay back in the pillows and said, "God, I thought they'd never leave. They mean well, but good grief."

Stepping closer to the bed, I said, "Lucille, I am so, so sorry."

Her brow furrowed. "For what?"

It was hard to fight back tears. Especially when she looked so small and vulnerable lying in that bed, her arm in a sling. I wanted to tear Toph to pieces.

"I made this so much worse," I said.

"You think this is your fault?" she said. "No, no, no." She furrowed a brow and scooted over on the bed, making a space for me. "Sit."

Easing onto the bed, I said, "Thursday—I shouldn't have provoked him. I pissed him off, and he took it out on you."

She shook her head, wincing. "I don't blame you. Toph's an asshole. I never should have gotten in the car with him. I made that decision. Not you."

"But I—"

"Shush," she said, waving her hand in dismissal. "Enough already. He drove like an idiot. He wrecked the car. None of this is on you. Do you hear me?"

I nodded as she lay her hand on my forearm.

"Thank you for standing up for me," she said. "You're the only person who didn't make me feel stupid."

My eyes filled with tears. I wished I could have done more, spared her all of this hurt.

"I mean, I still made a stupid decision," she said. "Several actually. But there's a difference."

"What happened?" I said. "I thought he left Thursday night."

Her brow furrowed. "He came back. He stayed in New Orleans and then came back to the house last night, apologizing for everything. He was his old charming self again, giving me some crap about how he'd been so stressed with work, and he knew he was being an asshole, and he wanted to fix things between us. He said he wanted to take me out to a nice dinner and talk."

She shook her head. "It was stupid to believe him, but I thought if I went with him, we could end this amicably." She scoffed. "He took me to this fancy restaurant downtown, and went through his whole spiel, and then I told him we should break up. He said I was giving up, pushing him away, and begged me not to leave." Her eyes looked sad. "For a minute, it was like he was his old self again, but I kept telling myself what you said: that this was a pattern, he wouldn't change. Controlling and manipulative is who he is." She shook her head. "I wanted to believe all this time that he was a good guy pretending to be a bad boy. But I had it all backwards."

She squeezed her eyes shut as I placed my hand on her good arm.

"He was calm when we left the restaurant," she said. "It was like he just switched all of his emotions off, like he was at a business meeting. He said, 'OK, that's it, then,' and he paid the check, and we got in the car to go home. At first he wouldn't talk to me in the car, but then he started threatening me, saying he'd given me this apartment, gotten me this job, and then he was yelling that I was ungrateful and that I was using him." Her hands trembled as she spoke. "He was in a rage, worse than I've ever seen him. And then closer we got to home, the angrier he got. He was driving so fast, and then there was another car, a horn blaring. He swerved to miss the car and ran off the road and crashed into a tree."

She shook her head. "I thought it was over. I saw that other car and thought we were dead."

"I'm so sorry," I told her.

"Stupid," she said. "I never should have gone with him. But none of this is because of anything that you did."

He'd been so callous on Thursday when he'd been talking about Lucille, as if she were in his debt forever. I shuddered, thinking of how terrified she must have been, trapped in a car with him and all of his rage.

"I can't help but feel like I set him off," I told her. "I shouldn't have antagonized him."

"He thinks everyone's antagonizing him," she said. "He has a massive chip on his shoulder."

I swallowed hard. She'd been truthful with me, and I owed her the same. "He said such awful things that day. And then he threatened you, and something in me snapped. Before I knew it, I'd punched him as hard as I could."

She arched a brow. "I don't fault you for that."

"But he said something." I paused, knowing I had no right to ask, but wanting her to know that I understood her fear. "He said you'd gotten into trouble, something that would hurt you if it came out."

She leaned back against the pillows, her eyes tired. "He's

not the first bad decision I made." She looked away, and then I realized that she was crying. "He throws these blowout parties, trying to 'make connections,' as he says. There was one I was at where there was all kinds of bad shit happening. Drugs, underage girls—when I realized what was going on, I left and never went to another one."

"Can you take that to the police?" I said, thinking this might be the easiest way to keep him away from her.

"I could, but I'd get myself in trouble, too." She frowned, leaning back in the pillows. "He asked me to send some 'reimbursements' to people the day after the party. Said his payment account wasn't working right and asked me if I'd pay his friends if he sent me money to cover it." She sighed and said, "Later I learned I'd paid a couple of underage girls, God only knows what for, but based on what blew up on his social media, I can guess."

"He made you an accessory."

"See? Stupid."

I shook my head. "We can talk to Andre. There's got to be a way to keep you out of it."

"Maybe," she said. "But the scandal alone would ruin everything. I can kiss that job goodbye."

My face felt hot with rage. I wanted to walk upstairs and strangle Toph. He'd done this on purpose, to keep Lucille entangled with him, to make sure she had something to lose if she left him.

"Does Jack know all this? Your parents?"

"Oh God, no," she said, her eyes widening. "But they might all find out soon enough. If it comes out, I'll deal with it. It was my mistake." She smiled weakly, her cheeks wet with tears. She was trying to put on a brave face, but she looked uneasy.

"We'll figure this out," I said. "The first step is to get you away from him and in a safe place."

She nodded.

The door clicked open behind me and Kate stepped inside, carrying two coffees. She handed me one and said, "Jack's outside. He wants to talk to you. I told him to stop being an idiot." Then she glanced at Lucille and said, "Sorry—I'd bring you one if you didn't have a head injury."

She paused, reading Lucille's expression, and then turned back to me. "What's happened?"

"Nothing," I said. "I'll be back in a minute."

As I shut the door, I heard Kate ask how she was feeling. Outside, Jack was leaning against the wall by the door. He looked exhausted, with dark circles under his eyes and three days' beard stubble.

He stared at me for a moment and then said, "Can we talk?"

"There's something I need to do first." I stepped past him and stalked toward the nurses' station.

"Enza," he called. "Wait."

"Ten minutes," I said over my shoulder.

Blood pounded in my ears, drowning out his voice and mine. There was one more thing I could do to help Lucille, to try and make up for my mistake. It might be a long shot, but it was worth a try.

If I didn't do this right now, I was afraid I wouldn't muster up the courage again.

Chapter Seventeen

ONE FLOOR ABOVE, Toph lay in his own hospital bed, in a room nearly identical to Lucille's. At first, the nurse at the information desk on Lucille's floor had been hesitant to tell me his room number. But when I'd insisted that his family was in Dallas, that they wouldn't be coming, her face softened and she looked sympathetic.

If she'd known what kind of person he was, she might not have cared so much.

It was a lie of course, that got me the information. I told her that he was a friend who was visiting, that I could be in touch with his family and tell them what they needed to know. It was surprisingly easy to speak those words, despite my heart hammering in my chest.

At last, she'd given me his room number and told me about his injuries. He had some nasty lacerations that had needed stitches; he had a broken collarbone and a concussion. His new flashy car had good airbags, which had saved his life but bruised some ribs. When I saw his face, all battered and cut to pieces, I almost felt sorry for him.

Almost.

His eyes were closed, his breathing shallow. Part of his ken-doll hair had been shaved above his ear, and he had a deep cut on his cheekbone. He looked smaller now, not so threatening anymore. A machine by the bed beeped steadily, displaying his vital signs. Two IV bags hung on a stand near his head, one for fluids and one for a painkiller that I hoped was not a substantial one.

He deserved to feel some pain.

I stared at him for a long while, thinking of how he'd hurt Lucille, how he'd so brazenly threatened her—first at my house, and then in public. And how many times before? He'd been so callous when he told me how he could ruin her, and looked as if he'd delight in doing so. In that moment by the lagoon, I'd hated him for treating her so badly, for thinking he could bully her into staying with him, for thinking he could hurt her and get away with it.

But men like him too often got away with it. They buried their crimes. They paid other men to make their sins go away. And then they started all over again. It a was a predictable pattern, and one that I refused to let play out with Lucille.

For a moment, I imagined the crash happening differently. It could have been much worse. Toph could have been a lot less lucky, and a lot more broken. If he hadn't survived, then there would be no more threat to Lucille. Her secret would remain hidden, and she wouldn't be afraid.

But Toph would most likely recover. His injuries were severe, but not life-threatening. He'd live to hurt another woman—because this was the pattern. Men like Toph never hurt only one person. They were never violent only one time, and they'd never back down until they met someone meaner than they were.

When he began to stir, tugging at his blanket, I stepped closer to the bed. His eyelids fluttered open and he looked confused, squinting in the dim light. My heart pounded so hard that it hurt.

"What are you doing here?" he said. His voice was raspy, his eyes bloodshot.

"Remember me?" I said.

"These drugs aren't that good." He snorted, then winced at the pain. "You hoping to get in another sucker punch?"

Nothing wrong with his memory, then.

"You and I need to talk," I said, keeping my voice cool and even. He needed to think that this was not a fit of anger, but a careful calculation. He wasn't the only one who could plan ahead.

His eyes narrowed, and he gave me his smug smile again.

"It seems you made some very bad decisions in the last week." I leaned against the bed and ran my finger along the IV tube.

His eyes tracked my movements, and his jaw tensed.

"You're going to be here a little while," I said. "With all these broken bones. But then you're going to go back to Austin. You're going to pack up all of Lucille's things from her apartment, and you're going to ship them to her here. And then you're never going to see her or contact her ever again."

"Why would I do that?" he said.

"First, because she doesn't want to be with you, and she told you that. That should be enough, but let's not kid ourselves. Second: you'll have a restraining order filed against you. Your bad decisions this week will have led to a number of charges, including DUI, assault, reckless endangerment, and— shall I go on?" I wasn't entirely certain of that last part, but he didn't need to know that.

He glared at me. I had his attention.

When I dropped my hand onto his chest, he grimaced, though he fought hard to hide it. Bruised ribs, indeed. "There are some charges we have no say in, but some that we might decide not to pursue, if the conditions were right. If, say, we agreed that you would never again contact Lucille." I pressed my thumb down until he groaned and turned his head to the side. "Do you understand?"

When he turned back to face me, his eyes were cold. "Fuck you," he spat.

I dug my thumb in deeper until he howled in pain. "Incorrect answer."

He gasped, leaning back in the pillows.

"Criminal suits bring unwanted attention," I said. "I can't imagine your family or your many business partners would appreciate that sort of spotlight." My finger slid along his sternum, which must have been quite sore from the impact from the airbag. "And civil suits can drag out for years. Do you really want to waste your time chasing after a woman who doesn't want you? Imagine what that will cost you."

"Whatever," he grumbled.

"You're not the only one with fancy lawyers," I said, keeping my voice even. "My father's lawyers will make a sport of coming after you. And so will the media." That was a complete bluff, but I had to try. Lucille had told me enough to understand that he'd made some headlines over the years and his father had paid enough to make his crimes disappear. But enough digging would reveal all sorts of secrets that he'd rather keep hidden, and I was banking on him feeling like this time, his money couldn't protect him.

"You're full of shit," he said.

I shrugged. "Seems that you hosted some wild parties.

Maybe invited the wrong people. You could make national headlines this time."

He glared at me, his eyes cold.

"Take a moment," I said. "You have a head injury."

His jaw tightened and I knew he was considering it. He must have done other horrible things. Lucille could get in trouble for helping him, but he'd be facing much more serious charges. And he knew it.

At last, he shifted his gaze to the window.

I pressed down slightly on his ribs. "Time's up. Do we have an agreement?"

He winced, biting his lip. "Yes," he said. "Now get the—"

"Excellent," I said, slapping his chest. His face twisted in pain and I leaned down close enough to smell the antiseptic on his cuts. "Say the words, Toph. I need to hear you."

"I won't contact her again."

"You will disappear from her life," I whispered. "Or I'll make you wish you'd died in that crash."

He glared at me as I stood and walked to the door, but said nothing more.

When the door clicked quietly behind me, I strode down the hall to the elevators, willing myself to hold it together, just for another couple of minutes. When at last the elevator came, I stepped inside and leaned against the wall. Finally, I could breathe. My heart felt like it would beat right out of my chest and onto the floor.

When the elevator doors opened again, I stepped out and went back down the hall to Lucille's room.

Jack was standing outside her door, his arms crossed over his chest.

"Now can we talk?" he said.

"Okay."

Walking slowly, he led me down the hall to a dimly lit seating area with a long bank of windows. It was empty, except for one gray-haired main who appeared to be sleeping in a chair in the far corner. Jack raked a hand through his hair and said, "Kate has informed me that I'm being a jackass."

"The word she told me was idiot."

His brow arched. "She used a variety of words with me, which I suppose is justified."

When I said nothing, he stared at me for a long moment, his gaze piercing. "I tried to call you," he said, his voice even. "I thought you'd want to know about Lucille."

"Why didn't you leave a message? I thought you were just calling to yell at me some more."

He sighed. "I'm sorry about that. I shouldn't have said those things."

"I was angry too, and hurt. Then when I did call you back, I thought you were ignoring me, trying to prove a point."

"Kinda had my hands full with Lucille," he said, not unkindly.

"I see that now." I sat down on the other end of the sofa, feeling exhausted now that the adrenaline had worn off. "You were afraid for her, and angry at me. I get it. I was worried about her, too."

"Why did you leave like that?" he said.

"You said terrible things to me. I couldn't stand the thought of spending the night in that house with you."

He looked surprised.

"Did you not expect a direct answer?" I said.

He crossed his arms and stared down at his boots. "Fair enough."

"You were so angry. I felt like you weren't listening to me. Like you didn't even want to."

"I'm sorry," he said. "I was wrong to blame you." He moved closer to me then, and took my hand in his. "Lucille told me everything after you left. I understand why you felt you couldn't tell me." He looked up at me then, his eyes as blue as glaciers. "But I don't want us to have secrets like that, not ever. I need you to trust me, or else this doesn't work. Whatever awful thing is happening, you need to tell me so we can try to fix it together."

"I thought you were leaving me," I said, feeling the sting of tears. "When I came back and the house was empty, I thought that was it."

He pulled my hand to his lips. "I'd never do that to you, chère. I wouldn't disappear on you."

"I should have told you about Lucille. I'm sorry for that."

"I know." Pulling me against his chest, he wrapped his arms around my shoulders and kissed my cheek.

"And I do trust you," I said.

He leaned his forehead against mine, pulling me close. His stubbled beard tickled my cheek as he said, "I'm not going anywhere."

WHEN WE WALKED BACK DOWN to Lucille's room, we found Andre and Kate standing in the hallway.

"What are you doing here?" I said to Andre.

"Jack's been here most of the day," he said. "Told him I'd take the night shift."

"I don't want to leave Lucille by herself," Jack said. "Especially with that asshole right upstairs."

Toph hadn't looked like he'd be walking around with ease anytime soon, but I figured that was Jack's call to make.

"I don't think he's going to be a problem anymore," I said, and they all looked at me quizzically.

I shrugged and said, "We had a chat."

Andre glanced down at my hands, as if looking for more evidence of a right hook.

Jack said, "You talked to him?"

"We have an understanding, yes. Though we should probably go over a few things with the sheriff here."

Kate smirked, sipping her coffee.

Andre arched a brow and said, "Anything I can do to help."

Jack shot me a look that said he expected to hear all of the details later.

"Don't worry," I told him. "I'll explain everything." This time, I wouldn't leave anything out.

Chapter Eighteen

"I LIKE this new stone cold side of you," Kate said.

We were sitting on the porch late Sunday morning, having coffee and discussing my chat with Toph in the hospital. I'd told her all the details, just as I had with Jack the night before. He'd been concerned of course, but had eventually admitted that my solution was better than his urge to shove Toph from the roof of the hospital. After everything Lucille had told us, it seemed the police both here and in Austin would have plenty to investigate in connection to Toph. That's the thing with people who think they're untouchable: they leave a long trail of broken laws and bad behavior. They can hide a lot with their money and their privilege, but the ones like Toph, who are arrogant enough to think they really are invincible—they usually get sloppy and leave a trail behind. You just have to dig a little to find where they crossed the line into what's prosecutable.

Social media's a pretty good place to start. And Toph loved crowing on all of his accounts, making himself look the bad boy part at every turn. There were lots of likes and shares, and nothing on the internet ever really dies.

"It seemed more effective than punching him again," I said.

She nodded. "You throw a good punch, though."

"You taught me well."

"Is Lucille going home today?" she asked.

"This afternoon, they said." Andre had texted Jack this morning, giving him an update. She'd stay with her parents through the end of the semester, likely finishing her coursework online. They wanted to keep a close eye on her for a little while, mainly because of her injuries, but also because of Toph.

"Jack's already trying to convince her to take the next semester off from school," I said. "Just to give herself time to heal." He'd gone over to see her right after breakfast and would likely be there until she was released.

Kate sipped her coffee. "Not a bad idea. Concussions can wreck you for a few months."

"She might be stuck here for a while with the whole family clamoring to take care of her."

She smiled. "That's not so bad. I wouldn't mind having this bunch fussing over me."

"Me either."

"Oh my God." She swatted me on the shoulder. "You big doofus. You already do." After a pause, she said, "At first I was really sad that you moved out here, and then the evil part of me thought maybe it would just be a phase, and you'd come back. But now I see how good it is for you. You built your own family, and it's a damn good one."

"Well, you're part of it, too." Even though I loved it here, it was hard being so far away from Kate. She'd been with me

through the toughest parts of my life, and some of the best—
we were stronger because of each other.

"Whatever," she said, teasing. "I can't compete with Sexy
Gray Suit Guy. I knew this day was coming the minute you
met him."

I snorted, thinking of that miserable day, when we sat
squeezed in that tiny church for Vergie's funeral, when the
storm raged all around us, shaking the windows and knocking
the power out. "There's no way you knew that."

"It was written all over your face," she said with a shrug.
"His, too."

"I might say the same thing about you and that guy you
beaned with the hair dryer."

She sipped her coffee, hiding her smile as she stared out
over the yard. "We'll see." I knew that thousand-yard stare—
she'd considered that possibility, too. Kate McDonnell was
smitten, and she was trying her best to hide it. She might still
be wounded, but she wasn't counting Andre out anymore.

"You should come back for Christmas," I said. "Maybe
have a little house arrest?"

She rolled her eyes, pretending to be annoyed, but her
cheeks had a hint of a blush. "Didn't you need my help with
something?

I laughed. "Yeah. Come on. Now's as good a time as any."

IN THE BACKYARD, we built a small fire in the fire ring that Jack
had dug out the winter before. It was chilly and overcast, and
finally starting to fell like autumn.

"You ready?" Kate said.

"Yep." The letter felt heavy in my hand. It had taken me an

hour or more to write everything inside, but it needed to be thorough. The letter had been Kate's idea—because how else can you talk to a dead person?

"This still feels silly," I said, sitting next to her.

"It worked for me," she said. "My therapist had me do it. I thought I could sum up everything I wanted to say to Benjamin with two words on a sticky note, but she made me work harder." She propped her feet up on a stump near the fire ring and stared into the flame. "Since I couldn't outright murder him, and since I didn't want to say all of these words to him and give him the satisfaction of knowing he'd made me have all of those complicated thoughts, it seemed like a good solution." She glanced at the letter in my hand and said. "Turns out I had lots of things to say. Now, I don't waste my time imagining how I'd tell him."

When I tossed the letter into the fire, it smoldered for a moment before the flames licked at the sides of the envelope. Once I'd started writing, the words had come easily. For years, I'd imagined the questions I'd have asked my mother, had we ever met again—and really, it came down to only one: *Why were we not enough?*

There were other things I'd tell her, of course: parts of my life she'd missed, parts of hers that were still a mystery, how her actions had hurt me for so long. These things needed to be said somehow, in a way that felt meaningful. Watching my words turn to smoke and ash felt like the only way that I could give the words weight. If they took up space in the world, at least for this moment, then they were real. They had meaning.

They were enough.

When the last bits of the letter had turned to ash, I pulled the stack of my mother's letters and postcards from the box. Sorting through them, I found the one postcard I wanted to keep: the one written to me. The one with no postmark and no address.

It was from the Texas hill country, where there was a field of bluebells.

I love you. I miss you. I carry you with me.

None of the rest mattered.

I handed it to Kate and said, "This is the only one."

"You sure?" she said, reading the back.

"I don't need them anymore." I dropped the letters to Vergie into the fire, and watched as the flames licked at their sides. The images on the post cards buckled and curled in the fire: the mission in Texas, where she helped the padres cook and tend to their vegetable garden; the remote ranch in New Mexico that doubled as an artists' retreat; the national park in Utah with the painted desert arches—I'd never know what my mother was searching for, what she couldn't find with us. I'd read them over and over, and memorized most of the words— that part of my mother's life would always be a mystery, but I no longer needed to understand all the details. Her choices were her own, just like mine were my own.

The only way forward was to let these parts of her go.

When the last bits of the letters were gone, I plucked two journals from the box and handed them to Kate.

She arched a brow and said, "These too?"

"I want you to take them," I said. "I'm keeping the older ones, but those are the ones that talk about my mom. Do whatever you want with them. I don't want to know."

She looked at me, puzzled.

"I'm dying to read about thirty-year-old Vergie and all of her adventures," I told her. "But I don't want the ones about my mother. I don't want to be tempted to read them anymore." Even if I read them a hundred times, nothing about that period of her life would be any clearer. If the books were here, they would haunt me, and I just wanted to be free.

She nodded, and handed me the one postcard I'd keep. I stuck it into one of Vergie's old journals and then placed it back in the box.

"I should probably get going," she said. "Go see if I still have a job."

We walked back up to the house and I helped her carry her pile of luggage out to her car.

"Come back for Christmas," I said. "I'll try to make it as boring as possible."

She smirked, shoving her bags into the trunk. "Not cut out for boring, remember?"

After a quick hug, she climbed into her car. Kate hated long goodbyes.

"Call me when you stop for the night, OK?"

"Sure," she said, putting her big Ray-Bans on. She waved her arm out the window as she headed down the drive and toward the highway. When she was out of sight, I went back to the porch and pulled my phone from my pocket. It would be nearly five o'clock in North Carolina, and my father would most likely be sitting in his study, poring over the newspaper with glass of iced tea. When I called him, he picked up on the second ring.

"Dad," I said. "I'm sorry I haven't had a chance to call you back."

After a moment, he said, "That's all right."

"You were trying to tell me some things about you and Mom. I'd like for you to finish."

There was a long silence, and for a moment I thought he'd hung up.

"I should have told you these things sooner," he said at

last. "I always knew that, but I just wanted to put it all behind me." There was another pause, and his voice lowered. "But what was best for me wasn't best for you. I'm sorry I didn't see that."

I'd always be disappointed that he'd kept things from me, but I wanted to believe that he didn't do it to hurt me. By staying angry at him, I was treating him as if he were the only person in the world with secrets. My mother had had them. Vergie had had them. It was impossible to ever know exactly what lay in a person's heart, no matter how well you knew them—because we all keep parts of ourselves hidden. There was a time when we knew how to talk to each other— a time when we didn't have currents of anger and disappointment tugging us apart like riptides. Something had been broken between us, but I didn't want to walk away.

"You can tell me now," I said. "I'm listening."

Chapter Nineteen

THREE DAYS LATER, Jack and I went back to the house on the canal. It wouldn't take much more to finish it, and Jack had been itching to add baseboards and crown molding in the two bedrooms. The house had been remodeled sometime in the last decade, but never quite finished completely. There were visible repairs that the previous owners had made, like a section of the ceiling that had been replaced and painted a slightly different shade of white. What this house needed was mostly cosmetic, and not structural, which was why we'd jumped on it.

When we'd done our final walk-through and made our master to-do list, Jack had said, "Who doesn't put in baseboards?" as if it were the worst injustice one could commit in a remodel. "It's like leaving the okra out of a vegetable soup." He'd shaken his head in that solemn way that translated to *Bless their hearts*.

"I know," I'd said. "Criminal."

Attention to detail was one of his superpowers.

Today, I put a new coat of paint on the ceiling of the smaller bedroom, where a the section of ceiling had been replaced. It was likely a leak that had caused the damage, since it was just an eighteen-inch square. The seam had been visible, so we'd patched and sanded it, and with a fresh coat of paint, you couldn't even tell it was there.

If only all rebuilding was as easy as the repairs we made in houses.

When the ceiling was finished, I went into the bedroom to check on Jack. He'd nearly finished installing the baseboards, which he'd stained to match the existing hardwood floor. There was one two-foot section that was still bare, next to the closet. Jack was on his knees, his back to me, and looked to be writing something on the last board.

When I slipped up behind him and said, "How's it coming?" he jumped.

"Just dropping the last piece into place," he said, shoving his pencil behind his ear.

"What's that you're writing?" He sometimes wrote calculations on boards, but that was when he was cutting.

"Oh, nothing," he said with a shrug.

When I peered over his shoulder, I saw his neat block writing stretched across the back side of the baseboard. "That's not nothing," I said, pointing.

He looked at me a bit sheepishly, a boyish grin touching his lips.

He'd written *Enza and Jack Mayronne, Bayou Sabine,* followed by today's date.

"Jack," I said, feeling my voice catch.

"What?" he said. "Builders do this kind of thing all the time. Back when Buck built houses, he used to leave a copy of the blueprints inside the house's newel post. Some people think it's good mojo, to leave a little piece of you behind."

I knelt down and touched the board. "You didn't write Parker."

"The board's pretty small."

Except that it wasn't. "Are you blushing?" I said.

"No."

I tousled his hair and said, "Oh, yes you are."

He smiled his crooked smile and shrugged. "I like the way your name sounds with mine."

Holding the board in position, he tacked one end into place with a nail, and then did the same at the other end. Two more nails and a few hits with the hammer, and it was done. A perfect fit.

It felt good to think of it being there, a permanent part of the house now. Etched into its bones.

"Did you do something like this at Vergie's?" I asked him.

His eyebrow arched as he stood up and brushed his hands on his jeans. "It brings good luck."

"Is that right?"

"You're still here, aren't you?" He helped me up and then placed his hand on my cheek. He kissed me until I slid my fingers in his hair, then he took a step back and grinned.

"Ready for a nice night in?" I said. "Now that we have the house to ourselves again?"

"I have all sorts of plans for you, chère. I think we should knock off early."

As we packed up the tools and took them out to his truck, he said, "You're still thinking of where it could be, aren't you?"

When I didn't answer, he said, "I'll show you one day. It's not covered up with plaster or paint."

He laced his fingers in mine and led me outside. We climbed into his truck and rumbled down the little road by the canal, the house growing smaller in the distance. Off to my right, a blue heron launched itself from a stump, its great wings propelling it just above the surface of the water. Its snakelike neck bobbed back and forth as it kept pace with us for a few seconds, and then it made a sharp turn and vanished into the cypress along the bank.

"You know," I said, "I like the way our names sound together too."

He smiled then, shifting the truck down into third gear, taking the curve by the lagoon slow and easy, steering us in a graceful arc. It wasn't hard to imagine all the curves that lay ahead, all the pieces of ourselves we would reveal—sometimes slowly, and sometimes in an instant.

There were some things Bayou Sabine might never reveal to me. There were things I would never know about Vergie, about my mother, about my father. I might never learn how my mother died, and I might never know what drove her and my father apart.

I was no longer in a hurry to learn these secrets that were not mine. If I was meant to know them, I would learn them in time. But in the end, knowing the reasons why wouldn't change the events that had happened. I thought again of the bottles hanging from the branches of the tree in the backyard, how they trapped spirits, the things we wanted to forget and keep away. I imagined Vergie and my mother speaking their secrets into the bottles, hanging them in the highest branches for safekeeping. Only time and the wind could release them, these whispers from the past, and every so often one would fall from its limb and shatter, and the truth might be revealed in a ghost of a breeze, in a dream.

George had been right: We can never truly know what's in another person's heart or mind. Kate would say we just do our best to interpret the data we collect from their words and our observations. We fill in the gaps as best we can.

What I didn't know could fill the Gulf. What I did know was this: I would stay in Vergie's little house by the lagoon until my life sent me someplace else. I would stay with Jack for as long as he would let me. I would let him love me for as long as he would, and love him back as fiercely as we could stand. About this I was certain; it was as real to me as the weight of his hand on my knee.

He grinned his crooked grin as I slid my fingers in his hair, and then downshifted again before placing his hand back on my thigh. He had a way of slowing us down to the right pace, and we were good together. We were good at building, at making things last.

Preview: Just the Trouble I Needed

What happens next in the Bayou Sabine series?

Sometimes a little trouble is exactly what you need. Kate didn't intend to go back to Bayou Sabine, but when Enza needs a favor, she can't refuse. A chance encounter with sexy sheriff Andre Dufresne gets her more adventure than she bargained for in *Just the Trouble I Needed*.

Here are the first two chapters:

Chapter One

THE KITCHEN LOOKED like the scene of a crime. It wasn't even my kitchen, but it made me sick just the same. A red puddle covered the floor at the point of impact, a sunburst of my famous marinara sauce. The casserole dish had broken into three big pieces, but I knew I'd be picking up ceramic splinters for the next week. Slices of eggplant and floppy lasagna noodles were strewn in front of the stove, but not nearly enough to have filled the dish.

My bottle of shiraz lay on its side, teetering on the edge of the counter by the stove. Thankfully, I had put the cork back in it before I went upstairs to take a bath. The bath had been my treat for surviving my first full day here in the land of giant mosquitoes and prehistoric reptiles. This week was supposed to be relaxing, but it was off to a terrible start.

For a moment I thought the disaster was my fault. In my rush to relax in the bath, had I left the stove eye on, absentmindedly placed the dish on top of it and caused it to explode? I'd been unfocused lately, most days feeling like I was in someone else's skin, someone else's life. Since stalking out of the research facility last Friday, I'd envisioned a lot of things exploding: the toilets in the employee lounge, the line of test tubes in my lab, even my colleague Ray, who constantly leered at me over the rims of his wayfarer glasses.

I'd sometimes fantasized about having a lab accident that would give me a supernatural ability that was both useful and a little dangerous. Some days I wished I was like that girl in the Stephen King book who could start fires just by squinting her eyes and concentrating. If I had that power though, I wouldn't waste it on baked pasta. No, I would use it on the pants of people like Ray. And my boss Jeffrey, who so easily told me my job was about to be eliminated, and my ex, Benjamin, who'd dumped me right before Christmas and still continued to call and text me, whining about his bad decision and its unhappy repercussions, all of which I could have predicted.

Too bad I hadn't been able to predict how he would mistreat me.

I thought I'd gotten over him, but when Jeffrey called me into his office last Friday and told me the lab's funding was being cut, the familiar teeth of betrayal began gnawing at me once again. The blood had risen in my cheeks as Jeffrey explained that they were cutting several positions, making them intermittent contract work instead. They might be able to bring me back in a consulting role, but it would be only part-time. No benefits. I'd spent the last hour of my workday staring into a centrifuge, watching samples spin and separate, and my rage had bloomed into a kind of recognition: I hated my job. There was a time when I'd liked it, but it wasn't a challenge anymore. I'd lost sight of what I wanted, stuck in the spin of the lab. But it had given me stability and predictability: two things I needed most.

I surveyed the kitchen, examining the scene. The stove's dials were off. A noodle squished under my toes. Then a single red paw print caught my eye.

"Bella!" I yelled, stomping into the living room.

It felt weird walking around and yelling in a house that wasn't mine, but Enza had told me to make myself at home. Enza, my best friend, had called me on Friday night. I hadn't planned to tell her about my job, because Enza's a fixer. She's a sweetheart, for sure, but her first inclination is always to offer support, quickly followed by plans to rebuild. She flips houses for a living, so she's used to fixing broken things and making them like new again.

I just wasn't in the mood to have her trying to fix me.

For the first time since college, I was uncertain about my future. Uncertain about what I wanted from it. When Enza called, I avoided the topic of work as long as possible.

"Are you seeing anybody new?" she asked. I could imagine her twirling that dark curly hair of hers around her fingers as she spoke.

"Not really," I said.

"Kate," she groaned. "You have to get out of that lab more often. You're too much fun to be a workaholic."

I tugged at the ends of my hair, thinking it was time for a cut. After a whole winter inside, it was a dark shade of blond —the shade that indicates no sunlight for a year. I didn't even get any tan lines last summer.

"I know," I said.

"Sometimes I picture you as a mad scientist, like a Jekyll and Hyde situation."

"I'm definitely feeling more like Hyde today."

"Seriously," she said. "You never take a vacation. They must owe you three months by now."

It was more like four. Which was how I ended up getting this week away. Jeffrey had hesitated at first, but if he hadn't conceded to my request, I'd been prepared to pack my lab up into a couple of banker's boxes and hustle out like the building was on fire, leaving my current project incomplete. Jeffrey didn't appreciate unfinished experiments. That had been my one bargaining chip.

"Don't worry," I said. "I think things are about to change."

"Sure," Enza said. I could tell from her tone how high her eyebrow was arched.

"No, really. I'm on vacation starting today."

Enza shrieked, and I held the phone away from my ear. "Tell me more," she said. "Where are you going? What's the plan?"

"No solid plans," I said.

Enza was chattering so fast I could hardly keep up. "I'm so happy," she said. "No one deserves a nice vacation more than you. After all the overtime, all the holidays, all the breakthroughs—you're the smartest person they've got and it's about time they did something nice for you."

I finished my glass of wine in one long swallow. "Nice doesn't accurately describe it," I said, and then I couldn't lie to her anymore. I told her about how Jeffrey had told me the grant money was being reallocated this year and then used that ridiculous word. *We're downsizing,* he'd said, as if they were moving the three-story lab to a smaller building, or clearing out all the old equipment that was no longer useful. As he talked about coming back in a part-time capacity, his pig-like eyes had darted past me as if he couldn't wait to get me out of the room.

Enza was quiet for a long moment. I poured another glass of wine, feeling just barely tipsy from the first.

"Hello?" I said. "Are you still there?"

"I have an idea," she said. "Jack and I are leaving town on Monday for a little getaway ourselves. Why don't you come here and house-sit? Forget about all of that work nonsense for a while and swim in the lake."

"Your lake is full of dinosaurs with big, pointy teeth. I saw how that movie ended."

"Come on, Kate. Get out of the city for a while. You need some peace and quiet. And some nature, for god's sake." What she was really saying: *You never leave Raleigh. You never take time for yourself. And put your big girl panties on.*

She wasn't wrong.

"It's hotter than hell down there," I said. And it was. Enza lived in Bayou Sabine, a little town close to New Orleans. She'd insisted I visit her last Christmas after my breakup with Benjamin. I would have just walked around in my underwear if her boyfriend and her entire family hadn't been there. She had a big Victorian house that she'd inherited from her grandmother, more square footage than I could ever afford in Raleigh. It was like a dollhouse: big rooms with high ceilings and carved molding, a dozen acres, and a little lagoon that looked like something out of a movie shot with a fuzzy lens.

"It's cool in April," Enza said. "This is the best time to come. You'd be doing me a favor. You can watch the dog for us."

"I don't know."

"I bet there's a sheriff who'd be happy to see you," she said. "See? Everybody wins."

I groaned, thinking of the perfect storm last December that had shoved me into the orbit of the town sheriff, Andre. He was about as far from my type as I could get, but not as easy to resist as I'd predicted. He was kind and warm, two things I'd learned that Benjamin was not. Andre made me laugh, and he beat me at Scrabble, two things that made him exceptionally rare. But he lived in a tiny town in Louisiana that had zero use for someone like me, a person who peered into microscopes and petri dishes all day. This was the worst thing about dating at my age: I was stable, comfortable in my career and content with my status as a homeowner, and a cozy distance from my family. The problem with being thirty-four was that most men I encountered were also in that position, which made it difficult for either party to give up their work or home life for the sake of romantic risk. It was easy enough dating someone in my hometown, but to find a man in a different location that would upset the balance of everything? That seemed impossible.

Andre had been a welcome distraction from my breakup. We'd left things on friendly terms, never giving a definition to whatever we had. It was fun, and I liked him. But I didn't see how either of us could leave our careers to be together. After enough weeks had passed, I'd convinced myself that our parting was for the best. After Benjamin, it was clear that my judgment had been compromised. The last thing I needed now was another man complicating my life.

Besides, Andre was Jack's best friend. That made things much more complex. If Andre ended up hurt, then Jack would hate me, and that would put Enza in a difficult position.

No, it was best to stay away from the sheriff.

"I don't need a matchmaker, Enza."

"Have you heard from him?"

"Stop," I said. "No sheriff."

"Fine. Sit by the lake. Work on your tan. Read that stack of dirty novels you've been saving."

I took another sip of wine, trying not to think of Andre. But there he was with his hopelessly tousled hair, his wiry forearms, and his eyes that darkened when he laughed.

Dammit.

"I'm looking up flights right now," Enza said. "Direct from Raleigh-Durham, less than three hundred bucks. How's eight next Monday morning?"

"Ugh. That's too early."

"Otherwise you have to wait until four, and when you wait that long, the airline has time to run late, have catastrophes, and get delayed. Just get yourself some strong coffee and a doughnut. Maybe a cab so you don't get road rage."

I started to protest again, but thoughts of the blue-green lagoon seeped into my head, and I felt the lush grass beneath my toes, the tingle of sunlight on my skin, and then I was reading Enza the numbers on my credit card.

And now here I was, staring down a speckled swamp dog in my best friend's living room. Her coat was mottled gray and brown, like granite. Her amber eyes held a mix of curiosity and ire. "She likes you," Enza had cooed only yesterday, letting the beast lick her face. "She's super smart, and a great watchdog. You'll get along just fine."

But I could tell that dog hated me. She didn't lick my face. She didn't nuzzle me on the couch. She squinted at me the way my great aunt did when my two rambunctious brothers and I came to visit, bringing more baggage than Amtrak with us. Enza said it took a while for the dog to form a bond, that she was protective of her and Jack, and therefore wary of interlopers.

"She'll come around," Enza had said. "And I think you could use a loyal companion, since you insist on avoiding the sheriff." Bella was a catahoula, a herding breed that needed ample time outside to romp around and unearth trouble.

When Jack and Enza had loaded up the car to leave, Bella had tried to herd them right back inside the house. She was clearly displeased when I was the one who went back inside with her.

"There you are," I said to the dog, my hands on my hips. "I saw what you did. Don't try to pretend it wasn't you."

Bella stood by the fireplace, peeking into my new leopard print tote bag that I'd bought the day I'd left the lab in an attempt to cheer myself up. She pricked her ears toward me, then looked away as if ashamed.

"Hey!" I said. "Get away from there."

Bella pushed her snout into the bag, still peering at me through one handle. She blinked at me once, woefully, and turned back to the bag, her ears flattened.

Her back arched as she emptied the contents of her stomach into the tote.

"Good god damn," I said.

The dog blinked at me and then stared at the wall.

"That was vintage, you little minx."

Bella snorted and shoved her nose into the bag. Her bobbed tail wagged.

I knew in that moment, as surely as I knew anything in my life, that I was not a dog person.

Chapter Two

I'D SWORN I wouldn't disturb Enza on her getaway, but this was an emergency. Bella had sprawled on her side by the fireplace, emitting monstrous sounds. I could only imagine the chemical reactions that were happening in that furry little body. Less than twenty-four hours in her house, and I'd broken the dog.

I sent her a text message: *Your dog hates me.*

After a few moments, she wrote: *Jack's dog.*

She barfed in my new tote bag.

Why?

Seriously? Dog people. *Because she hates me,* I wrote.

She's not a cat. She doesn't vomit for vengeance.

I groaned.

Did she get outside and eat some dead thing? Enza wrote.

She ate my eggplant lasagna. Do you think she needs a vet?

Your lasagna's not that bad.

You're hilarious.

Gotta run. Don't worry. She's had worse. She'll eat anything that sits still long enough.

I think we've made a terrible mistake, I wrote.

She'll like you more tomorrow. xoxo. Call Lucille if you need backup.

Lucille was Jack's younger cousin, who might as well have been his little sister. Jack's aunt and uncle had raised him right along with her after his parents had died. Enza had planned on inviting Lucille to house-sit before Friday's phone call changed that. Lucille had left me her phone number and said to call if I wanted company.

This getaway had become a disaster. I did need backup.

I texted Lucille: *Does anyone deliver pizza out here?*

She replied a few moments later. *LOL. Not where you are.*

Up for a girls' night out? Dog ruined my dinner and I'm starving.

Sure! I'll come pick you up. You're on the way to town.

What's in town?

Best seafood ever. Be there in twenty minutes.

Bella stared at me from across the room. She lay on her side, her legs splayed out as if she'd just tipped over like one of those fainting goats that go stiff as a board and crash to the earth out of fright. Her golden eyes were fixed on me as she let out a heavy sigh.

"Don't look at me like that," I said. "You brought this on yourself, you big piglet."

I went upstairs to change out of my pajamas. It was still warm out, so I chose a charcoal scoop-necked shift dress that came almost to my knees. I'd brought a pair of tall boots and two pairs of flats in red and navy, trying to keep to my two-bag limit. I slipped the red flats on and ran the flat iron through my hair to press the humidity out. My hair had become frizzy the moment I got off the airplane in New

Orleans, and no amount of heat or product seemed to tame it for long.

A half hour later, Lucille was at the door. She looked healthier since I'd seen her at Christmas, with fuller cheeks and red highlights in her hair. Tonight she wore slim-cut jeans, a beat up brown motorcycle jacket and tall brown boots. Being back here was good for her, it seemed. That, along with being rid of that jackass Toph whom she'd been dating when I last saw her.

"Hey," she said, giving me a quick hug. "What's the dog emergency?"

In the living room, I heard the jingle of Bella's collar against the floor as she turned her head to look at us.

"I'll tell you on the way," I said.

"Is that what's you're wearing?" She tilted her head to the side.

"Yeah, why?"

She shrugged, stumbling over her words. "Awfully fancy," she said. "We're going to a place where you toss peanut shells on the floor."

"This is the most casual outfit I have."

"Seriously? Don't you have pants?"

"Yeah, that I wear out in the yard." I'd gotten so accustomed to business casual that I was uncomfortable around people if I wore most anything else. Khakis were for gardening. Jeans were for college kids.

"So put those on," she said.

"But I wear them in the yard."

She blinked at me.

"I'm starving, Lucille. Can we talk fashion later?"

She smiled and shrugged as we went outside and climbed into her tiny blue Volkswagen sedan.

Lucille drove us along the main road towards town and pulled over at a white clapboard building with a big front porch made from weathered lumber. Colored lights crisscrossed through the beams and a chalkboard outside proclaimed *Fresh Catch + Cold Beer.* The windows glowed with orange-tinted light.

"It doesn't look like much from the outside," Lucille said, "But it's my favorite. And they have fried green tomatoes."

Inside, it was all wood paneling and diner-style tables that were almost certainly from the 1950s. The chairs, mismatched, were a dozen different colors, all vinyl with aluminum and rivets. The bar was off to one side, with a jukebox and a pool table in the opposite corner. The place was half full, so we chose a booth in the back, near the jukebox. I'd never seen so much denim and plaid in my entire life.

A waitress came to take our orders, and Lucille greeted her by name. They chatted for a moment while I looked over the menu. Lucille finally caught my attention and said, "Want to split a seafood platter as big as our heads?"

"Only if it has fried green tomatoes," I said.

The waitress, Gina, grinned and nodded. "Anything to drink, girls?"

Lucille asked for a beer. I asked for a martini. Gina sauntered back to the bar.

"Everyone's looking at us," I said.

"They're trying to figure out who you are," Lucille said.

"Should I make an announcement? Would that stop the staring?"

She chuckled. "Word'll spread soon enough. This is basically the only place to hang out around here."

Gina came back with our drinks. My martini was in a

lowball glass with an olive rolling around on the bottom like a marble. The glass was half full.

"I think she brought me a double," I said.

"See? Best place around."

"Cheers," I said and clinked my glass against hers.

"So what's new with you?" Lucille asked.

I told her about my meeting with Jeffrey, my job that was about to disappear. "They offered to bring me on as a part-time consultant, but I think I might hate that job anyway. So I'm taking this week to figure out if I just want to quit completely and start something new."

"Oh," she said.

"Enza thought a week away from the vortex might help me decide."

"It worked for me. Just took longer than a week."

"Are you still doing your master's program?"

"This is my last semester, so I'm down to thesis work and one class. I stay with a friend in Baton Rouge two or three nights a week."

"How's Buck?" I said.

"Much better." She smiled, like she'd almost put her past with Toph behind her. Enza had told me Lucille had stayed with her parents since the winter, helping her father recover from an accident. She was working on a master's in theater arts.

The jukebox whined an old Zeppelin song, the bass notes thrumming like a pulse. The crack of billiard balls split the air and a chorus of hoots erupted from the far corner. Lucille wiggled along with the music, sipping her beer and telling me about their spring play, a retelling of *The Tempest*.

On our second round, she said, "It was good to come back to something familiar for a while. You need that sometimes."

"I did the opposite," I said. "It's easier to make objective decisions if I step back a bit, you know?"

Lucille nodded. "Get away from the center of things."

"It felt like everything was falling apart. My job, my fiancé —but that's a whole 'nother long sad story about a cheating bastard."

Lucille frowned. "Well, you met my bastard. I don't know why I stayed with him for so long."

"Why do we stay? I think something in me is broken. Sometimes I think I just picked a bad match, but then I think it was my fault, too. I'm a workaholic. I know that."

"It's not your fault he cheated. I may be young, but I know that much is true."

I shrugged. "I drove him to it. I wasn't there enough for him."

"Nope," Lucille barked. "Not your fault. That's not how cheating works."

"Maybe."

"Not maybe," Lucille said, leaning closer.

"I like my lab, where everything's predictable. Ben was that in the beginning, but then one day he wasn't. And it wrecked everything."

She shrugged. "Unpredictable's not always bad. You'll find a better one, one who surprises you in the good way."

The music changed to something fast and Lucille pounded her fist on the table, making the glasses rattle. Then she stood up and said, "Come dance with me. I love this one."

"Everyone's already staring at me," I said. "I'm not going to make more of a spectacle of myself."

"Come on. Nobody in this place will dance with me because they're scared to death of Jack and my dad. And of Andre, of course. They all protect me so much I never have any fun." She stuck her lip out in a pout, tugging on my wrist. "Please," she whined.

"Maybe next time."

She groaned, staring up at the ceiling. Then she started dancing in a tiny circle, right next to me, raising her arms overhead, shaking her hips. "Fine," she said, exaggerating the movements. "I'll just be right here."

"Suit yourself." I sipped my martini as she twirled in her own bubble, letting the quizzical looks from the locals bounce off her like points of light from a disco ball. She wiggled against me, which seemed to just draw more attention to us, and I laughed in spite of myself.

"I see that foot tapping," she said. "Don't fight it."

When she shimmied to the side, the room narrowed to a point. And at the end of that point was Andre Dufresne, walking right toward us with just enough swagger to hold my attention. His badge, clipped to his belt, caught the light like a coin in a fountain and a flicker of surprise flashed over his face before he smiled. Andre, with the tiny wrinkles that showed around his eyes when he laughed his raucous laugh. He nodded a greeting, tilted his head to the side as he snuck up behind Lucille.

"Hey, Luce," he said, dropping his hand onto her shoulder. "Burning up the dance floor, I see."

She moonwalked past him and said, "I might have a partner if you didn't scare them all off with all that authority and whatnot. They all think you'll lock 'em up for touching me."

"And they're correct." He ruffled her hair like a big brother might. "I'll let you know when one of this lot's good enough for you."

"I can choose my own fellas, thank you," she said.

The song faded out and she took her seat at the table, winking at me. I took a long drink from the martini.

Andre turned to me and said, "Hi, Kate. I heard you were back in town." His hand rested on my shoulder for a moment, as if he wasn't sure if he should hug me.

"Dog-sitting," I said.

"Vacation," Lucille said, smoothing her hair back down. "Escaping the perils of the big city."

"Is that right?" he said. He'd rested one hand on his hip, one on the back of my chair. He smiled so his dimples showed. "It's good to see you again."

"You, too," I said, and something fluttered in my chest like a bird.

His eyes were greener than I remembered. His reddish hair was tousled, like he'd been driving all day with his windows down. It was just long enough to stand up in tufts, just a hint of curls. I bit my lip, thinking of how we'd sprawled out on the living room floor last Christmas, playing Scrabble and drinking bourbon way too far into the morning. I'd been staying with Enza, helping her survive the holiday collision of her old family with her new one, and out of nowhere Andre had appeared with his easy smile. I'd been completely smitten.

I'd also just broken up with Benjamin, so the timing of meeting Andre wasn't exactly great. We had chemistry, sure—but I don't do rebounds. They're selfish. I was a guest in my best friend's house, and the last thing I wanted to do was have a fling with her boyfriend's best friend and create more tension. Lord knows, Enza had enough drama in her life without adding me and my messed up love life to the mix.

So despite wishing I could tangle my fingers in the sheriff's hair and kiss him stupid that night last December, I'd gone back to my room upstairs and left him sleeping on the couch, Scrabble tiles littering the floor like confetti.

And now here he was, standing in a bar with no name, even more adorable than I remembered, staring at me like he was replaying every detail of that evening in his head.

"How long are you here?" he asked me.

Kate wiggled her eyebrows and I nudged her foot under the table.

"Just until Sunday," I said.

"Well maybe I'll see you around," he said.

"Maybe so."

"I certainly hope so."

Someone hollered to him from the bar and he tore his gaze away from me. He waved to Gina, who was holding a brown paper bag.

"Take out," he said. "Working late tonight."

"Ah, that's too bad," Lucille said. "Thought for sure you'd join us for the next dance."

"Rain check," he said, his eyes still fixed on mine. "You ladies get home safe tonight."

"Thanks, Andre," I said.

He turned back and said, "Good to see you again, Kate," and then strode towards the bar.

I watched him a little too long, his lean frame in the snug pants and shirt.

Lucille cleared her throat, then tapped the table in front of me.

"What?" I said.

She grinned and said in a voice one octave lower than her usual, "Good to see you again, Kate." She batted her eyelashes.

I snorted, feeling tipsy from the martini.

"He might be exactly what you need," Lucille said. "He

could make you forget about all the perils of the city, all your work nonsense."

"Lucille!" I said. "He's like your brother."

She scoffed. "He needs a vacation, too. You two would be cute together."

"You've been hanging around with Enza too long."

She shrugged. "We gals have to look out for each other."

But I couldn't argue with her. It wasn't like the thought had never entered my mind.

And sat there in the far corner, percolating.

And resurfaced in dreams that left me breathless.

Read more about Kate and Andre in
Just the Trouble I Needed.

Join My Newsletter

JOIN my team and you'll get my special author newsletter, Writing Down South. Click here to subscribe and claim your free book, *Beneath Our Skin: Short Stories about Wild Women*.

Acknowledgments

Many people helped make this book happen, in more ways than they might ever imagine. It's not easy being a writer, but you all keep me going.

First I have to thank Katie Rose Guest Pryal, the best beta reader a gal could ask for. I'm sure glad we found each other all those years ago—it's been delightful becoming a novelist with you.

A special thank you goes to Mike House and the Wildacres staff, who let me crash there in the most perfect writers' cabin in order to buckle down and finish this book. I couldn't have made my deadline without my time with you all.

To my family and friends: I'm thankful to have each and every one of you in my life. Thank you for always believing in me and encouraging me to keep doing what I love most. Your support means the world to me. To Mom and Dad: You two keep me strong and solid, and I'm lucky to have won you in the parent lottery. To Andrew: Thank you for reminding me to stop and savor the moments that matter most. I'm sure glad you let your gelato melt that day.

Thanks to Velvet Morning Press, for publishing the first edition of this book.

And thank *you*, dear reader, for traveling to the bayou with me. Hope to see you next time.

About the Author

Lauren divides her time between writing, teaching, and printmaking. She is the author of the Bayou Sabine Series, which includes the novels *Trouble in Bayou Sabine* and *Bayou Whispers*. Originally from South Carolina, she has worked as an archaeologist, an English teacher, and a ranger for the National Park Service. She earned her MFA in creative writing from Georgia College & State University, and her MFA in Book Arts from The University of Alabama.

She won the *Family Circle* short fiction contest, was a finalist for the Novello Festival Press First Novel Award, and was nominated for an AWP Intro Award. She currently lives in North Carolina, where she's at work on the next novel in the Bayou Sabine series. Sign up for Lauren's author newsletter, *Writing Down South*, at laurenfaulkenberry.com.

facebook.com/FaulkenberryAuthor

twitter.com/firebrandpress

instagram.com/firebrandpress

amazon.com/author/lauren-faulkenberry

bookbub.com/authors/lauren-faulkenberry

Made in the USA
Columbia, SC
22 January 2022

54629713R00162